ACKNOWLEDGEMENTS

First and foremost, I must thank my wife for her love and support throughout this adventure. A special thanks to Seton Hill University and Dr.'s Lee McClain, Al Wendland and Mike Arnzen for making the *Master of Arts in Writing Popular Fiction* program possible.

"THE PERFECT PATSY"

BY
MILT ANDERSON

For Rees & Susan,

Enjoy this installment of
Murder & Mayhem in the
Man Valley.

Milt Anderson

"The Perfect Patsy," by Milt Anderson. ISBN 978-1-60264-380-2.

Published 2009 by Virtualbookworm.com Publishing Inc., P.O. Box 9949, College Station, TX 77842, US. ©2009, Milt Anderson. All rights reserved. No part of this publication may be reproduced, stored in a retrieval system, or transmitted in any form or by any means, electronic, mechanical, recording or otherwise, without the prior written permission of Milt Anderson.

Manufactured in the United States of America.

CHAPTER 1

Wally Gustafson didn't have his usual dream where he was standing in the foaming water of the South China Sea, looking out over its vast emptiness, contemplating the long trip back home to safety and comfort, shuddering with fear of the thought he would never make it home at all.

This decade's old dream reconstructed the morning after a drunken binge in the village of Yafuso, a half-mile's distance from base. He lay in his mosquito-net-covered bunk knowing something was terribly wrong, but the headache and cobwebs in his skull wouldn't allow his thoughts to materialize. He'd been drunk before and sensed similar feelings, but this time dread hung over him, nudging him back into awareness. He became confused when he realized he was dressed in civilian clothes. A numbing chill marched through his veins at the sight of blood, thick and dark on his hands, wrists, and arms up to his elbows. What if, in his delirium, he had hurt someone? He later discovered that he had come to the rescue of a young girl being attacked by a drunken sailor.

But this headache contrasted from previous ones. His thoughts confused and frightened him. A teeth chattering-sweat enveloped him as if he was being cocooned in a frozen body bag. The pinging sound of raindrops pelting glass finally roused him. The faint, misty color of late autumn's dawn struggled through voile draperies and between the half-closed slats of window blinds. The image of a revolving ceiling fan—its paddles fashioned palm tree leaves—reflected in a mirror atop a French provincial dresser. The fan spun slowly making a squeaking noise as if on its last electrical leg. Wally lay frozen, studying the room that wasn't his. He shook his head trying to organize memory cells in his brain.

He shuddered, remembering the decades old dream and wondering why this dream came to him now. Wally checked his forearms for blood. He was relieved to find none . . . that is until he rolled over into a pool of the fuchsia colored liquid and looked into the glazed-over eyes of death.

CHAPTER 2

A golf ball made a pinging sound as it bounced and ricocheted between the underside of a '98 blazer and the concrete surface of the garage floor. J.C. Ducheck stared at the Titleist; his face long and drawn as if surrendering to an unseen enemy. Running late for his 10:00 a.m. tee time, J.C. thought today was going to be one of those days he'd rather forget. Minutes before, while maneuvering through the garage's obstacle course of accumulated memorabilia, he kicked over a pigeonhole case of nuts and bolts he had been methodically sorting for weeks. Getting hit in the head with a four iron, while pulling his bag from an elevated shelf, was the coup de grâce; it left a mark on the right side of his forehead resembling a ripe strawberry.

J.C. slumped into a wooden folding chair, surveyed the multitude of steel fasteners strewn across the floor, and watched the golf ball slowly dribble toward and then roll into an uncovered floor drain for a hole in one. A crooked smile slowly crept over his forlorn face; he couldn't help but wonder what would happen next.

That's when the phone rang.

J.C. reluctantly hoisted himself from the chair and weaved his way through the metallic rubble toward the obnoxious noise. Seven rings later he reached the phone and snatched the receiver from its cradle.

"Hello," he said in a voice that anticipated a recorded telemarketer.

"I got a problem. A big problem. I need your help."

"Wally, are you okay? What—?"

"I'm okay. I can't talk over the phone. Meet me at my place in fifteen minutes."

"But I—." The abrupt click of a receiver ended the conversation. "Son of a bitch."

J.C. predicted it would take nine minutes to drive Mononville's 5-mile diameter to Wally's house. He jumped in the Blazer and headed East on the Thompson Run Parkway toward the Lindenwood section of town. A few minutes later he approached the W&J Steel Plant where Wally had worked.

Nothing is as sad as an empty steel mill. And no steel mill is as sad as the W&J Steel Plant. Once, one of the largest producers of steel that forged the World War II victory, rust is now the only product of the plant's decaying carcass.

The plant's demise would be easy to blame on subsidized steel imported from Great Britain, cheap Japanese cars, or corporate or union greed, but W&J Steel's decay is as much a product of evolution than anything else.

The once modern plant was a beehive of activity for three shifts of thirty-five hundred men with five blast furnaces that stood tall, erect and proud. The blast furnaces, and therefore the plant fell victim to the basic oxygen and electric furnaces.

Wally worked as a scarfer for thirty years. A scarfer shapes, cuts and trims billets before they cool, a hot and demanding job that few wanted but Wally accepted without complaint. That's what bothered J.C. Wally didn't ask for help; he was a tough, self-reliant, proud man who took care of his own problems. J.C. knew Wally had to be in a real dilemma.

J.C. took the Balazia Street exit, turned right on Graham Avenue and headed for Polish Hill. Wally's house took root on the corner of McKee and Luce, two blocks from Rostraver, one of the city's main streets. J.C. parked around the corner. He jumped out of his vehicle and dashed toward Wally's house, kicking up shiny flecks of steel dust on the cracked sidewalk as he ran.

J.C.'s long legs took the twenty-foot cement stairway two risers at a time to a deep wooden porch. Two giant steps later, he flung the door open to Wallly's living room.

Wally sat sprawled in a threadbare emerald green recliner at the opposite wall. A half empty bottle of Bellows Bourbon and a revolver were on the coffee table in front of him. He squinted from the bright sunlight that J.C. ushered in.

"Wally, what's wrong?" J.C. said, closing the door.

The sound of J.C.'s voice relieved Wally slightly.

"What kept ya'? I could've driven to Tipperary by now." Wally dug his elbows into the arms of the chair trying to straighten himself from his slumped position. Deep furrows appeared on his normally smooth forehead. His ice-blue irises focused on J.C. "And what's that red bump on your head?"

J.C. touched the strawberry. "Oh, that's nothing, Wally I... cut the shit. What's the problem? And what's that gun doing on the table?" J.C. slid into a leather chair opposite Wally, studying his face, trying to determine his state of mind.

Wally didn't know how to start. His face hung long and his normal color went south also. The furrows between his sunken, bloodshot eyes deepened as he stared at the bourbon, the visual image of the early

5

morning seemed to make a permanent impression on his retina.

J.C. hadn't seen Wally like this since Wally's second wife, Helga, died seven years ago.

J.C. reached over the table and shook his arm. "Wally, what's wrong?"

Wally snapped out of his stupor, and in a low, slow voice, said, "Did you ever wake up and immediately know that something was wrong but didn't know exactly what?"

J.C. surveyed Wally's bloodshot eyes. "Yeah...after drinking. Did you go on one of your—?"

Wally had been known to *tip a few beers*, especially after coming home from two tours in Vietnam. I should say more than a few beers and usually every night. It was what the troops did. Drink, do your job and drink some more. Wally usually stayed away from the hard stuff; beer was his choice of abuse. He tried marijuana once after getting high on beer, but didn't like the results. Slowly, Wally decreased his drinking from every day to four days a week to three days a week. And, after a while the drinking was kept to a minimum. Except for special occasions, and then a weekend would disappear.

"No, that's not it," Wally said, shaking his head. "We only had a glass of wine—"

"We?"

"Yeah, Gigi."

"Who's Gigi?"

Wally bowed his head; his eyes welled up. "I've been seeing Giovanna for a couple 'a months after I broke up with Eleanor."

"Eleanor? I thought you were going with the widow Beechford?"

"She was too old for me. Reminded me of Helga."

"She's only forty-eight Wally. You're sixty-one.

"That's beside the point. She acted old; so did Eleanor. Gigi was . . . she was . . ." Wally covered his face with his massive, wrinkled, arthritic hands and sobbed.

J.C. extended his arm over the table and rested his hand on Wally's shoulder. "What happened, Wally?"

Wally told J.C. about his strange dream, how his headache was different from any other, and how he awakened in Gigi's bedroom with a feeling of dread.

"It was then I realized Gigi was covered in blood." Wally started to cry. "Shot... she had been shot."

J.C. sunk back on the chair's upholstered upright, his mouth agape, his eyes under arched brows searching the ceiling for an answer. He thought for a minute and said, "What the hell happened?"

"I don't know. I just don't remember anything."

"Did you call the police?"

Wally's facial expression turned to one of despair. He grabbed the Bellows and took a long draw. And in a positive voice, he said, "Absolutely not."

J.C. leaned back in his chair. "Why not?"

"Because I'd go to prison, that's why. I'm being set up."

"But you said you don't remember anything. What makes you think you're being set up?"

"That's the point. I don't remember anything. I don't even remember going to bed and that's the last thing I'd forget."

J.C. knew Wally's reputation with women. Wally came home from the war in nineteen sixty-nine when many of the public called the returning GI's baby killers, murderers, and other terrible names, but not the ones that knew him, especially the women. He stood six foot one in his jump boots and filled out his dress green uniform to the satisfaction of admiring ladies. They couldn't keep their minds or hands off him.

J.C. didn't pursue Wally's statement. He hesitated, thinking over the possibilities. He could only come to one. "What about suicide?"

"Suicide?" Wally pointed to the revolver. "No, not with my pistol."

"Your pistol! How in the hell did your gun get there?"

Wally shook his head in desperation. "I don't know. I guess her husband had to bring it."

"Her husband? Holy shit," J.C. threw his arms up in despair. "You didn't say she was married."

"Separated. Three months." Wally looked like he lost his last dime down a sewer drain. "I think I was drugged. He set me up. You are looking at the perfect patsy. I don't know any way out of this. I'm screwed."

"Why do you think it's so hopeless? Who's her husband?"

"Leonard Antonelli," Wally glared a stare of understanding at J.C. "Police Captain Leonard Antonelli."

J.C. slumped back into the chair. "Oh, that's just terrific. That's why I didn't know about her. You didn't tell me because she's married to a cop."

Wally didn't want to tell the others about Giovanna because their relationship might fail. His first wife, Arlene left because of his heavy drinking. He married Helga for stability. Wally thought a tough German woman would temper his past, but that failed also. Helga tried for years to bend the unbendable, but succumbed to despair. Wally got up and went to work every day believing he was not in the category of what he called the weepy-eyed veterans who claimed post traumatic stress disorder or other maladies attributable to the war. That's what citizens are supposed to do, he'd say, go to war when called on and do your job; it's expected. Some vets didn't want to become part of society and didn't want to work. They just wanted to be recognized by joining the veteran's mutual admiration organizations. That wasn't Wally. He wanted to be self-reliant and independent.

"Well?" J.C. said as he stood up.

Wally pushed the bourbon aside and said, "Call Harvey. He gets off work at three-thirty. Have him meet us at the bar."

———

Captain Leonard Antonelli stood six foot five and weighed two hundred and forty pounds. With the additional height of his hat, one that looked like it should be on a German S.S. officer's head, he barely made it through the door of Representative Darby Davis' Mononville office, a former book store previously owned and operated by the Taylor brothers. He rented the office, at taxpayer's expense of course, as his campaign headquarters for the upcoming election for the vacant U.S. Senate seat. He added an additional four desks for campaign workers, all young and pretty women, who were now staring admiringly at the Captain.

Ruggedly handsome, Leonard Antonelli attracted looks and propositions from ladies of all ages and stations in life almost every day. He couldn't restrain himself from glancing from table to table, smiling at the new recruits as he walked to Davis' office at the back of the office.

Antonelli walked through the normally open door and closed it behind him. He took off his cap exposing a narrow streak of silver that parted his coal-black hair. A two-inch scar descended from his hairline on his right temple. Davis looked up from a Playboy magazine he was reading. He wore a blue pin-striped suit, the jacket open exposing a wide girth and belly that cascaded over his belt. "Leonard, what brings you here?"

Leonard pointed to the magazine. "You must have this election all locked up."

"Yeah pretty much," Davis said, through an exhale of cigar smoke that wafted up past his balding head.

Davis was more than confident at the election's outcome. He slid into politics on the coattails of his father, Michael Davis, a World War II hero, earning the Medal of Honor at Pointe du Hoc on Omaha Beach at the invasion of Normandy. He was a lieutenant in what was then called Darby's Rangers—hence the name Darby for his only son.

Antonelli smiled. "I was wondering if you'll be needing security from my guys at your rally next Wednesday?"

"Now who would want to hurt me?" Davis said, extending his arms as if to include the universe and beyond. "I'm a respected politician, family man and churchgoer. What could be better than that? Why would I want security?"

Leonard canted his head.

"Probably three officers," Darby said, smiling, making his already chubby cheeks bulge even bigger. "By the way, while we're on the subject, how's it going with your wife?"

Antonelli slumped into a chair. "The divorce will be final in a month."

"Sorry to hear that Leonard."

"I don't care about the divorce; she wants to take a ton of my money with her."

"What can I do? Maybe if I get her a job she won't want so much."

"She's already a bookkeeper. Works for a number of businesses, but she wants more. She wants money, my money. I need some help with this woman that will convince her to get off my back."

"Let me think," Darby said, rubbing his chin. I know some of her clients. Maybe I can make some arrangements."

Leonard stood up and put on his cap. "Thanks a lot Darby, I appreciate it. You've always been there for me."

"And in the future also."

"I'll count on it," Leonard said, standing up. "I have to go now. Got to keep your city orderly."

"Take care," Darby said.

Leonard walked out into the admiration of the campaign workers.

CHAPTER 3

Streaks of late afternoon sunlight peeked around frayed
window shades, tracked over worn oak floor boards
onto a mahogany bar highlighting its wood grain through
puddles of amber liquid, exposed miniature black
potholes created by neglected cigarettes.

Ducheck's Bar is a typical neighborhood tavern in
Mononville, a leftover from the heydays of the 60's and
70's when times were good and the steel mills were
working full tilt. Now, with only a skeleton crew at the
coke plant, the only mention of the decaying industry
passed through the saddened lips of retirees, like the four
playing euchre near the seldom used shuffleboard.
Younger displaced workers, who used to pack the bar,
fled the area years ago.

J.C. leaned idly on the mahogany talking with two of
the regulars and Moldy, the bartender, when Harvey
Stuhl bolted through the door. Harvey scanned the area
and strode up to J.C. Wally, who had been watching the
euchre game, joined them at the bar.

"What's up J.C.? What's goin' on?" Harvey asked
enthusiastically, his huge glistening horse teeth chopped
up and down as he spit out his words. Large horn-
rimmed glasses covered his wide excited eyes.

Harvey is soft spoken and doesn't talk much—not your basic requirements for a code enforcement officer. Wally's nephew, Detective Paul Andrews, helped Harvey get a job with the city when he came to town ten years ago looking for work. Paul's reputation on the police force greased the path to the position. Of course Harvey's computer knowledge and experience with inspecting off post housing with the Air Force didn't hurt. Paul brought Harvey to Ducheck's after work frequently—that's how Harvey met J.C. Somehow the tall, dark haired, good-looking J.C. and the diminutive, ordinary looking Harvey quickly developed a friendship. Being in their early thirties was the only physical thing they had in common.

Wally slung his arm around Harvey and ushered him toward the rear of the bar. "Let's go in the back room," Wally said, "we can talk there."

J.C. picked up the Iron City Light he ordered for Harvey, grabbed his own bottle and followed the pair into the back room.

Fondly called a *lounge* years ago, the room provided an atmosphere where families could enjoy a home-cooked meal, sandwiches, or pizza away from the boisterous, crowded bar. An old leftover Wurlitzer juke-box glowed in bold primary color next to the kitchen's closed service window. The screens of three illegal poker machines danced with light displays. The electronic devices provided financial help for small clubs and bars like Ducheck's to survive.

J.C. followed Harvey and Wally to a large corner booth. J.C. slid in next to Harvey.

Wally didn't wait for pleasantries. He beamed a long hard look across the table at Harvey and said, "I need your eyes and ears at City Hall."

Harvey had developed a friendship with J.C. and Paul Andrews, but Harvey's relationship with Wally hadn't started to congeal. Wally was desperate. He knew the cards were stacked against him and didn't know when they would collapse. He needed help from someone on the inside of city hall. He couldn't put his nephew's job in jeopardy and had to rely on Harvey Stuhl, the antithesis of the person he envisioned would help him, but there was no one else.

Harvey blinked a few times resembling a spectacled owl. "What . . . Why—?

"You're the Code Enforcement Officer. You spend a lot of time in the building, right?" Harvey nodded. "You know how to operate computers?" Wally nodded in the affirmative as if waiting for the same response from Harvey.

Harvey hesitated and nodded.

Wally continued. "You have access to offices and computer files, don't you?"

Again Harvey nodded, nudging his bulky glasses back into place, "But I don't understand—"

J.C. interrupted. "That includes the police department?"

Harvey turned his head toward J.C. as an owl would. "Yes but—. What's that red bump on your head?"

Wally held up his hand in a halting motion. "I need to know what Captain Antonelli is working on, who he talks to, if he talks about his ex-wife Giovanna, if he leaves the station or goes off the clock."

Harvey had been taking a long draw on his beer and stopped abruptly, pulling his bottle away. The foaming liquid dribbled down his chin. "What about your nephew, Paul? He's in the police area more than I am. His office is right across the hall from Antonelli's."

"Maybe later," Wally said. "But I can't involve Paul at this time." Wally grabbed Harvey's hand. "I need your help now. It's important. Can I count on you?" Wally's desperation produced the side effect of sweat. He had previously relied on his service buddies for help, the ones he knew he could count on, the bigger stronger men who volunteered to serve. He didn't put Harvey in that category.

Harvey hesitated. The wash of Wally's despondency fell over him. He swallowed hard. Confirmation of Wally's and J.C.'s friendship hung thick in the air. Harvey swallowed hard again. Siphoning information from City Hall could be dangerous.

"I don't know, Wally. I could get fired. What's this about? Why all the secrecy?"

"You'll have to trust me. I can't tell you right now and I can't go to the police or involve my nephew. Not yet. I know this will be risky for you and, if caught, might jeopardize your job, but I wouldn't ask if it wasn't extremely important."

J.C.'s sober, pleading eyes fell on Harvey.

J.C. nodded.

Harvey studied J.C.'s face then dropped his head, looking at the floor. "Sure. What can I do?" he asked.

Harvey's answer brightened Wally's spirits, and at the same time piqued a sense of uncertainty. Wally wasn't sure Harvey could handle the job. But Harvey was the only help available—and agreeable.

Wally quickly grabbed a pencil and scribbled on a scrap of paper. He spoke in a firm, authoritative manner and jabbed the note at Harvey. "This is strictly confidential. You're the only one to know about this. Here's my cell-phone number. For the time being I need to know everything Captain Antonelli is doing. I want to know if he calls anyone into his office, if he sends anyone on a special assignment, or if he leaves his office. Call me the minute you know anything."

Harvey took the number and stuffed it into his shirt pocket. "Okay, sure Wally. But what's this about, I mean generally?"

"I can't get into it today," Wally said. "Meet us here tomorrow after work. I'll fill you in then. Right now, J.C. and I have a lot to talk about."

Wally's hint fell on Harvey like a sudden, cold rain. "I'll see you tomorrow then," Harvey said in a somber voice. He pressed his palms to the table as he slowly stood up. He nodded and then walked hesitatingly out of the room—as if a rubber band attached his ass to the booth.

"Why didn't you tell him?" J.C. asked.

"He'll find out soon enough. And besides, he might shit his pants if he knew what was going on."

"What *is* going on, Wally?"

Wally's head hung. He clasped his hands together, intertwining his fingers on each other, his knuckles white. In a somber voice he said, "All I know is, I'm in deep, deep shit." Wally raised his head and with his palms in an open position spoke in a raspy voice, "I didn't kill her. I couldn't have. I loved her." Wally pounded the table, dropped his head to his chest trying not to sob.

J.C. held Wally's forearm in a comforting manner. "I know you couldn't murder anyone." He looked away and started to grin. "Not a woman anyway."

Wally looked up and caught the expression on J.C.'s face and managed a faint smile which quickly disappeared. "I have to find a way to prove my innocence."

"What did you do with the gun?"

"I hid it where the sun don't shine."

"Shell casing?"

"It's a revolver." Wally said, slowing his words, thinking about his weapon. "Paul knows I have a pistol. He's seen it. He's an officer of the court. He would have to answer any questions under oath, if asked. The police will want to check it for being fired and to compare the bullets and whatever else they do."

"What'll you do?"

The proverbial light bulb seemed to light above Wally's head.

"I'll replace it," Wally said. "It's old and was never registered."

"They'll be watching you," J.C. said. "You can't—"

"That's where you come in. You're going to have a busy day tomorrow."

J.C. looked questioningly. "Doing—?"

"Don't worry, I'll have everything ready for you. Just a short trip to Fairmont will solve the problem."

Wally remembered seeing a notice in the paper about a gun show being held in Fairmont, West Virginia. It was essential that the pistol be replaced to keep him from becoming a suspect—at least temporarily.

J.C. shrugged his shoulders in surrender from Wally's unexpected request. "What about finger prints? Did you get rid of them?"

"No. People knew Gigi and I were dating."

J.C. took a slow draw on his beer. "What about the wine bottle and glasses?"

The *Oh Shit* expression poured through Wally's saucer eyes. He wrapped his hands around his head as if it were to explode. "Damn it, I forgot about them. I was nervous and scared. I didn't go into the living room where we drank the wine. I wanted to get the hell out of there... fast. I rushed down the hallway and out the back door. The wine bottle and glasses are still there. My fingerprints are all over them."

J.C. nodded. "We have to get them back for another reason." Wally pondered J.C.'s statement. J.C. continued. "From your description of what happened, you and Gigi were drugged. If the crime lab finds your prints on them and determines that there were drugs in the wine, it'll look like you drugged Giovanna and then killed her."

Wally leaned back against the booth and looked to the ceiling as if searching for divine help. "Antonelli will be watching me. I have to wait until dark."

CHAPTER 4

The waning crescent moon that hung over Palmer Park provided a faint fluorescence of light filtering through a sparse canopy of trees.

Wally trekked through the vegetation in a crouching motion, stopping periodically behind small bushes and evergreens, listening, cautiously examining his environment.

Earlier that evening, Wally parked his white '98 Ford pickup truck conspicuously in front of his house, snuck out the back door and met J.C. at the old Linden School playground at 2:00 a.m. J.C. dropped Wally off at the World War II cannon, on the east side of Palmer Park and planned to pick him up after the pilferage was finished at 3:00 a.m.

Wally continued westward in a zig-zag manner, creeping, walking, and every few minutes stopping to watch and listen as he had been taught at the J.F.K. Special Warfare Center at Fort Bragg, North Carolina. His mind wandered further back in time to Vietnam. He cautiously checked for tripwires that were attached to claymore mines or traps. Traps could be covered pits, deadfalls, logs or branches that would drop on or smash into unsuspecting G.I.'s with urine and feces covered shards of bamboo attached to them. Approximately eighty-yards from reaching Wally's goal—Reed Avenue and Giovanna Antonelli's house—a distant light from the west tracked through the trees. Wally froze behind the thick trunk of an elm, the luminance becoming brighter and closer moving gently up and down and suddenly turning south. That's when he heard the English speaking voices. Wally snapped back to suburbia from his decade's old reverie in the jungle. Wally finally determined that the voices were from a carload of rowdy teenagers heading home after a night of partying. He murmured grumbling noises of discontent before continuing on. A few minutes later, he knelt behind an azalea bush ten yards from Reed Avenue and directly across from Gigi's house.

Now came the hard part. Wally had to cross a sidewalk, a street, another sidewalk, and approximately forty yards of driveway to Gigi's backdoor—all in the open. Darkness was on his side however, as her house sat midway between two distant streetlights.

Wally, running like a man many years his junior, dashed across the street and up the driveway to the back porch. He crouched behind a lounge chair and checked the neighboring houses for any sounds or signs that would precipitate a call to the police. He waited a few minutes and retrieved a door key from under a small potted plant on the windowsill and unlocked the back door. He stopped, glared at the key, grumbled something under his breath and put it in his pocket. He pulled a pair of latex rubber gloves from his jacket pocket and stretched them on. He wiped his fingerprints from the doorknob with his handkerchief and closed the door behind him.

He reached into the inner pocket of his jacket and retrieved a small penlight flashlight. He directed the narrow beam of light around the kitchen reflecting off kitchenware and glasses producing flickers of light like many small dimly lit fireflies. He walked down the hallway toward the living room, pausing to look into the bedroom where Gigi lay. The faint moonlight shone through the window illuminating her light-skinned body; its aura looked as if her spirit was leaving her body in a luminous wisp.

Wally wanted to run to the police and let the chips fall where they may, but he couldn't. It wasn't in him to back off from a fight. He had to do the right thing, clear his name and find Gigi's real murderer. He walked down the hall, opened the linen closet door and grabbed a pillowcase. He continued to the living room where he retrieved the glasses and imported wine bottle, wrapped them in newspaper and stuffed them into the satin pillowcase. Retracing his steps in the hall, he froze in the bedroom doorway, dropping the pillowcase at his feet.

He leaned on the jamb and tried to compose himself and muster the strength needed to finalize his mission. He knew he had made a terrible mistake by not wearing gloves to open the back door. His fingerprints were on the key. If the key were pristine, the police would know the murderer had wiped it clean and that the murderer had to know where the key was. That would be Wally. The solution—he had to wipe his prints from the key and replace them with Gigi's.

Wally walked into the bedroom as if he had lead boots on, each step slow and painful. As he crept closer, the smell of death increased. He stared at the dried blood's blackness that surrounded her head like a large death halo, stretching out and saturating the bed linens.

Wally wiped his prints from the key, his hands quivering. He reached for Gigi's hand. He hesitated, his hand shook and the sweat squished under the latex. He finally forced himself to grab her fingers and make the impression on the key. Tears fell. Wally used the material of his jacket's forearms to dab the droplets away. He sobbed a prayer of good-bye, walked out of the room backwards, grabbed the pillowcase and double-timed down the hallway into the kitchen. He peeked out the window, slowly opened the door and stepped onto the porch where he replaced the key. He took off the latex gloves, wiped the sweat from his hands, put the gloves in his pocket and used his handkerchief to dry his face.

Wally had one more thing to do. Make it look like someone broke into Giovanna's house. He closed the door and, using his elbow, broke the glass next to the door lock. He previously made sure a shag rug was near the door to deaden the sound of falling glass.

With the pillowcase in tow, Wally walked like a zombie, retracing his steps through the park to the cannon where J.C. was waiting.

Light escaped from the vehicle when Wally opened the door. He slid in, laying the pillowcase in front of him, between his feet.

"Did you get them?" J.C. asked.

"Yeah. Let's go."

CHAPTER 5

Tuesday nights are usually quiet in Ducheck's Bar;
Tuesday afternoons are dead. Only Ten Quarts, a
Monday thru Saturday customer, sat at the bar in his
designated chair, the impression of his butt-cheeks
permanently imprinted on the old stool's leather covered
seat. He liked to be near the television where he watched
characters on "The Young and the Restless" making love
while he made love to Old Overholt.

Wally spent the last half-hour recounting the events
of last evening to J.C.

J.C. said, "That must've been tough."

Wally took a long draw on his beer. "Hardest thing
I've done in a long time. I've seen death before. This was
different. It was personal." He uttered each word as if he
was spitting out a bitter pill. Wally hadn't gone into detail
about the death he'd seen before, or the special ops unit
that he was attached to that had caused it.

"Why would Antonelli want to kill his wife?"

"Don't know," Wally said. "Maybe because they
hated each other or because he was a sick bastard."

"Maybe he couldn't handle the fact she was seeing
another man and was sleeping with him."

"That would give him a reason to hate me, but I
hardly knew him. Probably freaked him out, figuring he

could get two birds with one bullet." Wally took a long draw on his beer and looked off into space. "He sure did a good job. I've heard he's a miserable bastard. A lot of people hated him. Even his dog couldn't stand him. Committed suicide, I heard. Ran out in front of a Dodge Colt."

Wally's corny sense of humor broke the tension and drew a faint smile from J.C.

"Have you heard anything at all?"

"No. Maybe Harvey has," Wally said, glancing at his wristwatch. "He's a little wimpish. Do you think he'll be of any help?"

"Yes, I think so. Don't let his stature influence you. Looks are deceiving. He spent four years in the Air Force before becoming a code enforcement officer. He's done a good job and he has a toughness about him, maybe from being orphaned at a young age. Give him a chance."

Wally nodded. "What are you going to tell him?"

"We have to tell him everything if we want his confidence and his help."

One hundred and fifty five pounds of exuberance under a foretop of mousy-brown hair strode into the bar.

"Hi, guys. I came right over." Harvey jabbed his glasses against his head and slow-footed in the direction of the back room. "Are we going in the back room?"

Wally shook his head, pointing to an empty chair at their table. "Have a seat. Don't worry about Ten Quarts, he's oblivious. His favorite story is on the tube."

Harvey sat down and alternately quizzed looks at J.C. and Wally.

Wally rested his chin on his clasped hands. "Well?"

"Oh...Antonelli. He was at his desk most of the day. Didn't make any phone calls."

Wally and J.C. looked at each other as if Harvey's statement didn't make sense.

J.C. spoke. "You said most of the day. Did he leave the building?"

"No, just a few trips to the Mayor's office."

"Mayor's office?"

"Yeah, the mayor's office."

J.C. nodded. "Looks like Antonelli's sucking up for the chief's job."

"Sucked up all his life," Wally said. "He was a corporal eleven years ago. Now he's second in command. How's that for rapid advancement?"

Harvey squinted. His glasses slipped down his nose. "Why?"

"I didn't get details, but Paul intimated that Antonelli was chummy with the right people."

Harvey pushed his spectacles back. "Who?"

"He didn't tell me."

"What about the chief?" J.C. asked.

"Mononville's chief of police is merely a figurehead," Wally said. "Has been for years. Angus 'The Bull' Burke was castrated by early onset Alzheimer's years ago. He's just dressing the part until retirement."

Harvey jabbed at his eyeglasses again. "What's this all about guys?" He directed his question to J.C. who glanced at Wally.

Wally held his glass as if it were going to slide away. He leaned forward and started to tell Harvey the whole sordid tale. As Harvey listened, his eyes widened and strained to fill the generous expanse of his lenses; his expression froze in incredibility.

When Wally finished speaking, Harvey's face thawed and uttered the words, "What did you do with the body?"

Harvey's abrupt question, although logical and helpful, was disrespectful and washed cold over Wally. He hesitated before he spoke. "I left Giovanna in a peaceful sleep," he said in a brittle voice that seemed to strike from his eyes as well as his mouth.

Harvey, who had been hunched over the table, sat upright. "I ... I just thought no body, no crime. I didn't mean anything—"

"That's all right," Wally said, regretting his tone, "I know you meant well, but my job is to prove my innocence, not cover up a crime."

Harvey's body slumped into a relaxed posture. "What are you going to do then? How can you prove you had nothing to do with her murder before Antonelli comes a knockin'?"

"That's where you come in," J.C. said. "Letting us know what he's up to will be very helpful." J.C. hesitated. "Maybe you could check his files. See if he has one on Giovanna."

Harvey's eyebrows arched and his right eye pinched slightly closed at what one might consider a Herculean task. He paused, pondering the question. "Yeah, I could do that. But let me ask you a question, Wally."

"What's that?"

"Did Giovanna have a diary or letters that might incriminate Antonelli?"

The *oh shit* expression once again covered Wally's face. "I don't know," he said hesitatingly, thinking he didn't want to go back into Gigi's house for any reason. "She might have. She mentioned once that she kept receipts and records a ridiculously long time. She might have had a diary."

"Maybe you should—"

Wally interrupted Harvey. "I can't do it. I'm not going back in that house."

"Antonelli will really be watching Wally now," J.C. said. "By the way, can you casually chat with him to try to find out where he was the night before last?"

"Sunday night? Night of the murder? Yeah."

"Good. And do you know someone in the lab that you can trust who will test a bottle and wine glass for drugs?"

"I might be able to... I don't know. Maybe."

Wally thumped the table with his big paw. "All right then. We'll meet at the same time tomorrow."

J.C. glanced at his wristwatch. "I've got an errand to run tonight. Moldy's coming in at six." He grabbed Wally's attention by jabbing his thumb toward Ten Quarts. "Can you watch the bar until Moldy comes? I've got to get cleaned up."

Wally minimized J.C.'s question with a wave of his hand, "Absolutely. Besides, I don't want to go home anyway. No tellin' who might be waiting for me."

Harvey goosed his glasses and grabbed the arms of his chair. "I've got to go too," he said with a tiresome sigh. "Got a bedroom to repaint in my apartment."

Harvey and J.C. stood up at the same time and left, leaving Wally and Ten Quarts alone in the bar. Rather than trying to talk to Ten Quarts who, in his present state couldn't verbalize two-syllable words, Wally deceided to play some music. He walked to the reconstructed Wurlitzer, shoved a Washington into it and pressed the sequence of buttons, one, four, seven.

Wally slumped into his chair and took a long draw on his beer. A few seconds later the sound of the oldie's group, "The DelRonics", filled the room. He listened to his favorite group, staring off into space feeling the rhythm only they could provide. It wasn't until the third stanza that he started to sob.

Twas a wonderful day in September
That I knew my true love was found
And I know I'll always remember
That forever our love is bound
Pretending that you're still around

Ten Quarts, seemingly alert and responsive, turned around in his seat and peered through swollen, yellowish eyes at Wally. He then turned around and rejoined Old Overholt.

CHAPTER 6

Traffic on Route 79 South wasn't especially heavy at 7:00 p.m., mostly eighteen-wheelers delivering life sustaining essentials like Game Boys and iPods to shopping malls.

J.C. figured fifteen minutes driving time would bring him to exit #132 and downtown Fairmont. As he drove, he thought about Wally and tried to put himself in Wally's shoes. He couldn't comprehend what Wally must have felt finding the love of his life in that horrific situation. It must have shaken Wally's inner core; something never before being imaginable.

J.C. had heard bar-talk about Captain Antonelli, none of it good, and found it hard to believe that any man would murder his own wife and blame it on her lover, a perfect stranger. Maybe, he thought, Antonelli had some differences with Wally's nephew, Paul, and, with Antonelli's separation only three months old, found it the perfect time to inflict his misery on both of them.

J.C. respected and loved Wally who had become a father-figure to him. He knew Wally couldn't have killed Giovanna and would do whatever he could to prove Wally innocent, including buying a revolver—something he wouldn't do for anyone else—at a gun show in Fairmont, West Virginia.

Wally had provided J.C. with a computer printed description and picture of a replica of his revolver from a website he found. It was listed as an S&W model #14 K-38 Masterpiece 38 Special. Wally said it should be easy to find as millions were produced. The model was first introduced in 1947 and discontinued in 1982.

J.C. expressed concern about possible recriminations from buying the gun but Wally set him straight. Wally said gun shows in West Virginia operate on a *no questions asked, cash and carry basis* when buying a gun or even an assault rifle. No records were required to be kept, no background checks, no names, no waiting period—just cash.

J.C. turned off exit 132, onto route 250 at dusk when shadows were swooping down from the adjacent hills creeping over the West Virginia landscape. Three miles down the road he located the Marion County National Guard Armory. J.C. found a parking space across the road from the armory's jammed lot.

Five minutes later J.C. stood in a long line of men women and children—most dressed in either plaid or camouflage—waiting to pay their $5 entrance fee. A gray-haired woman, holding the hand of her grandson, wore a cap embroidered with *Benezette—God's Country* on its front. The little boy's slightly older sister wore an NRA hat.

The smell of raw tobacco coupled with the empty paper cups that the men were holding led J.C. to believe that it wasn't bubble gum that produced their lop-sided, bulbous cheeks.

J.C. endured the ten minutes it took waiting in line to make it through the entrance vestibule into the large exhibit area. The poster on the wall stated there would be more than 190 eight-foot tables. All were packed with guns, knives, ammunition, army surplus items, books, hunting supplies and other necessities of a civilized society. J.C. wondered where the mortars and rocket-launchers were. He surveyed the area and thought he would start near the entrance and criss-cross his way to the other side of the building, making sure to check every table for Wally's replacement revolver.

J.C. walked past dozens of tables looking for the pistol Wally needed to keep the constabulary from arresting him. In jail, Wally wouldn't have the time or the means to prove his innocence.

He noticed an M-1 rifle on one of the tables and remembered Wally talking about how he had been one of the last recruits to train on it, the most accurate rifle he had ever fired. Wally earned a trophy and numerous requests for sniper training for being the best shot in the basic training regiment at Fort Jackson, South Carolina. Wally said he refused the sniper training, but J.C. had his suspicions. The thought of buying the M-1 for Wally quickly disappeared as J.C. had only enough money for the revolver.

J.C. decided he needed a break after forty minutes of scanning seventy-five percent of the tables. He wandered through the tables to the food concession area where it looked like they were preparing for a wedding. City chicken, rigs-n-pigs (rigatoni and stuffed cabbage rolls), chipped chopped ham, jumbo and potato salad were on display. He waited five minutes to get served after asking for a soft drink and a dog. Walking away, he noticed Captain Antonelli at the end of the far line. He was easy to spot. At 6' 5" he stood above most of the crowd; the narrow streak of silver that parted his coal black hair was a dead giveaway. J.C. quickly headed in the opposite direction back to the table and continued his search, slurping his drink and stuffing his face with the frankfurter as he walked.

J.C. continued to check the tables for the .38 and watch Antonelli at the same time. Two rows away, he finally spotted the exact revolver Wally needed. He watched Antonelli leave the concession area and walk toward the other end of the building near the entrance.

J.C. purchased the revolver and browsed around other tables until he thought he saw Antonelli leave. He waited a few minutes until he felt it safe and headed for the exit.

J.C. was wrong. About twenty feet from the door he spotted Antonelli in a crowd. He thought the Captain may have glanced at him. He quickly turned away, sliding off into the crowd, hunkering behind the mass of a huge man dressed in cammo's until he reached the sidewalk. J.C. figured Antonelli probably didn't know him but wasted no time returning to his car. He quickly sped off, trying to leave as much distance as possible between him, the gun show, and Antonelli.

On the drive back, J.C. wondered if Antonelli would remember him at the gun show if Wally's murder case would ever make it to court. He might put two and two together and figure that he had bought a replica revolver for Wally.

CHAPTER 7

T he sound of ceramic scraping across brick broke the 3:00 a.m. silence. A gloved hand retrieved a key hidden under the potted geranium on the windowsill. A dark figure eyed the broken window and replaced the key. He reached through the empty pane and opened the back door to Giovanna Antonelli's house. Cautiously, the masked figure moved into the kitchen stepping on broken glass making crunching noises. He stopped and listened, waiting for his eyes to adjust to the darkness. He quickly pulled the shade on the only window in the room. He reached into an inside pocket of a knee-length black hooded raincoat and pulled out a small penlight flashlight. He followed the light's oval beam across the kitchen floor into the hallway and into Giovanna's bedroom.

Without hesitating, the intruder closed the door behind him and walked quickly across the room to the window. He twisted the plastic dowel rod closing the mini-blind and pulled the cord closing the drapes. He retraced his steps across the room and flipped a switch turning on the overhead light.

The intruder dashed to the nearest bedside table. He pulled out the top drawer and turned it over throwing the contents on the bed next to Giovanna's corpse. His hands raced through the debris as if playing the shell game—

feverishly trying to hide the pea from a greedy chump. Not finding what he was looking for, he grabbed the bed sheet and yanked it upwards, throwing the miscellany onto Giovanna's body. He repeated the same procedure with the remaining two drawers from the end tables making the bed his morbid worktable.

He frantically dropped to the floor and looked under the bed. Nothing. He raised the side of the mattress opposite where Gigi lie. He repeated the procedure near Gigi, flopping her body into the middle of the bed. Disappointed again, he ran to the closet. He thrust open one of the sliding doors, pulled the chain for the overhead light, and began inspecting the contents of the many boxes on the two shelves above the clothes rack. One by one he clawed through them throwing the empty boxes over his shoulder like an animal searching for food. He repeated this process on the other side of the closet and came up empty again. He turned both lights out and left the room. He paused in the hallway and headed for the living room.

At the end of the hall, and just before the living room, he entered a small windowless area Giovanna called her reading room. A couch and recliner took up most of the space on the opposite nine-foot wall. A hutch, crammed with books of all sizes and colors, sat atop a cherry desk. No other furniture, except for wall plaques and pictures, was present in the seven-foot deep room.

The dark figure closed the door, turned on the light and began rifling the desk. Pencils, papers, and other drawer contents found themselves momentarily airborne. Books didn't escape his wrath either. Each was opened and shook to possibly reveal any hidden contents. Finding nothing, he swatted at the plaques and pictures on the walls, checking for a hidden wall safe. He scuffed through the debris on the floor, turned off the light, and left the room.

The living room, although more than twice the size of the office, offered few hiding places. He overturned each piece of furniture, checked every pillow and cushion, sometimes cutting open the undersides of the chairs and couch. The stereo lost one of its twin speakers when he slammed it onto the floor, breaking it into a dozen pieces, after finding it a disappointment.

The framed pictures, mostly of Gigi, her face reflecting happier times, were smashed and the cardboard backing removed to reveal any hidden documents that might be behind the photos. The man had hoped to find what he was looking for by now and didn't want to spend a lot of time in the kitchen. But he trudged off in that direction alternately punching the walls with his fists, first with a left, and then a right, a left, right.

The first place he checked was the freezer section of the refrigerator. He opened all the aluminum and plastic wrapped packages. Next, he checked the bottoms of the vegetable and meat bins followed by a quick inspection under the unit with his penlight. He then checked the oven and the apace between the dishwasher and the counter, finding only dust bunnies.

The cabinets took the longest time—there were many and each had a protective shelf lining he checked under. The bread drawer, the linen drawer, between stacked trays and pans, all were hiding places. All had to be checked.

He sat down at the dinette table and started to peel a tangerine he appropriated from the fridge. He ripped away each piece of rind thinking about what he had to do if he didn't find what he was looking for. He didn't want to be under the investigative microscope. He would have to resort to a more desperate measure. While planning his next move, he looked over to his right and focused on a door. A pantry? Yes. He had initially thought that the door led to the outside.

His hopes brightened. He darted across the room. He opened the door to a small room jammed with shelving of stocked canned goods, boxes, jars and bottles. He rooted through all of them, finding nothing. After finishing his search, by checking the lining of a wall-hung ironing board, he realized he would have to go to plan "B" after all.

CHAPTER 8

B arbara Berthine pulled to a stop at the end of the driveway. She wrestled with gravity getting out of the old, red Dodge Colt. Her blue blouse and matching slacks strained to keep her flesh from billowing forth as she lumbered onto the back porch of Giovanna Antonelli's house.

Barbara cleaned Giovanna's house every third Wednesday at 8:00 a.m. As she fumbled for her key in her handbag, she noticed the broken pane on the kitchen door. She reached for the doorknob and noticed that the door was ajar. As she opened it, the morning sunlight shone over the kitchen floor and the strewn about contents that the intruder had left.

"Misses Antonelli," she called. "Misses Antonelli?" She repeated to no response.

She inched into the house, stepping on broken glass making a crunching sound. To her left, she noticed the pantry door open and its contents also on the floor.

"Misses Antonelli!" she yelled. "Is anyone here?"

Barbara stood motionless for a long thirty seconds before gathering enough courage to walk through the kitchen into the hallway. As she approached Giovanna's bedroom door, she stopped and leaned on the wall for support. She seemed drained, psychologically as well as physically. She finally gathered enough courage and, using the wall for support, shuffled to the bedroom door and peered in the room. It was dark; the drapes were pulled over the closed mini-blind. She studied the strange heap of clutter on the bed. And then she saw the arm. She held her hand to her mouth to keep from screaming, but she did anyway. She ran down the hallway, through the kitchen and out of the house not stopping to close the door. She drove two blocks away before stopping at a convenience store to call the police on her cell phone.

Harvey Stuhl walked down the hallway blowing on a hot cup of coffee when he noticed Sergeant Fiore gesturing excitedly with Captain Antonelli. The Captain ordered something to the sergeant as he ran out of his room and then out of the building.

Harvey approached the sergeant. "What's up sarge?"

"Captain's ex-wife...maybe. I don't know yet. A report just came in from an excited woman. Says there is a body in Giovanna's house."

"Misses Antonelli?"

"Looks that way. Hope not."

"Robbery?"

"Oh, that reminds me. Captain wants me to contact forensics. He's going to the scene to rope it off."

"Thanks." Harvey walked to his desk and punched in a number. "Wally, Harvey. Some woman called in a report. Found a body in Giovanna's house. Yeah, the Captain just left. Okay, see you later."

Wally knew the police would eventually want to talk to him about Gigi's murder, and hoped it would be sooner than later. Now he knew it would be sooner. He hated leaving her there that night, it was like leaving a fallen comrade behind—it just wasn't in his core. It just wasn't done.

He left his house through the back door, as usual, avoiding the main street. He walked to the corner of Alliquippa and McKee where he had left his car and headed for Ducheck's.

The 9:00 morning air was thick with humidity reminding Wally of Southeast Asia. He remembered seeing dead bodies, many in contorted grotesque positions, some with limbs blown off, faceless even headless. And he had dreams about them from time to time, but today his only thought was of Giovanna, his true love.

Wally thought he could be doing more to find the real murderer but he had to avoid the police. Maybe he should go back to Gigi's house and search for evidence; a diary, bank statements, papers or a file that would shed light on why someone would want to murder her. But he couldn't now knowing that Gigi's body was discovered. He had to stay away from her house at all costs to keep from being arrested.

But he knew he might be questioned. I'll just say, Wally thought, that we broke up a few days ago. Haven't seen her since. Why did we break up? Can't think of a reason. Even if I make up what I think is a legitimate reason, it will sound like I'm lying. The police will know I'm lying. But love doesn't lie. He hesitated, thinking of a way he might sound more convincing. I know. I'm old and sick. Surely they'll believe that. She's young and beautiful. She's... Wally stopped thinking about an alibi when Gigi's image again flashed into his consciousness.

Wally parked in Ducheck's rear lot and entered through the back door. J.C. was stocking the coolers with beer; he had already made coffee. Wally filled his favorite Steeler's mug with hot, steaming java and sat at the bar.

"Any new developments?" J.C. asked, his voice echoing in the metal cabinet.

"Yes, they found her.

J.C.'s eyes lit up like Charles Manson lamps.

Wally's nephew, Paul, entered the front door. He was a big man, not tall, six-foot one, but broad and muscular. He wore a dark blue jacket with gray slacks. A white shirt opened at the collar. A young uniformed officer walked obediently behind Paul, scanning the bar area like he was mentally digitizing information and storing it for future reference.

Paul walked up to Wally. "Uncle Wally. We've got to talk."

Wally nudged a barstool with his foot. "Have a seat."

Paul glanced at J.C. and then back at Wally before sitting down. He leaned toward Wally with sympathetic, soulful blue eyes. He looked into Wally's and said, "I've got bad news for you, Wally. Giovanna was found dead this morning."

Hearing Paul verbalize the fact that Gigi was dead seemed to make her death suddenly seem authentic. And since he had earlier become emotional thinking about Giovanna, Wally broke down, sobbing.

Wally momentarily composed himself. "What happened? How...?"

Paul stood up and reached for Wally's arm to lead him into the back room but Wally waved him off.

"Go on ahead, I'll be right back," Wally said. When Paul was out of earshot, Wally whispered to J.C. "Call Harvey. Find out what's going on at City Hall."

Wally took a deep breath, slowly slid off his barstool, and plodded toward the backroom. Wally wondered how he was going to handle this situation. The man who could be his son, the one who admired and adored him was the one that would take him in for questioning. The questioning of a murder. No, not just a murder, but the murder of Giovanna—his Giovanna.

Paul sat at the large, corner booth; the young officer was standing in front of the Wurlitzer flipping through music titles.

Wally slid in the booth opposite Paul. "What can you tell me about—."

"I can only tell you she was shot. Murdered. Chief Burke extended me the courtesy to break the news to you...and to bring you in for questioning."

"Questioning? Questioning for what? I didn't murder Gigi," Wally protested. He paused and then said, "This is Captain Antonelli's doing, isn't it?"

"No, Wally. It's police procedure. Questioning people close to a murder victim is standard policy. Others will be questioned as well as the investigation continues."

"Does that include Antonelli?"

"I can't say yet Wally. Let's take this one step at a time. I'm in your corner. I'll be watching your back."

Wally stood up. "Let's go. I'm ready."

"We have to stop by your place first. I have to bring in your pistol for testing by forensics."

Wally looked dumbfounded. "You don't think—?"

"No, Wally. It's standard procedure. And it will prove your pistol wasn't the murder weapon. It's for your protection." Paul wrapped his arm around Wally's shoulder. "Let's go, Wally."

CHAPTER 9

W ally burst through the large double steel doors into City Hall's police vestibule. "I hope this won't take long, I'm getting thirsty," Wally said, walking ahead of Paul into the lobby. "It's been a while since I was summoned to the *Gray Bar Hotel.*" They turned right at the receptionist's desk and entered the dispatch area. Wally stopped within five paces of the desk sergeant and waited for Paul to catch up.

Paul and Wally hadn't talked since their argument in the patrol car. Paul had insisted that Wally have an attorney present when questioned. Wally refused, saying he didn't have anything to hide. Paul pleaded that a lawyer was for Wally's protection because slips of the tongue are sometimes recorded in interrogation and would later be used against him.

"I didn't kill her!" Wally said. "No one can make me say any different or put me in a position that would make it look like I had anything to do with her murder. Besides, having an attorney present makes it look like I'm guilty."

Paul walked past Wally to the sergeant's desk; a large, dark, oak structure elevated a foot and a half above floor level amplifying the importance of the position of the man seated behind it. Paul cupped his hand around his mouth whispering details to Sergeant Fiore as to why

Wally was being questioned. Fiore wrote quickly, glancing up on occasion verifying what he had heard. After a few minutes, they nodded in agreement. Paul turned and walked toward Wally; the sergeant slid a paper in the typewriter and started typing. Paul glanced apologetically at Wally and motioned for him to follow as he walked off down a hallway.

———————

Paul stood in front of a two-way mirror looking into the interrogation room as if the mirror was a looking glass into the past. He remembered the days when Wally and his Uncle Ben, Wally's brother, took Paul fishing, to all the sports events, to the picnics and anywhere else they could when time permitted. He could see his mother, Rebecca, and Wally's first wife, Arlene sitting on the front porch of his home shortly before his fifteenth birthday. Ben and Arlene both died within a year. Paul remembered.

The observation room was small, not much wider than the six-foot mirror. Lieutenant Algie Steitzer stood next to Paul. It was common practice to have a witness present during a police investigation. Standing next to Steitzer made Paul nervous. He didn't like Steitzer at all. Paul knew that he was a suck-up and a close confidant to Captain Antonelli. He also knew Steitzer had covered up police misconducts and falsified evidence in the past under Antonelli's orders. And Paul knew Steitzer and the Captain were aware that he knew.

Paul watched his uncle being questioned by Detective Felix Stahlman. Paul knew Stahlman to be a good cop and a fair man and Paul didn't object to his interrogation of Wally, only Wally's decision to be there without representation.

The defiance on Wally's face as he was asked pointed questions, the wonderment he displayed at questions he considered absurd, and his resigned posture when the truth seemed to hit a nerve, showed Paul that Wally wished he had listened to him. An attorney would run interference for him, object to questions and stop the interview.

Paul worshipped Wally since childhood. And when Paul's father, Ben, died at a young age, Wally became a father to him when Rebecca married Paul's stepfather, Sam Andrews. Paul remembered Ben telling him of Wally's Vietnam War exploits, about the special ops unit he was in, the medals and commendations, and how he was captured and imprisoned in a bamboo cage. He escaped five torturous months later. He foraged for food and evaded the enemy for six weeks until finding a LRRP, a long range reconnaissance patrol, of the 1st Cavalry Division.

Wally didn't talk about the war and he wasn't talking now. Detective Stahlman was swearing, his face red. He wasn't getting the answers he wanted. Stahlman was known for his thorough interviewing techniques but Wally, although upset over losing the love of his life, remained cool under Stahlman's barrage. Obviously, Stahlman wasn't familiar with Wally's past. Wally had been interrogated by the best—and for a lot longer.

Paul could tell from the interview that Stahlman probably knew Wally didn't have anything to do with Giovanna Antonelli's murder. When Wally intimated Captain Antonelli's involvement, Stahlman's face seemed to connect with the possibility.

Did Wally know something about Captain Leonard Antonelli? Why didn't Wally tell Paul? Did Stahlman know something? And why wasn't Antonelli at the questioning? Paul hadn't thought about it before, but Antonelli *could* have killed his wife, the wife that filed a PFA, protection from abuse, against him and slept with another man—Wally. And then there was the past friction between Paul and Leonard about Leonard's police misconduct. He wouldn't put it past Antonelli to cause him collateral damage as well.

The four offices of Pennsylvania House Representative Darby Davis were strategically located throughout
the 212th Legislative District, but he wanted only one
office—in Washington D.C. as a U.S. Senator. Davis was
in a tight campaign with incumbent Democratic Senator
H. Roland Stampfer of Upper Townsend. Stampfer's
opposition to the war in Iraq prompted Davis to throw his
hat into the ring.

A door led to the back room of Darby's main office in
Mononville where the real business was conducted.
Darby's wooden swivel chair creaked under his two-
hundred and thirty pounds. He resembled a reclining
beached whale, his clothing straining under the forces of
gravity holding back the onslaught of flabby flesh. He was
studying recent polling figures that had him two points
ahead in the senatorial race when Patsy Ciccione, his
campaign manager, walked in.

"I was just over at the Court House checking on the
Steffy property," Patsy said, "and I heard Giovanna
Antonelli was found murdered."

Darby lurched forward in his chair. "What? Giovanna?" In a whispered voice he asked. "Leonard?"

"No, they think Wally Gustafson did it. The cops just
interviewed him."

Darby strained as he stood up—all five foot nine of
him—and walked to the front of the desk. "Not Wally.
He's not the type—"

"The police didn't think so either. They released
him."

Darby sauntered around his desk and stopped at his
high-back wooden chair. "Okay Patsy, I'll get back to you
later."

As Patsy headed for the door, Darby said, "Close the
door please." He waited for the door to snap shut and
picked up the phone.

Paul had been in Lieutenant Steitzer's office on many different occasions, this time it was different. Wally was a murder suspect and Paul knew how the long arm of the law worked. In this case the law was Lieutenant Steitzer and Captain Antonelli. They wouldn't rest until Wally was proven guilty. Wally was the only one on their radar screen.

But they would have to wait. After three hours of questioning and taking a polygraph test, which Wally passed with flying colors, Wally was released.

Paul and Wally left the building without saying a word; Paul pointed to his Chrysler. Wally sat stoic in the passenger seat looking straight ahead. Paul started the car and adjusted his seatbelt. He looked over at Wally and said, "Well, how'd it go mister know it all?"

"Not bad, I could have gone for a couple'a weeks, I suppose."

Paul put the Chrysler in gear and pulled away. "I don't doubt that you could Wally, but why? One unintentional slip of the tongue and it would be used against you in court, innocent or not."

Wally dropped his head in resignation. "Yeah, I know. I shouldn't have answered any questions without an attorney." He raised his head and pointed at the sky. "God knows I didn't do it; that's all that counts. That's what I was thinking, Paul. That's why I guess I went in there alone. I felt I didn't have anything to fear."

"So you won't be going in alone in the future?"

"Right, I'll get an expensive mouthpiece."

——— ———

Wally unlocked the door, walked through the living room, the dining room and into the kitchen. The metal door of the sink cabinet creaked as Wally opened it. He reached in and pulled out a bottle of Bellows Bourbon. He retrieved a shot glass from an overhead cupboard. Both the bottle and glass hit the table simultaneously. Before he sat down, Wally turned the radio on to a local oldies station.

That went well, he thought, pouring a double into the glass. The North Vietnamese couldn't make me admit to things I didn't do. What makes these tin badges think they could make me confess to a murder? A murder of the woman I loved. He downed the double and refilled it immediately. He threw down the double and remembered he hadn't eaten. He slapped a one-half inch portion of Braunschwager on wheat bread and splashed mustard on it. A slice of onion was followed by a layer of Triscuits and another slice of bread.

Wally ate, drank, and listened to the oldies for hours. He looked out the window as it was starting to get dark. He thought of Giovanna when he heard the lyrics to one of his favorite songs.

We'll meet again at the end of night
And savor again our love's delight
For at the beginning we knew it was right
Meeting like this at dusk's twilight

It was twilight time for Wally also, when his head hit the paper plate his sandwich had been on.

CHAPTER 10

From the looks of Giovanna Antonelli's study, you wouldn't have known it was tossed by a veteran police officer. After his 8X4 shift ended, Captain Leonard Antonelli began the task of searching his estranged wife's former work area starting with a black metal file cabinet. The bottom two drawers were checked relatively easily. They contained items left behind upon her hasty departure; sneakers, workout clothes, a fake potted plant, photo albums, and desk ornaments to name a few. The third drawer went even faster as it contained office materials: reams of paper, file folders, staples etc.

The last drawer contained many files under various folder headings. Antonelli had meticulously fingered through every file under listings one would find in the average home: receipts, warranties, medical, reunions, small appliances, etc. until 7:00 p.m. Not finding what he wanted he decided to take a dinner break.

———————

Luciano's bar business flourished in the 60s and 70s when the mills were producing three shifts of steel. But foreign subsidized steel, strained union-management relations, and failure of the steel industry to modernize their equipment made a dramatic change in the steel industry in general and on the local economy in particular.

That's when Les Rosetti learned to become a chef and turned Luciano's into an upscale restaurant. After a few slow years his parking lot was filled with Cadillacs, Lincolns, Jaguars and other expensive cars from the surrounding counties in southwestern Pennsylvania.

Les mimed his words as he talked to an elderly couple seated at a table at the far wall, near a latticed partition that separated the bar from the restaurant. When Les saw Leonard come in, he motioned toward Leonard's favorite table in the rear of the room.

Harvey Stuhl peered through the latticework past the frail couple and watched Les escort Leonard to his table.

Les pulled a chair for Antonelli and took his order. Les served his patrons personally, demonstrating that he was part of their extended family and gave them that *extra special touch.* The pasta stained apron added to the homey effect. Les went into the kitchen to prepare Fettucine Alfredo, Antonelli's favorite.

Antonelli sat at the rear of the room as all cops do, being able to see everything in view if a felony occurs, or from sheer paranoia from potential reprisals from previously arrested criminals. His eyes fell on Mayor August "Auggie" Majewski seated at a table with Paden Tucker and his wife, Matilda.

August Majewski sat upright, his back against the booth. The lower portion of his belly sprawled on the table as if it had avalanched from his torso. Tucker, a thin, squirrelly man with slitty eyes, sat on the other side of the booth with his chubby, ever-smiling, ever-agreeing wife.

What a pair, Antonelli thought, a corrupt mayor and a corrupt ass-wipe for state representative Darby Davis. He knew them very well. Well enough to be seated with them, but that might confirm tax payer's suspicions that they had more than a civil servant relationship.

Mayor Majewski literally fought his way into office holding control over the city with an iron fist. He browbeat and threatened members of council, demanded kickbacks and campaign contributions from city employees. He did, however, provide jobs and services with his political connections throughout the state. Majewski gave Antonelli his job and Antonelli was grateful. And the mayor controlled Antonelli by promoting him to the top police position under Chief Burke who didn't know what was going on due to his senility—a win-win situation for the Mayor and Antonelli.

Tucker, however, wasn't on Antonelli's Christmas card list. Antonelli considered him a parasite, feeding off Darby Davis' fame. Antonelli watched Tucker trying to impress his wife and the mayor, traits learned, he thought, from Davis who was a master of impression. But why did Davis take Tucker under his wing? Surely not because of his affiliation with Freddy "Fish Lips" Caruso, a lieutenant in the Labruscia family. Yeah right, he chuckled to himself.

Antonelli noticed a person with a familiar gait approaching him, Earsoff "Funny Bone" Tecza. He walked as if he had an injured leg, but at the same time his gait had a peppy strut to it like a wanna-be dawn tawn homee.

Without asking, Earsoff pulled a chair from Antonelli's table and seated himself. "Looks like the big shots are keeping an eye on us," he said, nodding his thin squirrelly face toward the Mayor and Paden Tucker.

Antonelli glared toward their table. "Yeah, Tucker's the Mayor's Weight Watcher's counselor. Checking on the fat bastard's calories."

Earsoff managed a laugh through nicotine-stained teeth.

"Care for a drink?" Antonelli asked.

"No. Just came in to drop this off." Earsoff pulled out a bulging, business envelope from his jacket, put it on the table and slid it over.

Antonelli grinned through the toothpick in his mouth, picked up the envelope and put it in his jacket pocket. "OK, I'll take care of this." He patted the bulge in his jacket.

Earsoff got up to leave.

"See you next week," Antonelli said.

Earsoff turned and managed an attempt at a salute. He walked to the Mayor's table and handed similar envelopes to the Mayor and Paden Tucker.

Antonelli smiled with each bite of Fettucine.

CHAPTER 11

Antonelli removed a plastic toothpick from the padding of the sun visor and picked remnants of spinach salad from his teeth. Now that his favorite meal had satisfied his hunger and provided a needed break, he was ready to go back to work searching Giovanna's study.

As Antonelli drove home, the streetlights' stroboscoping fluorescence illuminated his crooked smile and a 2" scar on his right temple. He knew he only had Giovanna's computer to check. If he couldn't find what he was looking for—nobody could. He turned off Marguerite Avenue onto Shawnee. Halfway down the block he pressed the transmitter on his garage door opener. He idled up the asphalt driveway to the attached garage. The door slowly opened as he approached the house, revealing a large, well-kept, double wide service area.

Three hundred horsepower slowly pulled the Chevy Nova into the large open space. Antonelli killed the engine and punched the transmitter on his visor closing the door. A dark figure dashed from behind a nearby evergreen shrub and rolled under the closing door and then under the rear bumper of the street rod. Antonelli exited the Nova and entered the house through a rear door.

Antonelli pushed the power button on Giovanna's computer. A few seconds later, the desktop appeared on the screen with icons revealing Gigi's interest in art, publishing, photography, music, and others. The time on the task bar displayed 9:30 p.m.

Antonelli wasn't a computer nerd by any means, but managed to open and scan files he thought were of interest. After an hour, and only scratching the surface of the multitude of files, he decided it would take too long to check all of them. And besides, he thought, techs at police headquarters could check the files at lightning speed and recover any files that were erased. That's when he decided to remove the hard drive and put it in a safe place. After all, the information he was looking for would *have* to be on it.

Antonelli confidently strode to the garage door and creaked it open. He flipped a light switch that started a fluorescent light fixture flickering and then snapped on illuminating the immediate area around the work bench. The man in black, who had rolled under the garage door, quietly sat on a folding chair at the far corner of the garage in relative darkness.

Antonelli sauntered to the huge bench and laid the hard drive on top of it. On the left side of the table, and toward its rear, he slid open a wooden panel exposing a door to a built-in safe. He knelt down and spun a sequence of four numbers on the combination lock and flung the door open.

Anntonelli didn't hear or see the man approaching him.

"So, that's where you keep your valuables," the man said.

Antonelli whirled around, instinctively reaching for his glock, but he had already taken it off. He was surprised when he looked at the man. "You?"

That's when the bullet struck Leonard in the middle of his forehead. Antonelli's body hit the concrete block wall microseconds after chunks of bone and gray brain matter. The blast echoed off the concrete walls for seconds.

The man walked through the fog created by the burnt gunpowder—the strong smell of cordite in the air—waving the smoke away from his face.

The sound of tempered steel broke the silence as the sharp blade of a Bowie knife left its scabbard. The man retrieved the chair he was sitting on and placed it near the desk. After struggling to display Antonelli's body in the chair, the man slit Leonard's throat.

He emptied the contents of the safe and placed them on the worktable. He seemed surprised at what he found: birth certificates, marriage license, house mortgage, professional certificates, and a small notebook. He glanced at the first page of the notebook, smiled and put it in his pocket. He threw the other papers at the corpse.

He glanced at the hard drive and then focused on it, his eyes opening in discovery. He thrust the hard drive into his other coat pocket and left.

CHAPTER 12

Lieutenant Algie Steitzer watched seconds ticking away through the nicotine stained bezel on the large wall clock. The hands registered 7:50 a.m. Algie started to sweat. Captain Antonelli was twenty minutes late for the 8X4 watch.

If the captain is off duty, or late, it was Lt. Steitzer's responsibility to take over—thus the scrambled nerves. Algie Steitzer was a suck-up's suck-up. He used his polished, low self-esteem to shirk responsibility from the day he left the police academy. It was obvious to everyone. The patrol officers spelled his first name A L G A E, referring to the *green moss* that grew on immovable shaded rocks in stream beds.

Algie made the last of seven calls to the captain's house. No answer.

He approached the duty sergeant's desk like he had on similar occasions and said, "Sergeant Fiore, I'd like you—"

Sergeant Allan Fiore reached for the folder of morning reports and duty assignments Algie was holding and finished Algie's sentence. "—To start today's watch," and then smiled a crooked smile as he grabbed the folder.

"I've called the captain seven times. He hasn't answered and—"

"Yeah, I know. You have to go check on the captain," Fiore said, trying to mask his sarcasm.

No algae would grow on the soles of Steitzer's shoes as he hot-footed it to his unmarked Ford Crown Victoria in the parking garage. A squeak of rubber reverberated against the cement walls as 300 horsepower yanked the souped-up—never-in-a car-chase—cruiser out of his priority parking space and out of eyesight from the men in blue.

He knew where to find the key. Algie tipped the 3 foot high terra cotta pot containing the climbing rose Giovanna bought last spring. He swept the key from underneath the huge vase, dusted off his hands, and opened the door.

The last time Algie entered Leonard's house he surprised Giovanna who had been working in her study. She said she didn't want to be disturbed and had disconnected the main phone line. She did this frequently, usually after fighting with Leonard the previous evening. Algie had never asked Leonard about Giovanna's behavior.

"Leonard," Algie called, almost apologetically not wanting to interrupt possible lovemaking. He moved to the hallway that led to the bedroom and called again. And again when he took a few steps into the hallway and looked into the empty study and into the bedroom. The bed hadn't been slept in. He appealed to the premises again, louder this time, walking past the living room and into the kitchen.

From the kitchen, Algie opened the door that led into the dark, windowless garage. He snapped on the light switch. Large shapes slowly strobed into view as the fluorescent lights flickered on the silver Chevy Nova, the desk, the *body* in the chair.

Algie involuntarily lurched backwards against the wall, trying to retreat from the horrible scene. His legs weakened and buckled as he slowly slid to the floor in a sitting position.

Five feet from him, Leonard Antonelli's body was displayed in a wooden folding chair. His throat was deeply cut from ear to ear, his head, held only by a few tendons, hung over the top rail of the chair at a 270 degree angle with his body and turned toward Algie. Leonard's glazed eyes were open and looking at Algie— with a bullet hole between them.

Algie tried to stand up, but couldn't. He half-crawled and floundered about finally lurching to the door. He managed to get to his feet. He staggered into the living room and collapsed on the couch. The phone was next to him but he couldn't pick it up. Not yet. He was frozen with terror.

He wondered what he had gotten himself into. Are the illegal activities he helped Antonelli accomplish coming back to bite him in the ass? Antonelli was his boss and he was connected. And Algie was under Antonelli's protection, but now Leonard was dead. How long could he last, he thought. I'm not shit to nobody now. He didn't even know the big guys on a first name basis. He felt nauseous. Alone. Wait a minute, he thought. I'm a cop. I'm now in charge of the whole force. I'll surround myself with cops and their protection. He looked at the phone, picked it up and called the station.

————

Harvey switched off the phone. He had just called Wally telling him about the meeting he witnessed between Antonelli, the mayor, and the squirrelly-faced man at Luciano's bar. He was standing at the file cabinet, running his fingers over the labeled tabs when a commotion broke out in the hall. He peered over his glasses as he walked out of the room.

A man carrying a broom shuffled toward him. "Bert," Harvey said to the janitor, "what's going on?"

"Kennywood's open."

Harvey turned around as if Bert was talking to another person. He wasn't.

"What...?

"Kennywood's open. Your fly's down."

Harvey's cheeks reddened as he straightened himself. "Kennywood?"

"Yeah Kennywood, it's a burgh thing. Bert's face sobered. "I heard Sergeant Fiore talking to Stahlman. He said Steitzer went to check on Antonelli and found him dead."

"Dead? What happened?" Harvey asked, pushing his glasses against his face.

Bert leaned forward and whispered, "Algie found him shot between the eyes. And get this. His throat was slashed from ear to ear. The Mononville Slasher is back".

"Wow," Harvey said. "The Slasher. I've heard about the Mononville Slasher." He walked back into the room and picked up the phone.

CHAPTER 13

Over a hundred years ago, when Mononville's one-room jailhouse moved to the newly built city hall, the chief of police might have fancied a new desk and a few chairs for his office.

Or hung a few pictures on the walls to compliment family pictures on his cluttered desk.

Or interviewed criminal suspects before him.

The room's present occupant, however, couldn't care less about the adornment of or the duties of his office. Chief Angus "The Bull" Burke suffered from early onset Alzheimer's disease.

Lieutenant Algie Steitzer had been instructed by Captain Antonelli how to take care of the chief and his office. His duties: bringing the chief his morning coffee, briefing him on important cases, tidying up his office, and making sure the chief was properly dressed for ceremonial occasions and important announcements.

Today was such a day.

Seated in front of the chief were Detective Paul Andrews, Lieutenant Algie Steitzer, Mayor August Majewski and Representative Darby Davis who looked like he was ready to take the stage and jump into his oratorical routine as to why he should be elected Pennsylvania's next U.S. senator.

Today the chief spoke first. "Gentlemen. I called you together today because—" Angus reached into his vest pocket and fumbled for a pair of reading glasses. He jostled them into place and started to read from a paper he had placed on his otherwise pristine desktop. "—One of our own was brutally murdered. Captain Leonard Antonelli was found this morning..."

The chief jutted his head forward the obligatory six inches that older people do in order to see or hear better. He then pushed the paper away trying to focus on the typed words prepared by Lieutenant Steitzer.

Representative Darby Davis nodded to Mayor Majewski who stood up, nodded in respect to Angus and said, "Excuse me chief. Maybe Lieutenant Steitzer should report on Captain Antonelli's murder since he was the first officer on the scene."

Relieved, Chief Burke quickly sat down

Lieutenant Steitzer sprung from his chair and took a position next to the chief facing the inquisitive faces in front of him. His voice cracked as he started the briefing by introducing himself followed by the time and location of the incident. His eyes engaged the chief as well as the audience as he started to put on a show for the mayor and Representative Davis. He referred to his rarely used note-pad as he explained why he thought it necessary to check on the captain. Steitzer embellished the facts, stating that Antonelli had received threatening phone calls. The truth is the calls were from a local ladies group and a Boy Scout troop, both soliciting funds.

The mayor and Representative Davis glanced at each other.

Algie described arriving at the captain's house, entering it—not stating how he was privy to the location of the house key— and surveyed the premises. His hands started to tremble as he read from the page that described the murder scene.

He stopped momentarily and grabbed an 18 x 24 inch poster board he had previously prepared and placed it on an easel a few feet in back of him. The drawing resembled an architect's floor plan showing the measurements and layout of the garage. With a small hand-held laser Algie pointed to the entrance doors, the vehicle, tool cabinets, and storage areas.

Darby Davis fired a concerned look at Augie Majewski when the red dot of the laser landed on the workbench. Algie explained that the safe in the bench was open and empty.

The look of concern on the representative's face quickly changed to one of surprise and shock when Steitzer described the presentation of Antonelli's body and the gaping throat wound.

"His head was hanging by only a few tendons!" The mayor almost jumped out of his chair. "Oh my God," he said. "The Slasher's back."

The mayor remembered the unsolved murders of the two reputed prostitutes in 1998. Hilary Jefferson was found in an alley in the red-light district of town with her throat cut so deeply that the head was almost severed. The next day, Roxainne Giannamore was found in a nearby alley in the same condition. The details of the wounds were kept from the public to avoid panic. The Slasher murders ceased after Roxanne's death.

"We have to stop this problem. This Slasher," boomed Darby Davis. The fact that Roxanne was the sister of Albert Giannamore who was associated with his aide, Paden Tucker, might reflect on his political career; and that always came first. "Are there any suspects?"

Steitzer said, "We're looking into it."

"Looking into it?" The mayor said, his voice reaching a crescendo. "What about Wally Gustafson? Wasn't he a person of interest in Giovanna Antonelli's murder?"

Steitzer fumbled through his notes. "Yes, we questioned him earlier—"

"And released him," Paul said. "Wally didn't murder Giovanna. There was no evidence to accuse him and besides, he passed a voluntary polygraph test."

Mayor Majewski clasped his hands together. "Maybe, maybe not. Maybe Wally didn't murder Givanna as you stated, detective. But that doesn't mean he didn't murder Leonard."

Paul started to open his mouth but stopped when the mayor raised his hand in a halting motion.

"Maybe Leonard freaked out and did murder his wife. Wouldn't that give Wally motive for revenge? Maybe Wally, in a rage, flashed back on a Vietnam killing field and reverted to his old ways. Maybe Wally's the Slasher."

The mayor hadn't forgotten Wally's military history. After all, he participated in the awards ceremony when former Mayor Richard "The Lionhearted" Sonafelt conferred letters of appreciation upon Wally.

"That's a lot of maybes," Paul said through gritted teeth.

The timing seemed right for Steitzer to take the bull—not Angus the Bull—by the horns. "We'll bring him in for questioning. I'll have—"

Paul interrupted. "As a favor to me and respect for my rank and service to the community, give me until seven o'clock to bring my uncle in."

Steitzer looked at the mayor for approval who nodded in the affirmative.

"Okay," Steitzer said. "I'll be waiting."

———————

The card room was located on the second floor of J.C. DuCheck's Bar. It was the previous owner's mother-in-law's apartment and separate from J.C.'s living quarters. The room was perfect for gambling. It had a private entrance that insulated it from the bar and, more importantly, the liquor control board agents. It also had its own bathroom and kitchenette. The room was one of the selling points when J.C. bought the bar. The only change J.C. made to the room was installing a secret entrance from his bedroom closet into the card room.

Only four people had a key to the apartment: J.C., Paul, Harvey and Wally, who just used his key to enter the apartment. Harvey had called Wally fifteen minutes earlier telling him about Leonard Antonelli's murder. Wally knew the police would be coming after him. He felt he had to leave home and sequester himself in a quiet place to give him time to figure out what was going on.

Wally walked through the kitchen, past the card table in the middle of the living room and stood next to the couch, looking through the slats of the Venetian blind. Harvey had told him earlier that he was going to be surveilled when he called about Algie finding the body. Wally twisted a plastic rod closing the slats when he decided no one was watching. He collapsed on the couch. He crossed his left arm over his eyes, shutting out the remainder of light and any bad situations that he thought might enter his consciousness.

This can't be possible, Wally thought. Leonard Antonelli has to be the murderer. Who else would want Giovanna dead? It was a perfect plan for Leonard to kill his estranged wife and put the blame on him. Wally was there and his pistol was there. Someone else had to be after him, someone who wanted him to suffer through the death of a loved one and the prosecution of murdering a police officer.

Wally's mind wandered. He imagined the murdering dark figure standing in a thick mist, his back turned so Wally couldn't see his face. An unseen enemy waiting to jump out of the darkness like Charlie, the name given to the Viet Cong by the American G.I.'s. Wally tried, but couldn't figure out who would perpetuate such heinous crimes.

Unable to think clearly, Wally spent the rest of the afternoon watching T.V. and playing solitaire.

CHAPTER 14

Wally was seated across from Paul in their favorite back room booth at Ducheck's. "I already know," Wally said. "Harvey called as soon as he heard."

"Did he tell you I have to bring you in at seven o'clock?"

J.C. walked around the corner carrying three Iron City Light's.

"That gives us two-and-a-half-hours to figure out who the real killer is."

Paul took a draw from his bottle. "I wish it were that simple."

"What's going to happen, Paul?" Wally's eyes reflected his nervousness.

"Procedure has to be followed. Steitzer will make sure of that. He *does* know the manual inside out. After all, he's had plenty of time to read it."

"What's the procedure?" J.C. asked.

As soon as the word procedure floated out of J.C.'s mouth, Harvey strolled around the corner into the back room. "Did I hear the word procedure? You must be talking about Steitzer." He pushed his glasses against his face.

"That's right," Paul said. "Procedure. First they'll interview you. You can talk directly to them, like you mistakenly did before, or have an attorney present,"

"What should I do?" Wally asked.

"Get an attorney," Harvey blurted. "Don't fool with these shitheads."

Harvey's statement surprised J.C..

"Definitely," Paul said. "I'll call Bernie "the attorney" Eisner. We'll wait for his direction before answering any questions."

Wally slowly shook his head. "But won't it look like I'm guilty if I need an attorney?"

Before Paul could answer, J.C. interjected, "Don't you watch Boston Legal? An attorney keeps you from putting your foot in your mouth. From digging a hole you can't escape—"

"All of the above," Paul said. "It's your right to have an attorney. Not to get you off from something you did, but to protect your innocence from what you didn't do."

Harvey pulled his shoulders back in pride. "I couldn't have said it better myself. And don't forget, Paul, if an attorney isn't present, the questioning can go on for hours and hours."

Paul nodded.

Wally seemed reassured. "What's next?"

Paul took another draw on his beer. "While they're questioning you, they'll be canvassing the area around Giovanna's house and interviewing neighbors. C S I techs will be collecting physical evidence, viewing, photographing and measuring the crime scene, and doing whatever else they feel is necessary."

"How long does this take?"

"The police work will take days. Your questioning should only take about fifteen minutes."

Wally looked puzzled. "Should?"

"They don't have anything to hold you on. Bernie will quickly determine that there is no evidence and ask if they're filing a complaint. When they say no, and they will, you're free to go."

J.C. threw down a shot of Jim Beam, one of the few shots of hard stuff he had ever drunk, wiped his mouth and said, "Well, we know Wally didn't murder Giovanna or Leonard. Who did?"

Harvey smoothed his hair. "We all thought Leonard murdered his wife. We were waiting for the cops to investigate and prove that he did, in fact, murder Giovanna. He took off his glasses and flattened his brows with spit. "And now this had to happen."

"It points the finger at me," Wally said. "It looks like Leonard murdered his wife out of jealously and I murdered him out of revenge."

Paul held up a finger as if he had an important statement to make. "It looks that way except for one thing." He looked around as if waiting for someone to verbalize what he was thinking. No one did. "The modus operandi." Paul waited another second. The others looked at each questioningly. "The methods were different. Giovanna was shot. Antonelli had his throat slashed."

J.C. grabbed Wally's arm. "I know you didn't murder anyone Wally," He then looked at Paul. "But couldn't the same person be responsible for both murders?"

Paul responded. "Any murderer could use a gun; it's a distant and impersonal method to kill someone. But a knife—?" He gestured with his hand like he was holding a knife. "—is very close and personal. And to slash someone's throat—" Paul wiped his imaginary knife across J.C.'s throat. "—takes a completely different personality."

"I don't understand," Harvey said. "Are you saying there are two different murderers?"

"Things aren't as they appear." Paul said. "It appears that Wally murdered Leonard. But we all know he didn't, right?" Everyone nodded. "And it appears that Wally is the nineteen ninety-eight Slasher, right?" They nodded again. "Then who stands to gain by framing Wally for Leonard's murder *and* by making it appear that Wally is the Slasher?"

"The real Slasher," Harvey blurted out.

Paul pointed a finger at Harvey. "One free drink for Sherlock Harvey."

"So the Slasher murdered both Giovanna and Leonard." J.C. said.

"Not necessarily," Paul said. The other three looked at each other in confusion.

"Someone other than the Slasher *might* have murdered Giovanna, possibly Leonard. He would have been the logical suspect. Jealousy of losing a woman to another man is a powerful motive. This would be the perfect opportunity for the Slasher to frame Wally by murdering Leonard in the same method as the Slasher."

Harvey indexed his glasses to his face. "So either way you look at it, we have to find who the real Slasher is. Where do we start? Oh, by the way. I saw Leonard before he was murdered." The others waited for him to continue. He was at Luciano's for dinner. I saw him take an envelope from a man."

"Who was he?" asked Paul.

"Don't know. I watched from the bar through a lattice partition. I couldn't see who it was."

"Who else was there?"

"The mayor and his wife. And a thin guy, I don't know who."

"That might be a lead," J.C. said.

"Maybe," Paul said. "We'll have to talk tomorrow. Wally is due at City Hall."

CHAPTER 15

H e sat in the far corner of the Chief's office waiting to
swoop in like a vulture. Instead of being covered
with feathers, ADA Jack "stealie-eyes" Markel's exterior
was covered with a Sears' $150.00 dark blue suit.

Lieutenant Steitzer took charge of the proceedings.
Detective Stahlman sat to Steitzer's left in a subordinate
presence.

Wally and Bernard (Bernie the attorney) Eisner sat
in front of the Chief's desk.

Paul had previously dropped Wally off at the station.
He wasn't invited for Wally's questioning and made
arrangements with Bernie to drop Wally off at Ducheck's
later that evening.

After Steitzer's introduction of those present, he
opened the top drawer of the Chief's desk and reached for
a tape recorder that the chief had used for interrogations.

Detective Stahlman grabbed the Lieutenant's arm
and shook his head as if telling a child *no-no* and
whispered a reminder that Wally was to be questioned,
not interrogated.

Jack Markel's stealie-eyes noticed Steitzer's
confusion and winced. He didn't like evening trips far
from the county seat to watch irresponsibility. District
Attorney Russ Kirby was retiring at the end of the year

and Markel wanted his position. That meant prosecuting *and winning* cases.

Lieutenant Steitzer cleared his throat with a high-pitched cough and directed his first question at Wally.

"Where were you Wednesday night, the seventh of August?" Steitzer referred to his notes. "From eight to midnight?"

Wally looked at Bernie. Bernie had previously instructed Wally to wait for his approving nod to answer any questions. Bernie nodded.

"I was at Ducheck's Bar from seven P M to midnight."

"The seventh of August?" Steitzer asked.

"That's correct."

Stahlman spoke as the Lieutenant was beginning to mouth his next word. "Can you provide us with names of witnesses verifying your presence at this establishment?"

With the Captain's position vacant, Lieutenant Steitzer was the logical successor, but he was incompetent and the mayor knew it. That left Steitzer, Stahlman, and Paul Andrews as possible replacements. But Paul was the nephew of the suspected Slasher. So why wouldn't Stahlman make his presence known with a county ADA who might put in a good word for him?

Stahlman seemed pleased with the provocative question he had asked—until he noticed the scowl on Lieutenant Steitzer's face.

Wally looked to Bernie for permission to answer.

Bernie took out a sheet of paper and said, "I have a list of the patrons present at Ducheck's Bar who will verify my client's presence from seven P M to midnight on the day in question." He referred to his notes. "The seventh of August."

Bernie reached over the desk and handed the sheet to the lieutenant.

The distance between the lieutenant's eyes narrowed as he scanned the list.

"Ludgie Matta? Rusty Evans? Ten quarts Petty?" He came to a name he didn't understand. "Stench! What kind of names are these? What kind of hooligans hang out at this bar...Ducheck's? And where are the telephone numbers where we can reach them?" Authority has its privileges and Steitzer, a religious right winger, would amplify anything he could to display himself in a righteous posture.

"Sorry Lieutenant," Bernie said. "We haven't been able to produce their telephone numbers until we determine their given names."

"You haven't determined their names yet?" Steitzer asked.

Wally leaned over and whispered something into Bernie's ear.

"It's just come to my attention that we do, in fact, have a name. It's Michael Evans AKA Rusty Evans, councilman from the fourth district."

The Lieutenant sat back in his seat, seemingly amazed at Bernie's answer.

Bernie continued. "And that answers your question as to the nature of Ducheck's clientele.

Flustered, Steitzer rummaged through his notes, looking for something that had apparently made a connection with his memory.

"Here it is," he said. "Do you own a handgun?" Steitzer looked at Wally.

Wally waited for Bernie's nod. "Yes."

"What is the make and model of your handgun?"

Bernie interrupted. "What's the relevance of Wally's handgun? Wally was questioned, given a polygraph test, and released after the Giovana Antonelli murder."

Steitzer managed a faint smile. "Leonard Antonelli was also shot, mister Eisner. I'd like to know the make and model of your client's handgun."

Bernie nodded.

Wally stifled a smile knowing he would be handing in a replica of his revolver. "It's a thirty eight caliber Smith and Wesson Model Fourteen K thirty eight Masterpiece."

"Is there anything else? My client has had enough for one day."

"That's all for now mister Gustafson. Don't leave town."

Wally and Bernie got up and started to leave.

"Oh, and by the way, Sergeant Fiore will follow you to your house where you will surrender your handgun."

Wally waited for verification from Bernie. Bernie shrugged his shoulders. Wally nodded in the affirmative. Bernie motioned with a tilt of his head and a motion of his hands that the meeting was over and they left the building.

Wally was glad to leave the police station, but the feeling was short-lived when Albert Giannamore rushed past Paul and up to Wally, calling him the Slasher and tried to grab him. Wally parried his advance with a martial arts move that spun Albert off to the side. Albert regained his balance and tried to attack Wally again only to be directed elsewhere. Paul, not wanting Wally to be involved, grabbed Albert with help from Sergeant Fiore.

"Hold it Albert," Paul said, standing between Wally and Albert, "Wally didn't kill anyone."

"He killed my sister. He has to pay. He's the Slasher."

A crowd started to gather. Paul motioned for a uniformed officer to take Albert away. "Relax Albert, we'll find the real killer."

"It's been ten years. You've been protecting him for ten years."

The uniform led Albert away who was still raving accusations. Wally looked apologetically at the mob that had gathered as he and Paul walked to Wally's car.

CHAPTER 16

B ernard Eisner hit the smart key unlocking the door to his Mercedes S 550 Sedan. The shiny black mocha paint reflected shimmering lights from the stars, the waning moon and the parking lot's overhead lampposts.

Wally entered the luxury car sliding over the rich, soft, black leather seat. He gazed at the many options he didn't have in his old Ford pickup: the black walnut and leather console with the manual stick shift, the eight inch command center display in the center of the dashboard that controlled the radio, the phone, the G.P.S. system as well as numerous vehicle settings.

Bernie noticed Wally's awe-struck gaze and smiled one of those smiles of affluent arrogance as he sped off. He pointed to the main screen. "That G P S system is very useful on trips. Saves me valuable time."

Wally sat speechless.

Bernie punched a button on the command center activating the radio to a pre-programmed classical music channel. "This phone is voice activated." He pushed a button turning on the phone and the radio went silent. "Only one can be operated at a time," he said, patting his shirt pocket. "I've got the phone in my pocket. The system uses wireless technology.

Wally bent forward, trying to read the words on the screen. "No shit! I heard about this stuff on computers. I didn't know they had 'em in cars."

"This is actually a computer operated system, Wally."

"How's it work? Can I call Ducheck's and talk to Paul?"

"What's the number?" Bernie said, opening the palm rest on the front of the consol.

Wally spoke the digits as Bernie punched them into the address book's memory, giving the number the name *DuCheck*.

Bernie touched the audio button on the command screen returning to classical music and turning off the phone. "Now you try it," Bernie said.

Wally looked at the screen. "What do I do?"

"Touch the telephone button," Bernie said. After Wally touched it, Bernie continued. "Now you have two options. You can rotate that silver dial," Bernie said, pointing to a dial in front of the palm rest on the consol, "or say call DuCheck's."

Wally followed Bernie's advice and repeated the command. He heard the phone dialing to his surprise

After two rings a voice answered, "Ducheck's Bar. J.C. speaking."

Wally leaned toward the vehicle's speakers. "J.C. this is Wally," he smiled at Bernie. "Is Paul there?"

"Yeah, he's here, Harvey too. We're waiting for you."

Wally spoke looking at the speaker. "We'll be there in a few minutes."

"See you then," J.C. said, and hung up.

"Touch audio," Bernie said. "That's how you hang up."

"I'm impressed. That's quite a gadget. Maybe that's the kind of technology A D A Markel and Steitzer should have at their disposal."

"Markel didn't have a good evening."

"Yeah, he looked pissed. Why'd he get upset?"

"Politics. He's an Assistant D A—doesn't want to be second fiddle to anymore. Wants to be the top man. He wore his best suit for nothing."

"And Steitzer and Stahlman are bucking for Captain—"

Bernie interrupted, "Captain is second loser. They're bucking for chief."

Wally nodded. Sadness swept over him as he figured his problems had ruined Paul's chances for promotion. "Those were some nicknames, weren't they?" Wally asked. "They certainly threw them a curve."

"Those names *are* different. It seems as if everyone in this city has a nickname. I hope we're not talking about a bunch of *Wise Guys*."

"Bar patrons seem to have strange nicknames and the way they talk does resemble the lingo of the *Goodfellas*."

"By the way Wally," Bernie said matter-of-factly. "How did you remember the make and model of your revolver? I bought a little automatic two months ago and I can't remember if it was a Remington, or a Marlin."

Wally hesitated. "I thought they would have asked about my pistol yesterday when I was questioned so I wrote the information down." Wally thought he glimpsed suspicion in Bernie's expression.

———

Moldy was tending bar at Ducheck's—putting in the hours and being a payroll deduction would be more like it. He was a people person to the point that he would be so engrossed in banter that customers would often serve themselves and leave the money on the bar to be collected later—after the world's problems were solved, the jokes had run their course and the laughter had subsided.

J.C., Paul and Harvey were playing cutthroat euchre at a card table near the shuffleboard when Bernie and Wally entered.

Bernie was the first to speak as they reached the table. "I think the bar is being surveilled," he said, motioning toward the front of the bar and Donner Avenue.

Paul got up from the table and walked to the window. He used his index and middle fingers to scissor open the slats of the nicotine-stained Venetian blind.

"Yeah," Paul said, "patrolpersons Karen Thompson and Claudia Bianchi." Paul turned to the group, thumbed to the street and said, "In a green Toyota Camry. Parked on the corner of Delaware, facing us."

"Let's go in the back room." J.C. said.

J.C. and Harvey pulled two tables together as Paul's eyes searched the room. Wally entered with a full tray of live *soldiers.*

Bernie sat quietly as the others took turns re-hashing what they had talked about earlier.

Harvey summed it up with one sentence. "We believe that the Slasher found the perfect opportunity to make Wally the perfect patsy."

"Okay," Bernie said, stroking his chin. "Sounds plausible, but for the sake of clarity let's analyze the situation a little further."

"We've covered all possibilities," J.C. said.

"You're possibilities might be a little biased," Bernie said, smiling apologetically.

Harvey started to speak. Bernie interrupted. "What if Leonard didn't kill Giovanna? I was handling their divorce and Leonard was happy with the arrangement and thrilled with the idea of getting rid of her. What if the same person killed both of them?"

"That doesn't make sense." Harvey blurted. "They were murdered in completely different ways."

"It's been done before," Bernie said, looking at Paul for confirmation.

Paul dejectedly nodded. "It's uncommon and rare."

"Okay," Wally said, "If it's not me and the same person killed them both... Why?"

"What commonality did they share that someone would want them dead?" asked Bernie.

"She was an accountant," Wally said.

"I don't think that would be reason enough," Bernie said. "That wouldn't involve Leonard. Not enough to kill him anyway. What else did she do?"

"She worked for Earsoff 'Funnybone' Tecza at the Comedy Club," Paul said.

"Comedy Club?" J.C. asked.

"Yeah, Chuckle's Bar and Grille," Paul answered. "Thirteen hundred block, on Schoonmaker."

"I still don't think—" Bernie started.

Harvey interrupted, "—Tecza also ran a prostitution ring."

Bernie seemed to slowly digest Harvey's words. "Was Leonard involved?"

Paul hesitated. He looked embarrassed and finally answered. "Maybe he provided the protection."

Bernie sat back in his chair and smiled. "That's the connection we were looking for. Maybe she did the books for Tecza's illicit business as well as his legitimate show business enterprises."

"Maybe she knew something," Harvey said.

"That's right," Bernie said. "She could have made bookings as well. Maybe she kept a file on the clients."

Paul took a draw on his beer. "Her apartment was tossed. Someone was looking for something."

"Maybe they were blackmailing someone," Wally suggested.

"Could be," Bernie said. "It's very possible. But let's look at if from another angle. Giovanna and Leonard hated each other. What if Giovanna was threatening to expose Leonard? Maybe she continued the blackmailing on her own and Tecza found out. Or maybe she was blackmailing Tecza."

Harvey spoke up. "Or an influential client who didn't want to be exposed?"

"That's a lot of maybe's," Wally said. "Could be any one of them. Meanwhile I'm the logical suspect with a lot of maybe's between me and innocence."

"What about the Slasher?" asked Harvey. "The two girls murdered by the Slasher ten years ago were prostitutes weren't they? What if Giovanna and Leonard discovered the Slasher's identity?"

Paul put the pieces together. "And the Slasher murdered Giovanna and searched her apartment for the incriminating evidence."

"What about Leonard?" J.C. asked.

"Maybe the Slasher figured Leonard had it."

J.C.'s eyes brightened. "Then murdered Leonard. Searched his house—" He looked at Paul for confirmation.

"His wife's study was tossed and his safe in the garage was open."

J.C. continued, "—retrieved the evidence and slashed Leonard's throat putting the blame on the Slasher, whom he thought would prove to be Wally."

"Who is the Slasher?" asked Wally.

"Good question," Paul said. "Everything seems to point to prostitution. That'll be a good starting point."

"We'll get together again," Bernie said. "We have direction now."

Wally seemed to relax a bit after hearing the logical discussion offered by Bernie and Paul. And an hour later, and a few more beers, Wally tapped his glass to J.C.'s in a toast. He was a lot more relaxed now.

CHAPTER 17

Wally left Ducheck's and headed for his truck. He paused on the sidewalk, looked up at the cloudless, starlit sky and felt relaxed. The sparkling heavens reminded him of a song by *The Latronics*, "Ten Thousand Stars In The Sky". Maybe the productive discussion that had just taken place or the nerve-numbing six beers he had drunk provided a sense of relief—he didn't care which.

He scanned the pin-pricks of light that formed the big dipper, Orion, and all the other constellations and knew there was order in the universe. Order, he hoped, that would eventually provide proof of his innocence.

And then Wally saw the car. The dark green Toyota Camry on Delaware Street. Its vision brought back the reality that he was still the predominant suspect in the two murders.

Wally's pickup was parked west on Donner, but he walked east to Delaware and approached the dark Toyota. He stopped at the passenger door, braced his arm on the roof and leaned down to speak to the woman riding shotgun.

"Are you lovely ladies lost?"

The close-cropped, raven-haired passenger raised an eyebrow. "No, we heard a lot of good looking *young* guys hang out at that bar over there." She motioned toward Ducheck's. "We were waiting for one to come out."

"A trip to your local oculist is in order, young lady," Wally belched. The auburn-haired driver giggled.

"Or should I say officer?" He slurred the word officer. Wally stared at her buxom chest. "I don't see a nametag, honey. What's your name and size of your address?"

"Officer Bianchi. And thirty-eight dee."

Wally stooped a little lower to look at the driver.

"Officer Thompson," she said.

"Whoa, what have we here?" Wally said, looking at the passenger. "Is that Ann Margaret over there?" In the dark, Wally managed to see the driver blush, the color of her cheeks almost matching her short, wavy, auburn bob. He was infatuated by her beauty. An angel on earth, he thought.

"None of your business," Bianchi said. "Leave us alone. We're just doing our jobs."

"And what might that be?" Wally asked. "Not leaving me alone? Watching me? Looking at me like I was some kind of monster? Even the little kids run from me. A Chihuahua pissed on my foot this afternoon."

Thompson seemed sympathetic until Wally mentioned the dog. She laughed out loud.

Wally managed a chuckle. "Ann Margaret can laugh. That's nice."

"Shouldn't you be getting home about now?" Bianchi asked.

"So you can get back to your job, huh? Sitting here in your Japanese car tailing me and watching every move I make. I will be going home now," he said looking at Karen Thompson. "If you want, you can wait inside, Ann Margaret."

She smiled.

Bianchi hit the power window button. Wally jerked upward and backward, avoiding the rising window. He watched the window close. He cupped his hands around his mouth and in a loud voice said, "I'll take that as a maybe."

Wally walked back to the pickup, waved for the surveillance team to follow and drove off.

The Toyota followed.

———————

Back in the day, parking spaces in the 1300 block of Schoonmaker Avenue were a rarity with a multitude of businesses and services in the area. Tonight, however, Paul easily glided his Chrysler 300 to a premium spot.

In the 50's, the building was a former men's clothing store when Earsoff "Funny Bone" Tecza won it in a poker game. He changed its facade by removing the plate glass windows and covering the entire front of the store with red brick. Above a black steel door, and near the roofline of the one-story building, a sign with sequential flashing lights lit up the darkened street. The words "Chuckles Bar & Grille" were painted on it.

At 10:05 p.m., Paul opened the door to a *blast of the past*. The interior decorator was either dead or in an old folk's home. Earsof Tecza must have fallen in love with the art deco of the 50's when he immigrated to the U.S. from Russia.

Triangles and rectangles painted in bright colors adorned the walls. The bar was in the front of the large room and to the right of the entrance. All the barstools had different colored seats, supposedly to match the clothing of the *women of the night* who once occupied them.

The stage where the comedians performed nestled in the back of the room. The comics would burst through small double doors in the center of the stage and perform their acts. A small electronic marquee that identified each comedian hung above the door. Two large masks, not two drama masks where one was tragedy and the other was comedy, but two identical comedy masks, hung on opposite sides of the marquee.

Western theatre was born in Athens, Greece twenty-five hundred years ago. If Thespis of Attica could see the acts that were performed on the Chuckles' stage, he would spin in his grave like a whirling dervish.

The audience area, comprised of twelve tables that seated six each, was located between the stage and the bar. People would tip their glasses on good jokes and boo on the bad ones. Tonight the tables were empty, except for one that four euchre playing retirees occupied.

Paul walked with the usual cop's authority to the bar.

The bartender, a chubby old man with an equally chubby face that revealed a hard life beyond his years, leered at Paul as he approached.

"What can I do for you pal?"

"Where's Funny Bone?"

Chubby's face turned to a look of distain.

"Don't know pal. And who's asking?"

Paul flipped open his leather ID holder revealing his badge. "Detective Andrews is asking. Where is he?"

Chubby unfolded his arms, straightened them and casually placed his palms on the bar. And in a matter-of-fact way said, "None of your—"

Paul didn't wait for the bartender's retort. He grabbed chubby's white shirt in the middle of his wide chest with and a handful of hair that should have been on his head, and yanked him half over the bar.

The barkeep's eyes opened wide, revealing astonished chubby eyes. He raised his arm to point and Paul reacted as a beat cop would—he punched him with a short, crisp shot to his left eye.

The old card players turned around.

"Son of a bitch!" he said. "I was just trying to show you—"

"Where?"

"Back room," he said, waiting for Paul to let him point the direction.

Paul pushed chubby back as he released his grip on his shirt. He reached into his jacket as if ready to pull his weapon if the bartender tried anything funny like reaching under the bar for a club or a gun. He didn't. He pointed in the direction of the back room.

Paul crisply walked in the direction the bartender had pointed. He walked through a curtain on the right side of the stage and down a hallway. The door on the right had a sign on it that read *office*.

Without knocking, Paul burst into Earsoff Tecza's office.

Tecza sat behind a six-foot wide oak desk on the opposite side of the room. Surprised, he looked up through his large lenses surrounded by thick and dark horn-rimmed frames. A mop of thick, unkempt curly salt and pepper hair hung over his forehead.

"Excuse me," he said through pursed lips.

Paul flipped his badge as he surveyed the rest of the windowless office. To his right, a brown leather couch was positioned between two oriental end tables cluttered with liquor bottles. Probably a casting couch, Paul thought. And who would want to sleep with this bushy haired, ferret-faced twerp? A clothes closet and shelves with cameras and video equipment occupied the other side of the room. Possibly for comedy tryouts or, more than likely, for taping porn movies.

"Police. I'd like to ask you a few questions."

"And I'd like to take over Hugh Heffner's job when he retires. What the hell—?

"Giovanna and Leonard Antonelli," Paul said, looking for Tecza's reaction.

"Oh," Tecza leaned back in his chair. He nonchalantly clasped his hands together. "Aren't you the guy from 'The Village People'?" he said, smiling coyly.

"Giovanna did your books, didn't she?"

"How many cops does it take to screw in a light bulb? None. It turned itself in."

Smart-ass little bastard.

"Captain Leonard Antonelli provided protection for you, Didn't he?"

"You have a ready wit. Tell me when it's ready. Look. I'm really getting a chuckle (he emphasized the bar's name by raising his hands and fingering quote symbols) over you. But if you'll excuse me I've got better—"

"Look," Paul said, raising his voice. "My uncle is suspected of committing their murders. He didn't do it. I think you know—"

"Is he under arrest?"

"No."

"Why did the police arrest the turkey?" Tecza didn't wait for an answer. "They suspected him of fowl play."

Paul ran around the desk, grabbed Tecza by his shirt with both hands and lifted him out of his chair. "You son of a bitch. I want some answers. I don't think you have the balls for murder, but you're connected somehow."

Tecza gingerly removed Paul's hands and straightened his shirt, "Oh, I'm connected all right. And I'm smart. I was going to be a cop, but I decided to finish grammar school first."

Paul grabbed Tecza again, but this time forcefully yanked him from side to side and dragged him across the room. Tecza's hair flopped with Paul's force as he was dragged to the doorway and through it, and smashed into the opposite wall.

Tecza's glasses were hanging from one ear.

Chubby, the bartender, and the euchre players froze their attention on the battling duo.

"How many cops does it take to throw a suspect down the stairs?" Tecza said. "None. He fell."

Paul noticed the audience. "I'll see you again, slime-ball. When no one's around."

As soon as Paul left the bar, Tecza smiled and motioned to the chubby bartender.

"Rusty, get me five sheets of paper and some pencils."

Rusty ripped five pages of paper from a tablet he kept behind the bar and gave them to Tecza.

Tecza gave one back to the bartender and passed out the other sheets to the euchre players. "You all saw what just happened here," he said, motioning toward his office and he hallway. "Write down what you saw and heard. Nothing more. Nothing less."

One of the old euchre players looked puzzled.

"Don't forget to date it and put the time down," Tecza said, pointing an accusing finger. "And don't forget to sign it. Write your address and telephone number also."

Rusty, the chubby barkeep, nodded in confirmation of what Tecza had said.

"That's right. I'm going to sue the lousy bastard," Tecza said through tight lips. "The police department and the city too. When this is over, drinks are on the house."

Three of the four euchre players smiled mostly toothless smiles. The fourth gulped the last mouthful in his mug.

When the written statements were finished, Tecza collected them and walked down the hallway and into his office. He threw the statements on his desk, picked up the phone and punched in a number.

He waited a few moments and then spoke, "Wally's nephew was just here."

"Yeah, Andrews."

"He wanted to know what I knew about the murders."

"Nothing. He did mention the Slasher."

"The bastard pushed me around and threatened me."

"Yeah I got statements."

"I got time. Same place?"

"See you there."

Tecza left his office and walked into the bar. "See you guys later, I got a meeting."

CHAPTER 18

Detectives Joe Pastori and Jack Stahlman got the case at 9:15 a.m.

Earlier, while on routine patrol, Officer Mark Proctopovich had been flagged down by two boys with fishing rods.

The taller boy, thin with red hair cut close military style, ran up to the driver's side door of the squad car. The other boy, shorter and squattier, jumped up and down in front of the vehicle, his dark bangs flopping up and down with each leap. They jabbed their fingers excitedly toward the Monongahela River, each ranting their tale interrupting the other until Officer Proctopovich quieted their exuberance with a halting motion of his hand.

"There's a dead man down by the river!" the taller boy squealed.

A few minutes later Pastori and Stahlman were heading north on Tyrol Boulevard toward the Knoxville section of town, a former steel producing area that provided the steel that won World War Two.

Joe Pastori, the younger member on the team, was driving. He made detective just six months earlier.

"Do you think Paul's uncle had anything to do with the murders?" he asked.

Stahlman didn't like rookies asking a lot of questions especially when they didn't pertain to the case at hand. "No. Not the type. Good guy."

"I heard he was really gnarly in Nam."

Stahlman slowly turned his head toward Pastori and looked at him as if to say, *what the hell do you know.* "Oh?"

"You know. Special Ops stuff," he said, grinning a wannabe smile. "Close combat. They carry special knives."

Stahlman shook his head. "You watch too many movies."

"He got a bunch of medals for something," Pastori shot back.

That's true, Stahlman said to himself. No one ever thought of Wally's past. He didn't fit the profile. Wally just wasn't that kind of guy.

"Or was he?" He said in a whisper.

"What's that?" Pastori asked.

"Turn right on McMahon."

Stahlman remembered coming to this very place as a youngster with his teen cronies for a cool dip on a hot summer's day. He remembered the jokes about the polluted river like doing the breaststroke to push away the Monongahela whitefish and brown trout (local terms for condoms and feces). He felt lucky that he hadn't contracted a contagious disease.

Skeletons of remaining buildings stood like fractured tombstones on the horizon as Pastori turned onto Delaware Street. As they got closer, and turned onto River Street, the scene became clearer. An overhead train trestle rose high above a cruiser with its red and blue lights flashing. A patrolman leaned against it.

Stahlman instructed Pastori to park in back of the cruiser.

The officer on scene had already taped off the crime scene. He strolled over to meet Detectives Stahlman and Pastori.

"Officer Mark Proctopovich," he announced. "Didn't touch anything I just taped off the area."

"Good work, officer," Pastori said.

Stahlman didn't like rookies trying to take over. "Interview the kids," he said to Pastori.

Pastori looked stunned. He looked around. "Where are they?"

"I don't know. Find 'em." Stahlman raised the tape and walked under it toward the bloody scene in front of him.

The body of a man was perched on the trestle's ironwork, seated on a horizontal I-beam with his torso leaning on a cross-member. He looked like a tired fisherman taking a nap in the summer sun.

Blood covered his white shirt and pooled in his lap from the gaping gash across his neck. From ear to ear.

And the strangest thing was the exaggerated pair of lips painted on the corpse's bloodless white face with ruby red lipstick, not on but around the corpse's lips and much larger, forming a grotesque smile like the Joker.

Stahlman looked at officer Proctopovich.

Proctopovich shook his head as if it was the most heinous thing he had ever seen.

Stahlman pulled out a pair of rubber gloves from his inside jacket pocket. He carefully walked closer to the corpse watching where he was stepping, not wanting to disturb any potential evidence.

He reached around the smiling figure and patted his back pockets. He found the man's wallet and slid out a photo driver's license.

Stahlman read the name aloud, "Earsoff Tecza."

CHAPTER 19

While looking into the Ford's rear-view mirror, "Cagney and Lacey", a popular 80's TV show featuring two women detectives, popped into Wally's mind.

Officer Thompson and Bianchi were following him; Bianchi was driving this time.

Nice to have two good-looking females surveilling me, he thought, especially Thompson. What's her first name? Claudia? No. She's the one that thinks I'm guilty. Karen, that's her name. Karen Thompson.

Giovanna's face suddenly appeared onto Wally's consciousness. How wonderful life could have been with her. This murderer, this sadistic madman has to be found. Tecza's the logical connection to the murders. He ran the prostitution ring. Two prostitutes were slashed. Wait a minute. Hold the phone, he thought, that wouldn't be good business for a pimp—killing off his business. He hadn't thought of that before.

Wally's reverie ebbed as Ducheck's Bar came into view. He pulled in front of his favorite watering hole and watched the unmarked Toyota Camry slowly pull up in back of him. He thought he saw one of Karen Thompson's blue eyes wink at him.

That was enough motive for Wally. He pushed open the pickup's door and nonchalantly slid off the seat, like a young cowboy gliding off his horse, trying to impress a young girl at the county fair. He strode confidently in front of their car, onto the sidewalk and headed for the passenger's door when the toe of his shoe clipped a raised portion of sidewalk and he tripped, momentarily losing his balance.

The façade of the "Marlboro Man" vanished. A retired steelworker appeared.

Karen giggled. Wally was smitten by her smile, her full lips surrounded teeth as white as the porcelain on a new stove.

"Hello ladies," he said, looking only at Karen. "Kinda' early to start working, isn't it?"

Caudia's head dropped into view. "We're just finishing our shift. We were up all night on surveillance."

"Is that right?" Wally directed his question to Karen.

"Claudia was surveilling you. I was watching you. Kind of protecting you," Karen said.

"Well, well," Wally said, kneeling down, leaning closer. "You could have knocked on the door. I would have let you in."

Claudia started the car; put it in reverse and eased back, letting Wally know the chit-chat was over.

Wally's arm brushed the side of the Camry as it edged back. He stood up, straightened his shirt, smiled and motioned a two-fingered salute to Karen.

As Wally opened the door to Ducheck's, he turned around for a last glimpse of Karen. The surveillance car drove off. A Crown Vic took its place. The two women were being relieved by another pair of officers.

J.C. leaned over the sink, rinsing glasses. Ten Quarts sat at the end of the bar playing Gin Rummy with Moldy.

"What's up?" J.C. asked.

Wally slid onto a stool and pointed to the coffee pot. "I've been thinking. The more time I try to analyze this situation, the more confused I get."

"Like how?"

"When Giovanna was murdered, I really wasn't a suspect. I took the gun, glasses and wine bottle from her bedroom. No one knew I spent the night with her except the killer."

J.C. motioned for Wally to continue while pouring a cup of coffee.

"We were expecting Leonard to pin the murder on me because he had known that I was there. But he didn't know because he didn't come after me. Then he was murdered and the blame for his demise was now on my shoulders."

"That's what we talked about last night, isn't it? Tecza has to be involved."

"That's just it," Wally said. "Why would he murder his prostitutes? He's a tightwad. He wouldn't cut off part of his income."

The door opened. Paul stood in the doorway; the aura of morning sunlight enveloped him.

Wally motioned to an adjacent seat. "We were just talking about Tecza and his involvement."

"What about it?" Paul asked.

Wally repeated his theory.

Paul nodded in approval. "You're right."

J.C. started to pour a coffee for Paul. "This isn't your day off, is it?"

"No. I was just suspended."

"By who? For what?" Wally asked.

"Steitzer. For roughing up Earsoff Tecza. And get this, I may be a suspect in his murder."

J.C. spilled the coffee he was pouring and Wally choked on his.

"What?" J.C. asked.

Paul went over last night's events at Chuckles and how witnesses would perceive his actions as threatening.

"How. Why—?" Wally started to ask.

"A couple'a kids found him this morning under a train trestle at Sparrows Point."

Wally breathed heavily. "Was he slashed?"

"Ear to ear. Same as Antonelli. The only difference is," Paul made a circular gesture around his lips, "he had an exaggerated smile painted on his face with lipstick."

"Why?" J.C. asked. "Because he was a comedian?"

"Don't know," Paul said. "Maybe a profiler could figure it out. Too weird for me."

"What about your suspension?" Wally asked. "What's—?"

"I'm suspended with pay until Internal Affairs investigates."

"Investigates?" J.C. asked.

"Whether or not to file a complaint with the district justice." Paul noticed the puzzled look on J.C.'s face. "The first steps of any criminal prosecution take place before the minor judiciary. That means I can be arrested with or without a warrant."

"What can you do? Can you beat this?" Wally asked.

Paul shrugged. "Tecza made a slip of the tongue last night. He said he was *connected*.

"To the mob?" J.C. asked.

"I'm going to find out," Paul said. He got up and started to leave.

"How can I help?" Wally asked.

"Don't know yet. I'll meet you here this evening. Maybe I'll have something by then." Paul left.

CHAPTER 20

Paul drove into another time zone—Mononville's past. Rusted steel mills stood in the background of mostly vacant businesses, storefronts, and decaying tenements. During the 60's and 70's, the South Side flourished along the three block expanse of route 906, between 17th street and 20th street, also known as Parente Boulevard. At least twelve bars opened at 7:00 a.m. to catch the midnight shift; some stayed open all night providing prostitutes for the 4 X 12 crews. Most businesses, pool halls, and gambling joints wrote numbers as a side line.

The Four Aces Club, called by many former gamblers The *Five* Aces Club, sat in the geographical center of Mononville's entertainment area. The club was also the meeting place of the local mafia and office of its patriarch—Vito LaBruscia.

Paul steered the Chrysler 300 into the club's parking lot, the location of a former dress shop. Vito had the boutique burned down and bought the property for pennies on the dollar from an old widow.

As Paul walked through the lot he noticed a bald young man with tattooed arms walk to the corner from the front of the building where he had been standing. He was obviously a lookout, having already notified the club's doorman.

Years of acids and pollutants of by-products from the processes of making steel had darkened and stained the flagstone and wood that covered the front of the building. The acids also etched a dull translucent sheen to the long rectangular glass window above eye level and across the front of the building.

Paul stood at the doorway and waited for permission to enter. Within seconds a chubby hand pushed aside the black curtain that covered the window and motioned Paul's acceptance.

Paul opened the door and took a step into the bar but stopped short of the immense figure of Joey "Bags" Sappone. He got the nickname from the large darkened bags underneath his eyes, presumably from his golden gloves days—thirty years and two hundred pounds ago.

"What 'chu wan detective? You 'ere on official busness?"

"No. I came to see Don Vito."

Joey's chubby face contorted into an expression of *no way, copper.*

"It's about my Uncle Wally. He's in trouble. I think Don Vito can help him. It will only take a minute."

Joey seemed to empathize. "Wait right 'ere," he said, pointing to an imaginary spot on the floor. He got the attention of a skinny gray-haired man sitting at the corner of the bar by snapping his finger. "Right 'ere," he said, pointing to the spot with emphasis.

Joey waddled to the back of the bar and, swooshing aside a black curtain, entered a hallway.

Paul stood on the imaginary spot where he was instructed to wait. Three men sat at the bar. Closest to Paul was a skinny gray-haired man with a bulbous red nose. The man in the middle sported died black hair covered with a thick, greasy substance. The man at the end of the trio and next to greasy made eye contact with Paul but quickly looked away.

Paul wondered if this "wise guy" wasn't wise at all, or maybe he was just timid, or, the thought crossed his mind that he looked like he might be working undercover by trying to avoid suspicion.

Paul turned his attention to a large card table where seven men had been playing poker. From the looks on their faces, it appeared they were trying to project mind reading energy through their eyes into Paul's brain and read his thoughts.

The card players' trance was broken when Joey walked past them. He motioned for Paul to raise his arms to be patted down. Paul complied and then Joey thoroughly checked him for weapons and listening devices. Finding none, he motioned for Paul to follow him.

As they walked past the curtain and down a hallway, Paul smelled the stench from restrooms on his right and stale beer and pungent odors of hard liquor from a storage room on his left. The office was at the end of the hall on the left.

Joey tapped on the door with his knuckle. A weak voice, presumably spoken in Italian, authorized their entrance.

The old man sat behind a mahogany desk cluttered with manila folders, papers, a whiskey bottle, glass, and a large ashtray with a smoking cigar in it. His balding head sat atop a dark blue suit that a younger might have worn twenty years ago. His sleeves, longer than his thin arms, covered half of his wrinkled arthritic hands. He folded a ledger closed as Joey escorted Paul into the office.

"Pauley," Vito said, leaning back in an old wooden swivel desk chair. "How have you been? I haven't seen you for a while."

"I'm fine Vito, and you?" Paul said, wondering if Joey "the bags" had refreshed Vito's memory or if Vito's eight-decades old memory was still functional.

Vito's gesture offered Paul an upholstered chair in front of his desk.

Paul sat down after Vito's glance dismissed Joey.

Vito leaned forward, crossed his arms on his desk, cocked his head, and in a voice and tone that anticipated an answer he already knew, said, "Are you here about the recent murders?" Before Paul could answer, he said. "The Slasher is back, isn't he?"

"My uncle Wally's in trouble, Don Vito. He didn't murder Albert's sister. He's not the Slasher."

"Walter Gustafson. I knew his father, Sven." Vito leaned back in reminiscence. "Good man. Honest. Used to deliver coal during the depression."

"My superiors think he's the Slasher. So does Albert."

Vito shot forward in his seat. "That's impossible. He's a good man like his father. War hero. Family man. I told Albert about Walter and to lay off."

"Thank you, Don Vito." Paul went over the scenario that Wally avenged Giovanna's death by killing Leonard.

"But he can't be the murderer," Don Vito said. "Wally was under surveillance when Tecza was murdered."

Paul sat quiet for a moment, thinking. How the hell did Vito know Wally was under surveillance? Who's giving Vito information? I've got to be careful. No, I've got to get Wally and myself out of this mess.

"They're trying to pin Tecza's murder on me."

Vito looked surprised. "Really? How did they come to that conclusion?"

"I went to talk to him last night. He got shitty with me and I roughed him up a little."

"Witnesses?"

"Yeah."

"Doesn't look good for you Pauley. Maybe I can help?"

"When I was talking to him," Paul said, emphasizing the word talking, "he threatened me by saying that he was *connected.*"

"We had a business arrangement, that's all. He wasn't one of us, if you know what I mean."

"I understand, Don Vito. But the business he was in is related to the murders of Giovanna and Leonard Antonelli."

"But that doesn't involve us."

"Eventually, the police might think that it does." Vito waited for an explanation. Paul continued. "Nine years ago, two prostitutes were murdered by the Slasher. Everything was quiet until Leonard and Giovanna split up."

"I don't see a connection."

"Wally didn't murder Giovanna, he loved her. Leonard didn't either, although it appeared that way. I thought blackmail was the reason they were murdered."

"Why would you think that?"

"Because Giovanna's apartment was tossed. And when we found Leonard, his safe was open and empty. I thought of the possibility that Giovanna or Leonard might have been shaking down Tecza for a bigger piece of the pie. But when he was murdered..." Paul waited for Vito's reply.

"So the blackmailer and the Slasher appear to be the same person."

"Looks that way," Paul said. "And he seized the perfect opportunity to set up Uncle Wally."

"And you for the murder of Tecza," Vito said, nodding in appreciation. "But how does that involve my family?"

"If you remember, one of the prostitutes was the sister of Albert Giannamore."

Vito nodded.

"Albert was working for you as Tecza's liaison. My superior will eventually want to know more, I'm sure."

"And you might help him reconstruct this whole scenario."

"I don't want to, but I will. But I've been suspended for now. All I want is to lift the guilt from my uncle and me. If you don't know about the blackmailer maybe someone's not been truthful with you. For two innocent people as well as your own security, I ask you to intervene."

"I will have someone contact you about this matter," Vito said, waving his hand in a dismissive motion. "We can't meet again. Freddy Caruso will contact you."

Paul got the message, got up and left the room. As Joey walked Paul to the door, Paul felt that Vito really wasn't involved and that his visit wasn't in vain.

CHAPTER 21

The prediction of a thunderstorm by Channel 4's 6:00 p.m. news seemed to be coming to fruition. Streaks of light that lit up the sky became brighter and the rumblings of thunder turned into booming clasps.

The wind picked up blowing leaves and loose debris across City Hall's parking lot. Lieutenant Algie Steitzer sallied from his Volkswagen, locked it and scurried toward the building that gave him his identity. Once inside, he brushed off his lightweight tan jacket and dark brown pants. He stood in front of the wall-mounted building directory and, while looking at his dim reflection in the glass, combed and smoothed his hair, a ritual he performed daily.

The building's empty, dark and gloomy interior provided a more ominous feeling to Steitzer than the weather had outside. He hadn't been to an evening meeting with the mayor; they were usually reserved for Captain Antonelli. He felt nervous. There was no one to tell him what to do. Well, the mayor soon would.

The elevator doors opened on the third floor to a dimly lit sixty-foot long hallway, lighted only by four fifteen watt wall sconces evenly spaced across its length. A brighter light shone through the translucent glass door of the mayor's office at the end of the hall.

Steitzer tentatively walked down the hallway stopping momentarily as if someone was following him. The phantom turned out to be the reverberating sound of his hard leather heels making contact with the marble floor. He walked toward the light at the end of the hallway like a lost ship following a lighthouse's beacon—to home and safety.

When he reached the door to the mayor's office he hesitated, turned around to look at the steps he had taken and, almost reluctantly, opened the door and walked into the light. The reception room was empty. The secretary left promptly every day at 4:00 p.m. before the mayor conducted his *off the record* business. Her desk was opposite the entrance and to the right of the mayor's door. Her main job was controlling admission to the mayor's office. Tonight the door was open.

"Come on in Algie," the mayor's husky voice called out.

Steitzer walked to the open door and stopped. He crooked his neck around the door frame and gingerly rapped his knuckle on the door. The mayor encouraged Algie's entry with a motion of his short, stubby arm. As Algie entered, Majewski pointed to a chair in front of his polished mahogany desk.

August Majewski swiveled the computer monitor away from Steitzer's view. The screen was divided into four quadrants, each with a view from a separate video camera: the top left quadrant showed the waiting room; the top right, the police entrance to the building; the bottom left, the briefing room; the bottom right, the hallway Algie Steitzer had just walked down.

The mayor clasped his chubby fingers together across his paunchy stomach and reclined in his high-back leather upholstered chair. By force of habit, he raised his arms overhead and then clasped them behind his neck, giving the impression he was pointing to the wall in back of him adorned with ornately framed pictures of himself shaking hands with every important local and state politician that came within one hundred miles of Mononville—even the President of the United States.

In his present posture, Majewski looked up at Algie with his large, black eyes and, after a few uncomfortable seconds said, "You've been doing a good job Algie."

A pink glow covered Algie"s cheeks as he fidgeted in his seat. "Thank you sir."

"I've got to fill Captain Antonelli's position by the end of next week. You're one of the top candidates. I need someone who can handle the responsibilities that Antonelli had." Majewski canted his head while waiting for Algie's recognition of what he was saying in cryptic, political wording.

Algie leaned forward in his chair. His facial expression turned from bewilderment to serious. "I've worked very closely with Captain Antonelli. I can take care of Tecza's business."

"I'll have someone contact you about that matter, but I was referring to his murder. We need a conviction."

"We really don't have any real evidence, just—"

"How long have you been on the force?"

"Fifteen years sir."

Majewski started thumbing through a short stack of papers on his desk. "Hmmm. The only officer with more time in grade is Paul Andrews."

Algie Steitzer nodded. "I'll see what I can do to expedite—"

Majewski pounded his desk. "It better be quick. Have Internal Affairs file a complaint against Andrews with Justice Conte. And not just Andrews either. Wally Gustafson has to go down also. This is a problem. A big problem for a lot of people."

Majewski's face contorted into an ugly mass of eroded jellied flesh, his black eyes beamed out a message that was aimed at Algie's innermost core. "I don't want someone else taking care of this problem. You know what I mean? It could get very ugly."

"Yes sir." Algie didn't wait to be dismissed. He got up and started for the door.

"Algie," the mayor said. "Don't screw this up. Some very important people will be watching what happens. Get that complaint filed."

Algie nodded and continued out of the office, reception room, and into the darkness of the hall.

CHAPTER 22

A darkness more than night crept into the back room of Ducheck's Bar and hovered over Wally Gustavson.

"It's not fair," Wally said. "Paul didn't have anything to do with Tecza's murder."

J.C. took a draw from his beer. "Bummer. Doesn't make sense. Paul has a terrific record on the force, why would his superiors suspend him?

"I can't let this happen to Paul. Harvey said Leonard was seen with Tecza the night before taking an envelope from him. Looks like payoff money. Someone higher up had something to do with Tecza's murder. We have to find out who."

"What can you do?"

"Yeah, what can you do?" Paul asked as he strode around the corner. He held a shot of Jim Beam in one hand and an Iron City Light in the other. "You don't have any credibility, Wally. Don't forget you're a suspect also. They think you murdered Leonard." He bit his lip. "And that I murdered Tecza."

"That doesn't make sense," J.C. said. "Leonard and Tecza had their throats cut. They were murdered by the Slasher."

Paul's face screwed up after throwing down the shot. "They'll say Wally murdered Leonard and that he's the

Slasher. And I murdered Tecza in the same manner to take suspicion away from Wally."

J.C. looked puzzled.

"Because I knew Wally was under surveillance," Paul said, sitting down. "That would give him a perfect alibi."

Wally wrung his hands. "I—" he started to say.

"But there's hope," Paul said. "When I was roughing up Tecza he made a slip of the tongue by saying he was connected. I took it to mean to the mob so I went to see Vito LaBruscia this afternoon. He says he'll help."

"Can't hurt one little bit to have his help," J.C. said.

Wally managed a faint smile that quickly disappeared. "Can you trust him? He's a criminal. He may be behind this whole mess."

"He knows me. He knows and respects you and your father, Wally. I think I can trust him."

"Trust who?" Harvey's squirrelly voice preceded him as he popped around the corner carrying a Coor's Light. "You can't trust anyone. Not even the ones you work with."

The room quieted. All eyes focused on Harvey.

"I just drove past headquarters," Harvey said, pulling out a chair and sitting at a table next to the occupied booth. "I watched Steitzer walk in the main entrance." He exaggerated the word "main".

Paul dropped his head. "That means the mayor called him in. Steitzer wouldn't go there on his own."

"So, what's that mean?" J.C asked.

"That means the mayor wants blood, a sacrifice for his continued political career." Paul looked into the eyes of each, Wally last. "Arrests will probably be made Monday, followed by a press conference and a full investigation."

"Shit," Wally said.

J.C. watched Wally squirm in is seat. "Don't worry Wally. We have two days to find the murderer."

Paul pointed his bottle toward Wally. "Wally doesn't have to worry. A thorough investigation will clear him. I'm the one with the problem."

J.C.'s pleading eyes fell on Wally and the tilt of his head seemed to say, *now's the time.*

Wally knew J.C. was right. He hoped it wouldn't have come to this, but Paul had to know.

"I was with her."

After a second, Paul's head jerked toward Wally. "What?" he said, as if he hadn't heard what Wally had said.

"I was with Giovanna that night," Wally said, his eyes welling up as he looked into the other's faces for understanding. "I woke up next to her." He started to cry.

Paul looked out the window, into the darkness of the night.

"I couldn't tell you," Wally said. "It would have put you in a bad situation. You're an officer of the court."

Paul leaned forward. He ran his hands through his blond hair. An expression of understanding covered his face. "Tell me now Wally."

In between sips of beer and pauses of remembrance, Wally regurgitated the facts of Giovanna's murder.

"Your pistol?" Paul asked. "How did your pistol get in Giovanna's bedroom?" Wally shrugged.

"What did you do with it?"

"I put it where the sun don't shine."

"What about the revolver that forensics tested? Where'd it come from?"

J.C. spoke up. "A gun show in West Virginia."

"I asked him to do it," Wally said. "I gave him a printout of the weapon's description."

"That's good thinking," Paul said. "But I wish you would have told me."

"At the time I thought Antonelli murdered Giovanna," Wally said. "And he might have. But the point is I thought you would have been in danger if Antonelli had an inkling that you suspected him and were helping me."

"Now we're both under the microscope," Paul said. "It'll be hard to prove that we're innocent with the whole police force watching us."

"We *do* have some evidence," Wally said.

Paul nodded. "The glasses and the wine bottle?"

Wally beamed a smile. "I kept them of course."

"I hate to break it to you, but the evidence from the bottle and glasses won't hold up in court."

"Why not?" Wally protested. "It was imported Italian wine."

"Because there is no chain of evidence," Harvey said.

J.C. looked confused.

Paul raised a finger. "The court won't recognize any evidence that isn't substantiated. We could have laced the evidence with drugs."

"Oh," J.C. said.

"But," Paul said, "we still need to see what drug was used. It could help us find out who is involved. But it will be next to impossible to get them analyzed."

Harvey thumped his fist on the table. "Why?"

"You've worked at the station for what, ten years?" Paul said. "You can't ask someone to jeopardize their job for a few minutes work."

"Isn't there someone in the lab you can trust," J.C. asked.

"Yeah," Wally interjected. "Who works there? Maybe I know someone's father."

Paul scratched his head. "Let's see. Elliott Masci is the supervisor. Anthony Brown replaced old man Hopkins ten years ago and..." He rubbed his temple. "Phil. Yeah, Phil Thompson replaced Stretch Cunningham a few months ago on a provisional basis."

Harvey took a draw on his beer. "Provided he gets his master's degree first. He goes to night school at Seton Hill. Has three months to go."

"Thompson?" Wally asked. "Is he related to Patrolman Karen Thompson?"

Harvey looked surprised that Wally would know any young officers on the force. "Brother. Younger brother."

"Hmmn," Wally said under his breath. "Ann Margaret's brother."

"What's that Wally?" Paul asked.

"Nothing Wally said, getting up. "Maybe I can find a way out of this shit after all."

CHAPTER 23

The sound of a pop (soda) can bouncing across the brick paved alley broke the stillness of the night.

The man who accidentally kicked it had parked his car four blocks away near an all night convenience store. He wore a rolled-up ski mask that resembled a watch cap and a long black trench coat. He walked east on Schoonmaker Avenue for two blocks being careful to avoid being seen. He dashed between two vacant buildings to the alley behind.

He wasn't familiar with the area especially the littered alleys. Overturned trash cans, discarded toys, bricks from the dilapidated buildings, and other debris were strewn about and all were obstacles he had to encounter. The evening's dampness exaggerated the smell of urine and rotting garbage.

A light flashed through a third floor apartment window above a former sporting goods store. The man pulled his ski mask over his face and darted into the loading dock of the former Stern's Furniture Company. After a few minutes, he continued down the narrow back street and into the next block. Midway down the alley, passing the thick smell of pizza sauce, he started to examine the rear of the buildings. He stopped in front of a door. The sign above it read: "Chuckles Bar and Grille".

He pulled a three foot prybar from the inside of his coat and, after carefully checking the area, jammed it between the wooden door and sill. He yanked on the bar ripping the door open. He dashed inside and pulled the door shut. He clicked on a penlight flashlight and retrieved a length of wire from his coat pocket. He placed the prybar horizontally across and on top of the doorjambs. He wrapped one end of the wire tightly around the bar, the other end around the doorknob, securing the bar against the jambs preventing the door from being opened from the outside.

Feeling relieved that he was safely inside, he headed down the hallway. The penlight illuminated the sign on the office door. He opened it to the thick odor of cigars and whiskey. He checked for windows and finding none flipped on the light switch. He dropped the light into his pocket as his blinking eyes scanned the room. He strode to a large oak desk that was centered at the far wall across from a brown leather couch.

He yanked open the middle drawer and rustled through its contents. Not finding what he was looking for, he pulled the drawer from its compartment and overturned the debris on the floor. He opened a small drawer on the upper right side of the desk above a swing out typewriter. He hesitated as he looked into it. He picked up a small chrome plated .25 caliber automatic with ivory handles. He thumbed a slide switch above the grip and a clip dropped from the bottom of the handle. He checked to see if it was loaded with cartridges. He slapped the clip back into position and put the pistol in his pants pocket. He checked the contents of the small drawer as well, emptying its contents on the floor.

The man in black opened the left drawer where files were kept. His gloved fingers flipped through the tabs pulling out four manila files. He folded them and slid them into an inner coat pocket. He checked various notes on top of the desk and under the pad, putting two of them into his coat's inner pocket. He swiped his hand across the rest of the notes flinging them airborne. He rotated the rolodex to a certain point and ripped out a listing from the letter "J" and stuffed it into his pocket also.

He sat on the leather couch and glared at the opposite wall. It was divided into two sections: a five foot wide closet and a shelving unit of equal dimension. The shelves stretched from ceiling to floor; books, magazines, a camera and video equipment occupied its space. Clown outfits, old vaudeville zoot-suits, comic props like golf clubs, juggling pins, a baseball bat, clown shoes and boots, and other assorted items occupied the closet. Police hats, caps, homburgs, an Indian headdress and other various head gear were on a shelf above the clothing rack.

He stared at the closet and then at the shelves. Back and forth. Back and forth. He walked to the far side of the shelving unit as if he noticed something unusual. He felt along the vertical edge, next to the wall, looking for something. All of a sudden he ripped a number of books from the fifth shelf to the floor. He pulled a lever that had been concealed by the books. He tried to push and then pull the unit. Nothing. He bent down and repeated the process on the second shelf. He found a second lever and pulled it. He easily swung open the shelving unit.

The area behind the shelves consisted of floor to ceiling wooden pigeon-holes occupied by video cassettes. Almost every space was filled; there had to be a hundred videos categorized in alphabetical order. The man in black ran his gloved fingers across the letters selecting various ones until he had plucked out eight. He stacked them on the desk. He rooted through the debris on the floor, pulled out a roll of scotch tape and bound the eight tapes together.

That's when he heard the front door close. He turned out the light, but not before grabbing a baseball bat from the closet. He moved to a position in back of the door, pulled the ski mask over his face and waited as the footsteps came closer.

A faint light from the bar area slipped into the room as the door opened. The man in black swung the bat hitting the intruder on the head. He dropped like President Bush's approval rating. The man dropped the bat, walked to the desk and picked up the tapes. As he headed for the door, the intruder said something in Russian and grabbed the man's ankle. The man tripped, landing next to the Russian who grabbed him. They struggled. The Russian put an arm lock on the man and almost had him subdued until the man pulled the .25 auto from his pocket and fired. The Russian leaped backwards, grabbing his right side while screaming in Russian. The man grabbed the tapes and dashed into the hallway. He twisted the retaining bar to a vertical position and pushed the door open.

He retraced his steps through the alley much more quickly on the return trip relieved that he left with what he had come for.

CHAPTER 24

Usually on Saturday mornings, Wally woke up late—and with a hangover. But not today. The screen on the digital clock showed 8:30 a.m. After a shower and a shave, Wally spritzed with his favorite cologne.

He thought a light blue shirt with a white collar would accent his blue eyes and also go well with dark gray slacks. He felt he had to present himself in the most favorable light to prove his innocence. It was crucial that he enlist the aid of Karen Thompson. He hoped he was right, that even though she was surveilling him she found him to be a likeable rascal. He grinned into the medicine cabinet mirror.

Wally raised a slat on the Venetian blind with his finger and peered through the opening. He saw the dark green Toyota Camry parked across the street. Claudia Bianchi sat in the driver's seat looking off into space with an expression on her face that looked as if she were on a Caribbean island sipping a Mai-tai while relaxing in a hammock. Karen sat in the *shotgun* seat, reading a book.

The love of Wally's life, Giovanna Antonelli, died four days ago but that didn't stop Wally from being attracted to Karen Thompson—that was Wally. He could love two women at the same time, maybe three at times, but he stayed loyal to only one at a time. Giovanna was still his primary love and he wanted to solve her murder even more than proving his own innocence.

Wally slammed the door leaving the house, the noise jerking Claudia back from the Caribbean to McKee Avenue in Mononville, Pennsylvania.

Wally strode across the street as if he owned it and sauntered up to the passenger side of the Toyota.

He leaned over the passenger's open window, bracing himself with his left arm on the roof and said, "Whatcha reading?"

Claudia managed a faint smile in front of disgust.

Karen closed the book revealing brightly colored flowers and the words *Annuals of North America* on the cover. "Nothing much. Just research for my garden."

"Like to garden, huh? My first wife liked to garden. That is, until a snake bit her."

"Oh, that must have been awful."

"Yeah. Bit her right on the ass."

Karen glared under her eyebrows at Wally's expression. "You're kidding, right?"

"Nope. Copperhead."

"Aren't they poisonous?"

"Next to the rattlesnake they're the most poisonous snake in the area."

"Did she die?"

"Nope. We made it to the hospital in time."

"Great. She was lucky. Did you say she was your first wife?"

"Yeah. Arlene. The marriage didn't last long after the snake bite incident."

A surprised look landed on Karen's face. "That's gratitude. You had just saved her life. What happened?"

"She was pissed that I immediately drove her to the hospital. It was never the same between us."

"That doesn't make sense. What else could you have done?"

"She wanted me to suck the poison out of her wound."

Karen's expression changed from one of doubt to one of being taken advantage of. "No, you're kidding me."

Wally chuckled. "She ran off with an interior decorator." Karen's suspicious look prompted Wally to respond. "That's true. Arlene would rather decorate a house than live in it."

"You said first wife. Was there a second Mrs. Gustafson?"

"Helga."

"What happened to her?"

"She was bit on the ass by a copperhead."

Karen burst out laughing, deepening the dimple on her right cheek. Her hand covered her mouth as she muffled her guffaws. Her eyes became watery.

Wally's smile evaporated and then gloom covered his face. "Cancer. Seven years ago."

Wally knew by the look on Karen's face that he had twisted her emotions enough. "I wonder if you could help me for a minute?"

"What do you want?" Karen said, almost choking on her words.

Wally's request seemed to stifle Claudia's vacation once again.

"I have this strange looking flower growing in my yard. I wonder if you can tell me what it is."

"I don't know," Karen said. "I *could* get bitten by a copperhead." Wally bent over in laughter. Claudia managed a smile.

"Really," Wally said. "I've been trying to figure out what this thing is for months."

"What's the big deal," Claudia said, squirming in her seat. "A plant's a plant. Isn't it?"

Wally had to think fast. "My cat's been sick lately. I think she's been nibbling on the plant."

No verbal response was heard from the two policewomen, but both their mouths contorted in the form of sympathy.

Karen looked at Claudia as if asking for permission. Claudia shrugged her shoulders and arched her brows as if to say *what the hell.*

Karen opened the passenger door and squirmed out of her seat. Wally graciously extended a helping hand that Karen accepted with a shy smile. Claudia stayed in the car.

Wally extended his arm toward the house. "This way, please." He felt better that Karen had accepted his request and that Claudia wouldn't interfere.

They walked to the back of the house, out of sight of the Toyota, and stopped in front of a peony bush a few feet from his back porch. Wally pointed to it.

"That's a peony bush," Karen said, seemingly amazed that she had been duped and seemingly terrified at the same time.

"I know it is. Sorry. I had to talk to you alone." Karen started backing up, as if retreating from a big mistake.

Wally sat down on a stool trying to become less threatening. "I'm in trouble. Big trouble. I had nothing to do with Giovanna's murder. I'm being set up. I need help. I need *your* help."

Karen started to turn and walk away, but stopped. She slowly turned her head toward Wally. "Why do you think you're being set up?"

Wally felt a jolt of relief. He told Karen the story of his living nightmare from beginning to end.

"And that's the whole story. Do you believe me?"

"I know your nephew Paul very well. I couldn't make myself believe the rumors I heard about him. And something else. Steitzer had Internal Affairs file a complaint with Justice Conte. He's going to issue a summons. Claudia told me."

"Damn, I thought that might happen. What about me? Do you believe me?"

"What you're telling me makes sense. You are in trouble," she said in a sympathetic tone. She waited for a few moments and said, "I believe you."

"Will you help me? And Paul?"

Karen looked into Wally's eyes studying him, "What can I do?"

CHAPTER 25

The vacant lot where the Mononville Junior-Senior High School once stood caught Paul's attention. He remembered being in the seventh grade and bullied by a group of upperclassmen. Being an only child, Paul was easy prey for them. They waited for him after school and took advantage of his innocence by pushing him around, taunting, and hitting him. Not wanting to fight back, Paul took alternate routes home. One day the bullies caught him in front of old man Kachmarik's corner store and, while pushing Paul around, the store's large, plate glass window became broken. Paul denied breaking the window and of course the bullies blamed Paul who couldn't muster a defense because of his fear of them. It took many months to repay the money from his weekly allowance. That wasn't the hard part for him. He felt betrayed, not only by his schoolmates and friends that didn't believe him, but by his family as well.

The old memory hung in the car while driving to Wally's. Hopefully they would find answers that would steer them on the right path to proving their innocence. But the sight of the lot where he spent much of his youth made him nervous. Was this ominous sight a sign of his future he wondered? Was he destined to always be proving his innocence? He knew he needed help, and fast—but he didn't know how fast it would come.

A behemoth-sized black Lincoln Town Car—Paul didn't know what year, but an older model—pulled alongside his vehicle. The driver tooted the horn and motioned with his hand for Paul to pull over. Paul could tell that he was a large man with a huge head that filled the entire window area, but couldn't identify him because of the sun's glare on the window. Paul pulled to the curb and stopped. The Lincoln inched alongside and stopped. The passenger window slowly receded into the door revealing the man's identity. Paul's despondency seemed to evaporate at the sight of Freddy Caruso. Paul knew Freddy had a nickname, all the wise guys did, but he couldn't remember it. That didn't matter though. Vito was keeping his promise. Hopefully, help had arrived.

"Follow me," Freddy said, "Wait ten minutes after you park before you come in." And then he sped off.

Paul followed a speeding Freddy through school zones and stop signs, yellow and red lights through the lower East-side until Freddy pulled in front of the Chateau Lounge on Page Street and parked. He wrestled himself out of the Lincoln and lumbered into the bar.

Paul drove around the corner and parked in a tunnel under a deserted railroad bridge. The tunnel was blocked off, the road once led to a plant that manufactured wire and wire products. At one time the plant employed eleven hundred workers. In the late eighties the number was down to seven. Now it was empty.

Paul walked up the sidewalk in the footsteps of yesteryear steelworkers to the Chateau where they had usually stopped in for a shot and a beer, or maybe a game of cards before going home.

The sunlight that followed Paul into the dark bar slowly dispersed as the large, oak door closed. Al "Big Head" Minardi looked over the top of his spectacles as he poured a draught into a tilted glass. He motioned with a tilt of his head and eyeballed the door at the back of the bar.

Paul nodded and walked toward the back of bar, passing two tables of card players; one a Euchre game, the other Knock Rum. Paul walked through the swinging door without knocking.

Freddy Caruso sat on a ten-gallon lard can. He hovered over a table with a spoon in his left hand and a fork in his right. A large plaid bib, held in place by his third chin, partially covered his chest. Paul was temporarily taken aback by the sight, picturing in his mind Freddy in a loin-cloth, a bone impaled through his nose stirring a large black pot with a white man in it who looked suspiciously like Paul.

Freddy finally moved, motioning with his fork to a chair opposite him.

"What—?" Paul barely got the word out of his mouth when a short, stout woman with dyed black hair that sat on her head like a bird's nest interrupted by plopping down a large dish of spaghetti.

"Here you are sonny? Just the way mamma made it." She retrieved two sticks of butter from the fridge and placed them next to a basket of sliced Italian bread before leaving.

Freddy's meaty paws manipulated the fork and spoon. He twirled the strands of spaghetti into a miniature haystack, stabbed a piece of meatball and thrust the entire meal for a pigmy into his mouth. The mighty morsel filled Freddy's pie hole; his cheeks bulged as he chomped, his chubby lips forming an operatic oval and then pursing together like a fish out of water. That's when Paul remembered Freddy's nickname—"fish lips". Freddy "fish lips" Caruso.

Freddy shrugged his shoulders. "My sister. Got her a job here. Makes the best pasta."

"She cooks here?" Paul asked. "This isn't a restaurant. How'd you—?"

"Never mind," Freddy said, holding another combination of field and turf near his mouth and snatching it from the fork like a fish darting for a baited hook. Freddy was caught once again—caught in food addiction.

Paul waited for Freddy to dispose of the half-chewed morsel. Freddy's eyes closed and a faint smile spread across his sauce-covered lips as he happily chomped away. He seemed to be somewhere else until he finally swallowed his first *hit.*

"She helps out," Freddy said through a burp. "Cooks burgers and makes sandwiches." He nodded toward the door off the bar. "Besides, Murph owes me. Big time. But you're not here for that are you?" Freddy dove back into the pasta using the utensils like a prisoner trying to dig a hole to freedom.

"No, Vito said—"

"That's Don Vito to you," Freddy said through slushy clomps of pasta and ground meatball.

"That's right. Don Vito," Paul exaggerated the word *Don* and then continued, "said he might have some information for me."

"First of all, Don Vito wants it understood that ventures into Tecza's personal life are in no way connected to the Vito LaBruscia Family," Freddy waited for Paul's confirmation. Paul nodded. "You understand, right?"

"I will take Vito's word on this, but it's hard, knowing the connection between Vito, I mean Don Vito, Albert Giannamore, and Earsoff Tecza."

"Business. Only business."

"But murder crept into that business with the murders of Roxanne Giannamore and Hilary Jefferson. Albert Giannamore, Roxanne's brother, worked for Don Vito. And I remember that no one was arrested or even suspected of their murders."

"That's true. There were no reprisals because the family wasn't involved. Gabish?"

Paul's anticipation of Vito's help dwindled with his understanding of Freddy's logic.

"But," Freddy said, "Don Vito asked me to tell you that Albert Giannamore worked for someone else as well."

Paul's hopes soared. He almost jumped out of his seat. "Who?"

"That, I cannot tell you. You'll have to find out for yourself."

"But he's the murderer! I have to know his name. Don Vito said—"

"Don Vito said he would help. And he just did. Don Vito cannot betray a trust. The rest is up to you. This person may or may not be the murderer. You have to find out on your own who Albert worked for."

"But—"

Freddy waved his hand in a dismissive movement. "We're done. Good bye."

Paul started to open his mouth but Freddy's expression stopped any further conversation. Paul left the Chateau Lounge with a feeling of relief. Don Vito had come through like he said he would—but not all the way. Paul had to go the distance and find out who Albert Giannamore worked for.

CHAPTER 26

The end booth provided a sheltered, yet unobstructed view of the restaurant's entrance. She could see anyone who left and who entered. And that's what Karen Thompson wanted while she waited for her brother, Philip.

Karen remembered coming to Swooney's Restaurant with her father years ago when she was a young child. The Swooney's Special was the most popular sandwich in the valley and the near freezing draught beer usually packed the bar with the brewski brotherhood and thirsty golfers from nearby courses—truly a workingman's restaurant and bar.

Karen hadn't been to the restaurant since the new management leveled the old building and built the new modern one. The first thing she noticed was the high ceiling with lavender eighteen-inch metal heating and air conditioning ducts. Horizontal pipes snaked their way through ceiling trusses and strategically placed shorter vertical air ducts, that the air emanated from, hung like tentacles from a giant octopus.

The large ductwork contrasted with the six delicate wrought iron lighting units hanging from the ceiling. Approximately eight feet wide, each unit had tree-like branches supporting metallic flowers on its extremities with stamens, pistils and teardrop lights.

French motif seemed to dominate the restaurant. Posters of French women, either dancing or posed, decorated the walls. An eight by six foot expressionistic painting resembling Charlie Chaplain hung centered over the entrance opening. The scene showed him sitting at a table sipping wine with an old haggard woman. Under the image were the words:

In victory you deserve champagne.
In defeat, you deserve it.

Napolean

Karen had more on her mind than the restaurant's ambience. She had hastily made arrangements with Philip to meet her and perceived him as apprehensive to the late invitation; but she knew he would come. She was his big sister, the one he looked up to; the one who helped get him the job in the department.

And it wasn't easy getting him in the lab. Phil had a year left to get his degree in chemistry and a minor in forensic science at Seton Hill University. His excellent grades and Karen's recommendation landed him the job. He graduated two years ago and is presently working on a thesis for his master's degree.

A waitress, resembling the woman in the painting, slunk into the restaurant from the bar. It was her second trip for Karen's order. She looked as if she had a hangover, her pouchy red eyes and her posture gave the impression of regret. Karen unfolded her hands, palms up, and cocked her head sideways. The waitress spun on her heels and retreated to apparent safety into the bar.

Karen checked her wristwatch for the eleventh time as Philip entered the restaurant. He bobbed his head and craned his neck until he spotted Karen.

He strode toward her booth, his eyes glued on his sister, his face reflecting a built-up concern.

"What's up sis? Is something wrong?" he said, sliding into the seat opposite Karen.

"Does something have to be wrong to have lunch with my brother?"

"Of course not." Philip looked at Karen sideways, out of the corners of his eyes. "So what do you want?"

Karen chuckled. "Well, I do have a favor to ask. But I really wanted to see you. You've been busy with work and school; a Saturday lunch seemed like a good idea."

"Yeah, it's hectic sometimes. We have to get together more."

Karen's big sister smile was interrupted by the third appearance of Sweeney's *never to be employee of the month* waitress. She flipped her pad and pencil at the ready. And then she noticed Philip.

He was handsome by anyone's standards: his dark wavy hair contrasted with bright blue eyes on a rugged well proportioned face. His wide smile showcased a set of perfect pearly-whites.

The waitress suddenly mustered a bit of personality while gazing at Philip and slowly read the lunch specials from the back of her pad.

"Can you give me a few minutes," he said.

The waitress beamed at Philip without answering.

Karen and Philip stared at each other. Karen said, "We'll be a few minutes."

"Oh," the waitress said. She glared at Karen and before she turned to leave, she flashed a smile at Philip.

Karen picked up a menu. "We should decide what to order," she said, winking. "I think she'll be back soon."

Microseconds after they chose club sandwiches and tea, *employee of the month* hovered over the table, pen in hand. After taking their order she slow-footed away.

"How's the job going?" Philip asked.

"Great. Been doing surveillance lately. That's what I—"

"Who's your partner?"

"Claudia."

Philip looked puzzled. "Claudia Who?"

"Claudia Bianchi."

Philip's expression didn't change.

"Used to be Claudia Sappone."

"Joey Bags Sappone's sister?"

"That's her. We've been surveilling this guy. He's really not the type—"

"He's connected, isn't he? How'd she—?"

"Listen," Karen said, forcefully. "That's politics, not for us to concern ourselves over.

Philip started to open his mouth. Karen raised her hand. "About this favor. Can you test a bottle and two glasses for drugs?"

"Sure. Just drop them off at the lab—"

"No, not the lab. This is for me. Can you test them at the university?"

Puzzlement returned to Philip's face.

"This is between us," Karen said, her head nodded in the affirmative.

"Sure, but why—?"

"Can't tell you now. I'll give you the details later."

Pouchy eyes returned with their lunch tray.

CHAPTER 27

Freddy "Fish Lips" Caruso and Sergei Sokoloff introduced themselves and agreed on the present weather
situation in Al "Big Head" Minardi's apartment above the
Chateau Bar. A few minutes later Paden Tucker climbed
the dark staircase.

Like a mosquito to a light bulb, Tucker's desire for
celebrity became obsessive. Being Darby Davis' right
hand man put him in the spotlight and he loved it. But
not tonight. Meeting with Freddy Caruso and Earsoff
Tecza's replacement had to be on the que tee. There had
to be no affiliation with the *family* or any illicit business,
especially prostitution. Tucker slithered in the room and
closed the door so quickly barely any light or scent of
ravioli escaped into the hall.

"Freddy," Tucker said, "I thought Albert would be
here."

"He's not. You're five minutes late."

Sergei and Freddy plopped on a threadbare blue
velvet couch. Freddy extended his arm and invited Tucker
to a similar upholstered chair across from them. A coffee
table littered with ashtrays and empty I.C. Light beer cans
separated them.

"I thought I was being followed."

"Think you're on 'America's Most Wanted' or something? Who would want to follow you?"

"You know I have to keep a low profile," Tucker said. "We have to disassociate—"

"Yeah, yeah, I know," Freddy said, waving his hand in a dismissive motion. He pointed to his right. "This is Sergei Sokoloff, Earsoff's cousin."

Sergei stood up and shook hands with Tucker. He carried 150 pounds on a thin, five foot ten frame. Ice blue eyes contrasted with salt and pepper hair. "Nice to meet you," he said in a Russian accent.

Tucker nodded. "I understand you're Tecza's only family member that's left. Can you legally take possession of Chuckles?"

"Absolutely," Sergei said, pulling a document from his leather jacket pocket. "Earsoff and I had a reciprocal agreement with each other's wills. In other words—"

"Yeah, I get it. You covered each other's asses. I understand. The question is: did Earsoff explain our arrangement?" Freddy asked, alternating his digit finger between himself and Tucker.

"Earsoff told me of the arrangement. But I—"

"But what?" Freddy asked.

"I don't know if I can do this. This is dangerous. I—"

"Nothing to it," Tucker said. "Earsoff said you had a small operation in Webster. This is the same, just a lot bigger."

"My business was never broken into. And I was never shot."

"What!" Tucker and Freddy said simultaneously, looking at each other.

"I had a key and went to Chuckle's last night to check on Earsoff's business, where I was beaten up and shot," Sergei said to Freddy. Sergei looked scared. "I didn't know if—"

"If we were pushing you out?" Freddy said, raising his voice. "We don't want your business. We don't want involved in any way. We just want a cut." He looked at

Tucker. "Didn't Algie tell you—" He stopped when Tucker raised an index finger to his lips.

"What happened?" Tucker asked.

"I went in the bar and turned the lights on," Sergei said. He paused and then continued. "I helped Earsoff occasionally. He gave me a key. When I heard what happened, I came right over."

"Did the police notify you?" Tucker asked.

"No. Rusty the bartender called me."

Tucker's face contorted in disgust. Freddy rotated his finger in a circular motion prompting Sergei to continue.

Sergei put the document he had been holding back in his pocket. "The bar looked okay, so I went down the hall to the office. That's when he hit me."

Freddy leaned forward. "Who hit you?"

"Don't know. Didn't see him until after."

"After what?" Tucker asked.

"I must have been out a little while. Hit me in the head. Baseball bat I think. Anyway, when I came to I was on the floor and he was leaving. I tripped him and he fell. We struggled and I was getting the best of him until he shot me."

Sergei opened his jacket and lifted his shirt. He pointed to a red spotted bandage on the left side of his stomach. "Just a flesh wound. Through and through. But it scared the shit out of me."

"What happened then?" Tucker asked.

Sergei's eyes widened. "I stopped. I let go of him and fell back to the floor."

"Did you see who it was?"

"No, he wore a ski mask."

"What did he do then?"

"He picked something up he had dropped and left."

"He took something!" Freddy barked, "What did he take?"

Sergei held his jacket partially open. "After I checked and bandaged my wound, I checked the office. A silver twenty five automatic Earsoff kept in his desk was missing. Probably shot with it. And the rolodex was open and a page was torn from it."

"Where was it torn from?" asked Tucker.

"The letter J."

"What else?" Freddy asked.

"As far as I can tell... eight video tapes."

Tucker held his forehead. "Eight video tapes? Holy shit. How do you know there were eight?"

"There were eight empty slots."

"Empty slots? Where were these tapes?"

"The bookshelves were pulled open. Slots for tapes were built into the wall.

"We'll look into this," Freddy said. "You can go now. We'll be in touch."

Sergei left and disappeared down the dark staircase.

"Shit," Tucker said. He stood up and slowly walked to a window overlooking Page Street. He seemed to be thinking; his right hand held his chin, his left rested on his hip.

"You can say that again," Freddy said. "Don Vito's gonna be pissed. Why didn't the cops seal off the bar?"

"Too late now. Valuable information is missing. The question is: what is the information and why was it stolen?"

"This could shut down the operation," Freddy said. "Bad for business. Heads will roll."

"Why did the thief steal only selected tapes? He's not just a thief. This person has an agenda."

"Blackmail? Maybe this guy's the Slasher?"

"Naw. Maybe. Maybe he is the Slasher. But what's the connection with the tapes?

"You better find out quick. Call your contact on the force. Ask questions," Freddy said, and left.

Tucker continued to stare out the window.

CHAPTER 28

The faint moonlight enhanced the white paint on his Ford pickup putting Wally, he thought, in the spotlight. He parked near the 1200 block of Schoonmaker Avenue, a few doors away from Nuzzachi's Pizza Shop and across the street from Chuckle's Bar and Grille.

Wally thought he might be wasting his time, but he felt he had to do something; there were too many unanswered questions and Chuckle's seemed like a good starting point. After all, he thought, Earsoff Tecza ran a prostitution ring; he had to be *connected* to stay in business. Maybe someone would show up and lead Wally to that connection.

Business looked good for Nuzzachi's. Two delivery cars were running non-stop, but only a few customers stopped for a pickup order. They left their lights on and motors running for a quick getaway.

A light green older model Buick pulled in front of Chuckle's. Wally straightened in his seat when the driver turned his lights off. He craned his neck to see who got out of the car. The sequential flashing lights on Chuckle's sign were off and the moonlight highlighted a small framed man with salt and pepper hair wearing a leather jacket. The man walked toward Chuckle's door checking to see if anyone was watching. At the door he fumbled with his keys, unlocked the door and went in.

Wally wrote down the man's description and 9:15 the time he entered the bar. He wasn't Rusty, the bartender. He wondered who the man was. Who would have keys? A relative maybe?

Ten minutes later, another small man walked toward Chuckle's from the other direction. As he got closer, Wally readily recognized the squirrelly face and slity eyes that belonged to Paden Tucker. He hunkered in Chuckle's doorway and knocked on the door. After the third knock, the door opened a crack and then widened for Tucker's entrance. Wally recorded the time: 9:26.

Sergei Sokoloff's fingers stopped flipping through the manila folders when he heard knocking on the door. He grabbed the baseball bat that yesterday had introduced itself to his head and walked into the hallway. Another knock. He quickstepped to the bar and picked up the phone. He punched in a few numbers, hesitated and hung up. He cautiously walked to the door and squinted through the peep hole.

"Mister Tucker? Is that you?"

A deep voice answered. "Yes. Open up."

Sergei flipped the deadbolt knob. Paden Tucker pushed the door partly open and slid into the bar, quickly closing the door behind him.

"What kept you? I knocked three times."

"I was scared," Sergei said in a high pitched voice. "I didn't know it was you. I was going to call the police."

"What!"

"I didn't. I—"

"Good," Tucker said, locking the door. "Where are the tapes?"

Sergei led the Tucker toward the office, stopping in the hallway. He pointed to the back door. "That's where he got in." Sergei showed Tucker the marks made by the prybar. "I installed this earlier," he said, tapping a new deadbolt with his finger.

Tucker nodded and walked into the office. The expression on his face had features of both amazement and fear. "Have you been to the hotel or talked to Wanda yet?"

"I called her earlier. She's taking care of business."

"Do you know of anyone who had threatened Earsoff?"

"No. I don't know of—"

"Who was he blackmailing?"

"Blackmailing? I don't think he—"

"Sure he was. Why would he have video tapes?"

"I don't think so Mister Tucker."

"Well I do. Captain Antonelli was involved also. His safe was empty and his throat slashed like Earsoff's."

Sergei dropped his head. "I want to find out who did this honest, but I don't know anything."

"What's missing? Let's start with that."

Sergei picked up the right side desk drawer. "Earsoff's pistol was in here. A chrome-plated, twenty five caliber automatic." He slid the drawer into the desk's cavity and slammed it shut. He pointed to the rolodex. "An address from the letter J was ripped out," he said, pointing to a remaining portion of the sheet."

"Know anyone with the last name starting with the letter J?"

"No." Sergei said, picking up the desk pad. "He kept notes under this pad; nothing important was left behind."

"What else?"

Sergei stumbled through the rubble to the empty shelves and pulled the unit open. "This is where Sergei stored the tapes."

Tucker's eyes widened. "Holy shit. Look at all those tapes," Tucker said, gesturing with a panoramic motion of his arm across the width of the shelves. "There's got to be a hundred tapes there."

"Eighty-six. I counted them."

"How many missing?"

"Eight. Five H's, two R's and one D."

Tucker plopped in a chair. He seemed to search for words. "That makes ninety three total. Right?"

Sergei counted on his fingers. "Right."

"You were familiar with Earsoff's operation, weren't you?" Sergei nodded.

"You know some of the girls?" Another nod.

"Who do you know with the last name starting with H's or R's?"

Sergei rubbed his forehead for a minute. "None. Nobody."

"Call Wanda and find out." Tucker composed himself, stood up and walked to the tapes. He fingered through the D's, pulling out selected tapes and stacked five on the desk. He repeated this procedure for the M's and the T's until he had a total of seventeen tapes.

"Hand me that bag," Tucker said, pointing to a blue gym bag. Sergei handed him the bag and Tucker stuffed the tapes inside and zipped it closed. Tucker picked up the bag and headed for the hallway. "If you find anything that incriminates Representative Davis or Mayor Majewski, secure it off premises and call me immediately."

Tucker now walked toward the front door. He stopped short of the door, nodded in the affirmative and waited for Sergei's reply before leaving.

———

Wally's eyes focused on the black steel door waiting for Paden Tucker to leave Chuckle's. Wally wondered what the bar looked like. He'd heard of its reputation while frequenting various bars and, of course, from the locker room at the W&J Steel Plant.

Wally's mind wandered back to the sixties and the bars in the Far East. He remembered the smell of cheap perfume mixed with alcoholic vapors and the sound of American pop music playing in a dimly lighted atmos-

phere. *You gotta dolla G.I.? You numba one boy son. Dolla for jukey box? You buy me beeru?*

Wally's mind snapped back to the present when the steel door opened and Paden Tucker made a hasty exit at 9:55. Wally waited for a few minutes until Tucker disappeared into the night before getting out of his truck. Less than a minute later, Wally knocked on the black steel door.

"Did you forget some—"

"Yeah, I forgot to get a lot of answers," Wally said, pushing his way through the doorway.

CHAPTER 29

On Sunday mornings in Mononville, most people drive their cars to places of worship—but on this Sunday Bernie Eisner's black Mercedes headed for Ducheck's Bar where the only prayers to be heard were those of finding answers to unsolved murders.

"Are they here yet?" Bernie asked.

"I noticed Paul's Chrysler in the alley as we drove past," Wally said. "He was supposed to pick up Harvey."

"Good," Bernie said, gliding the German made driving experience into a stall in the bar's lot. He grunted climbing out of the car. Bernie made the same noise retrieving his briefcase from the rear seat.

Wally led the way to the back door, his steps crunching on the lot's gravel. Bernie took a second to turn around for a last admiring look at what United Steel Company's retainer had paid for and beeped the vehicle's chastity belt locked.

Wally knocked on the back door.

J.C. pulled aside a curtain on the door's window and peered out. He had to be careful. In Pennsylvania, public bars that didn't sell food were prohibited from selling alcohol on Sundays. Even though they were going upstairs to the card room and not the bar, liquor control board agents might assume otherwise. That wasn't the reason for the secrecy. They had decided to provide anonymity for the people who helped and shared information. J.C. motioned them inside with a wave of his hand.

Wally reached for the doorknob at the sound of the metallic deadbolt snapping open. "We parked in the lot," Wally said. "Didn't want to congest the area."

J.C. swung the door open. "Good idea."

Bernie and Wally followed J.C. up the staircase and into the card room.

Paul and Harvey mulled over a game of gin at the card table. As the others were seating themselves, Paul asked, "Did anyone follow you?"

"Not a chance," Wally said. "I snuck out the back door and jumped old man Sullenburger's fence to the alley, then cut through Harmon's yard to Ontario Street where Bernie was waiting with black beauty."

Harvey's puzzled expression prompted J.C.'s explanation. "His Mercedes."

"Oh." Harvey mumbled, seemingly relieved.

Bernie pulled a yellow legal pad from his briefcase and clicked open a gold-plated ballpoint pen.

"Let's get started," he said. "Paul, exactly what did Freddy Caruso tell you?"

"He said Albert Giannamore worked for someone other than Don Vito LaBruscia."

Bernie scribbled on the yellow pad. "I take it he was relaying this information directly from the Don?"

Paul nodded. "That's right. Freddy said Don Vito instructed him to give me this information, but not a name." Paul paused. "He also said that Don Vito nor any of his people had anything to do with the recent murders."

Bernie tapped the cleft in his chin with his pen as if he had an idea. He looked at each person in the room. "Why would Don Vito say Giannamore worked for someone other than himself?"

J.C. volunteered an answer. "Because the Don doesn't want to be involved?"

The others nodded.

Paul had taken a sip of beer and banged his glass down. "Don Vito has too many illegal ventures going on. He doesn't want to be under the law's watchful eye."

"That's true," Bernie said. "But why would he drop a dime on Giannamore."

"It's not Albert Giannamore," Paul said. "Don Vito's pointing the finger at whomever Giannamore also worked for."

"Bernie smiled. "I wouldn't take the word of a *Don* so eagerly my friend. Remember who we're talking about."

Paul nodded and sat back in his chair. He knew a lot about Don Vito's history—the prostitution, loan sharking, beatings, and murders—all from police records and information from his father, Wally's brother.

Wally must have read Paul's mind. "I wouldn't believe a crooked word Vito said. But even snakes run from danger. He's pointing the way." Wally had a wealth of information to share tonight, but decided to wait until the others offered their ideas and suggestions.

"Okay," Bernie said, "Who are we looking for?"

J.C. scratched his head. "Lieutenant Steitzer?"

"Steitzer?" Paul said. "He's a crooked cop, not a murderer."

J.C. tried again. "The mayor?"

"I don't think so," Bernie said. "They're probably involved on a low level, but we're after the Slasher, aren't we?"

Everyone nodded.

Bernie continued. "Then let's go back in time and gather the facts. Are there any prostitutes around that worked with the murdered girls?" Bernie directed his question at Paul.

"I'll get on it," he said. "I'll go to Wanda's Place tomorrow morning.

"That will be a start," Bernie said. "By the way, refresh my memory. Who were the girls that were murdered?

"Roxanne Giannamore and Hilary Jefferson," Harvey blurted.

"That's right," Bernie said. "Giannamore. Albert's kid sister. Maybe he knows something or—."

"Or the person he worked for knows something?" Wally asked.

"Ditto," Bernie said.

"How can we get Giannamore to cooperate?" Wally asked.

"Impossible," Paul said. "Mob's code of silence. He knows what would happen to him if he talked."

Bernie held up a finger in a halting motion. "Not so fast. It will be difficult but not impossible." Paul looked at Bernie for an explanation. "If we determine who Albert worked for, we can squeeze that person for information."

The smile on Paul's face reflected Bernie'a logic. The police would routinely *turn* one suspect against the other for a lighter sentence or no sentence at all. "That could work. All we have to do is determine who Albert worked for."

"Paden Tucker comes to mind." Harvey said.

Everyone looked at him.

Harvey looked around. He shrugged his shoulders. "I work in the file room. I've seen reports where Tucker was implicated in minor misdemeanors. Albert's name too."

Paul put his beer down. "I don't remember seeing any of those."

"You're a detective. You wouldn't work on misdeemeanor cases," Harvey said. "Anyway, they were dismissed, as usual."

"As usual?" Bernie asked.

"Yeah. With a wave of Judge Carson's hand."

Bernie nodded.

"Who's Paden Tucker?" asked J.C.

"He's the skinny, squirrelly guy that marches in all the Veteran's Parades," Wally said.

J.C. smiled. "You mean the guy that wears his Legionnaire's hat crooked; marches out of step and his pants are high, expecting a flood?"

Wally nodded. "That's him. All one hundred and fifty pounds of bullshit stuffed into Johnstown pants and a Legionnaire's hat."

"What did he do?" J.C. asked. "And why would Albert Giannamore work for him?"

Bernie interrupted. "He's a power broker."

"Him?"

"He's a member of every club and veteran's group in town," Paul said. "If he's in the Polish club and you hear him talk, he's Polish. The same with the Ukrainian Club, the French Club, Italian Club, Slovak, Hungarian, Croatian—"

"We get the picture," Wally said. "He's a member of everything and bullshits the politicians into believing that he has influence in these organizations."

J.C. held his hands open for an answer. "What does he do for a living? Does he have a job?"

"He doesn't work for a living," Wally said. "He gets appointed to organizations by his political buddies. Right now he has some position with Triple A."

Paul pushed an Iron City bottle toward the center of the table and tapped the top. "And before that he was some kind of representative for a brewery."

"Doesn't seem like a steady income," J.C. said.

"His wife works," Paul said. "She owns the 'Grapefully Yours Wine Shop'."

Paul's statement caught Wally off guard. "I hadn't thought about that before," Wally said. "That's where the drugged Tuscan Ridge Wine could have come from. But we'll deal with that later. I have some new information." He motioned to Bernie. "Bernie, I don't know if you should hear this, but I might have pushed the envelope a little in obtaining it."

Paul held his head and muttered in a low voice, "Oh no."

Bernie took a long look at Wally and at the other faces in the room. "Just answer yes or no to my question. Did you get this information from a person?"

"Yes."

"Did you ask this person questions?"

"Yes."

Bernie looked over the top of his glasses at Wally. "Did this person answer your questions?"

Wally's face broke into a wry grin. "Yes."

"Good," Bernie said, now give us the information you received at this question and answer session."

Wally explained why he went to Chuckle's Bar and Grille. He referred to a sheet of paper for the times Sergei and Paden Tucker arrived and left. He left out the information about how he entered the bar and how he extracted the information from Sergei Sokoloff.

"Sergei Sokoloff is Earsoff's cousin. He's taking over the bar and the operation."

"The operation?" J.C. asked.

"Prostitution. Wanda's place," Wally said. J.C. looked puzzled. "Cozy Nook Hotel on the outskirts of town."

"Jacob's Creek area?"

Wally smiled. "That's right. You been there? Been nookified?"

J.C. put his hands up in a defensive posture. "Not me. I just heard talk."

"Talk is cheap," Paul said, "How much did you pay?"

J.C. grinned. Everyone laughed.

Wally changed the tone of the conversation. "Seems our esteemed and decorated Captain Leonard Antonelli was involved by providing the protection."

Paul nodded as if he knew it to be true. The raids on Wanda's place always came up empty, as if she had been tipped off.

Wally lowered his head and bit his lip. "Giovanna was involved. She did the books."

Paul reached a big paw around Wally's shoulder. "Sorry Wally. I know how much you loved her. But hey, she was only the bookkeeper. She wasn't—"

"She was dirty. She was the bookkeeper, the second bookkeeper," he said, his eyes filling with moisture. "She broke the law."

"Antonelli probably made her," J.C. said.

"But she did."

Paul changed the subject. "That's why her place was tossed. She had to have Wanda's records."

"Antonelli's place was tossed too, wasn't it?" Harvey asked.

"Looks like blackmail," Paul said. "Whoever tossed Giovanna's place didn't find what he was looking for, so he went to Antonelli's."

"Did he find anything?" J.C. asked.

"A hard drive was missing from Giovanna's old computer and Leonard's safe was open. I think it's obvious."

"Tip of the iceberg," Wally said. He detailed the story of how Sergei was beaten and shot by an intruder who took hidden videotapes and an address from the rolodex.

"Hidden behind swing out shelves," Paul said, surprised.

Wally said, "Eight tapes. Five H's two R's and one D and an address from the letter J. By the way, what was Albert Giannamore's sister's name?"

"Roxanne," Harvey answered.

"There's the R," J.C. said. "What about the H?"

"The other girl's name was Hilary," Paul said slowly. "And the D...? Could that be for Darby Davis?"

"Whoa," Bernie said. "Hold on a minute. You're not suggesting—"

"We're just asking questions," Wally said. "Paden Tucker works for Davis, doesn't he? There's a connection. Someone is being blackmailed. Someone with a D in their name."

"I wouldn't go accusing—"

"We're not Bernie!" Paul said. "We're looking for the truth."

"What about the J?" asked Harvey.

"A girls name maybe," Paul said. "I'll check it out at Wanda's tomorrow."

Harvey spoke up. "Wasn't the J a missing index card from the rolodex?"

Wally checked his notes. "That's right."

"Aren't people indexed by their last names?"

Wally and Paul looked at each other. "That's right," Paul said. "Could be Jefferson. I'll check that out also."

"You've got that hearing tomorrow," Bernie said to Paul. "Don't get into any trouble before then."

"I didn't do anything. Wally didn't either. I think the person with the first name with a D or J has something to worry about."

"Let's get out of here," Wally said. "Think things over and get a fresh start tomorrow."

"One more thing," Paul said. "I was issued a summons last evening. A patrol cop dropped it off."

"When?" Bernie asked.

"Tomorrow. Eight O'clock."

"I'll pick you up at seven."

CHAPTER 30

A young man stood on the corner in front of the Four Aces Club. The light from the street lamp reflected off his bald head revealing a heavily tattooed neck and upper arm.

"Hey Guido," Freddy Caruso said, knocking knuckles with baldy.

"Nice to see you Mister Caruso. Don Vito is expecting you."

Guido didn't have to signal the doorman, Freddy's voice could be heard a block away. The black curtain that covered the window rose over an eyeball. The door opened to Freddy.

Freddy walked in the bar against the acrid smell of whiskey and cigar smoke.

Joey "Bags" Sappone slid off a barstool and grabbed Freddy in a bear hug before Freddy had taken three steps. For a man over three hundred pounds, Joey was surprisingly agile. Joey kissed Freddy on both cheeks.

Three men who were sitting with Joey acknowledged Freddy.

Mark Manfreado, a thin gray-haired man with a bright red bulbous nose offered his hand and obligatory hug. "How's it goin' Mister Caruso?"

"Good to see you Rudy." The *wise guys* called him Rudy—short for Rudolph the Red-nosed Raindeer.

John Landucci was next in the greeting line. Freddy"s hug was exaggerated to each side avoiding Landucci's greasy, dyed black hair. It was combed straight back against his head, looking almost painted on.

"What's new slick?" Freddy asked.

"S.O.S. Mister Caruso."

Joey motioned to the third man with mousey brown hair and small, steely eyes. He wore a Hawaiian shirt over blue Dockers.

"You remember Walt. I have him working with Albert now."

Walter "what's a matta you" Matta stood up and offered his hand. "Pleased to meet you Mister Caruso."

Freddy smiled. He grabbed Walt's hand and yanked him into a bear hug, wrapping his arms around his back— a procedure used by the wise guys to check for recording devices.

"Pleased to meet you too," he said laughing. "Hey, we're family here. Loosen up. I've heard you've been doing a good job with pick-ups for Rudy. Working for Albert will be less stressful." Freddy asked Joey. "How long's he been here? Two, three months?"

"Four months."

Freddy slapped Walt on the shoulder. He started walking away singing *The Jefferson's* theme song "Movin' On Up". He continued singing with the melody, breaking into a dance into the hall that led to the office.

As usual, Joey knuckle-rapped the door to Don Vito's office and, as usual, an Italian word authorized his entrance. The partial vacuum created by the opening of the door sucked strong cigar smoke into Freddy's face, instantly irritating his eyes.

The old bald man sat comfortably in an upholstered leather chair. He flicked his cigar ash into a large, thick glass tray.

"How was the meeting?" Don Vito asked. "Is Sergei gonna' play ball? Five percent over what Tecza paid?"

"Yeah, five," Freddy said. "Sergei's not the problem." Freddy hesitated.

"Problem? Is there a problem, Freddy?"

Freddy told Don Vito about the break-in and theft at Chuckle's Bar and what was taken because the bar wasn't secured by the police after Tecza's murder.

"Eight video tapes!"

Freddy stepped back at the old man's outburst. He composed himself and slowly went over the fact that five videos were taken from the H's, two from the R's and one from the letter D.

Don Vito pondered the letters Freddy mentioned. He slammed his fist on the desk. "Shit. This will be bad for business if this gets out. Secret tapes. Who authorized secret taping?"

"I don't know. Albert and Antonelli took care of the business."

"That stupid cop! He had to have his hand in it. I never trusted cops. They don't know shit about crime. They can screw up a one car funeral."

"Tucker was pissed too."

"About the cops not checking the bar?"

"Yeah, but more about the missing tapes."

Don Vito rubbed his chin. "I wonder—"

"I followed him after the meeting."

"Who?"

"Tucker. He went to Chuckle's Bar."

"Really?"

"Parked a block away."

"Good work Freddy," Don Vito said, waving his hand in a dismissive motion that signaled Freddy to leave.

As the door closed, Don Vito picked up the phone receiver and punched in a number. He held the phone to his ear. After a few seconds he said, "We have a problem."

CHAPTER 31

The drive to Seton Hill University didn't take long, only thirty-five minutes. Located practically in the middle of the town of Arnzen—a mid-sized town comprised mostly of corporate concrete buildings—the campus couldn't be more out of place. It covered over 200 acres of southwestern Pennsylvania forested splendor with nineteen buildings perched on a level plateau.

Philip Thompson's feelings elevated in direct proportion to the grade of the driveway as he drove the winding driveway that meandered the quarter mile to the campus. It wasn't just the beautiful scenery that elevated his mood but the total campus atmosphere. The faculty, students, and staff were like family to him.

Phil arrived at 9:00 a.m., two hours earlier than his 11:00 a.m. microbiology class. He had called Saturday for the Monday morning appointment to enlist the aid of Dr. Wendell's expertise and was lucky to catch him in his office.

"You might have to break the bottle," Dr. Wendell said, "if we can't find a swab long enough to reach the bottom." He rustled through one of the drawers in a wall cabinet.

Dr. Wendell chaired the chemistry department at the university and started the forensic science department, satisfying the clamor created by the various crime scene investigation shows on television.

"Why do you suspect Rohypnol?" Wendell asked. "There are plenty of sedating drugs on the street."

Phil didn't answer. He led a simple life, studied hard and stayed mostly out of the mainstream of the school's social life. "I don't know. Just a starting point. I heard the name on television."

Wendell continued. "Rohypnol or 'roofies' are the in thing today, but there's also chloral hydrate, known as mickey finns, gamma hydroxybutyrate, known as GHB, Triazolam, trade name Halcion, scopolamine, burundaga, and ketamine."

"I haven't heard of any of them."

"How about some of the street names like liquid ecstasy, liquid x, grievous bodily harm, easy lay for GHB, and special k for Ketamine? And Rohypnol, the drug you're interested in, is called roofies, roaches, larocha and the forget pill."

Phil looked stricken. "Do we have to test for all of them?"

Wendell shook his head. "Flunitrazepam—that's the trade name for Rohypnol—is the most popular so let's start with it. This sedative is in the benzodiazepine family. You know it as Valium, but it's ten times more potent."

"Is it dangerous?"

"Very. Especially when mixed with alcohol or other drugs it can lead to depression, aspiration, or even death. And it causes retrograde amnesia limiting recall for the victim."

Phil looked surprised. He wondered why his sister wanted this test to be a secret.

"How long has this drug been around?"

"It was reported in Europe in the late seventies. Started here in the nineties. Gay bars. Now it's in high schools and on college campuses. Inexpensive at two to four dollars a pop."

"I didn't know it was so widespread. How can we detect it?"

"We'll use Gas Chromatography Mass Spectrometry for a final determination. But first I'd like to try this Valium field test kit." Wendell held up a black pouch. He zipped it open and took out two ampoules and placed them on the table in front of him.

He took the bottle and glasses and sprayed a fine mist of distilled water into them. He sloshed the liquid around in the bottle making sure the sides were coated. He finally found a long swab in the cabinet and wiped the glasses and the bottom and sides of the bottle with it. He repeated this procedure with a second swab. He placed both swabs in a small oven and set a temperature and time setting.

"We'll let that dry for a while," Wendell said, "and use the dry powder on each swab for both tests."

The sound of a faint bell rang signifying the end of the swab's drying time. Wendell placed both swabs in a small holder and then broke the two ampoules and dripped their contents into a small glass dish. He inserted one of the swabs into the mixture and a lavender color appeared.

A smile stretched across Wendell's face. "Wa la. We have Valium present." He wrung his hands in pleasure. "Now to confirm the finding for flunitrazepam," He looked at Phil," I'm talking about Rohypnol. We'll use Gas Chromatography Mass Spectrometry.

Noticing that Phil looked a bit overwhelmed, Wendell said, "This will become second nature to you once you complete your masters. Right now your work is mostly D.N.A. and fingerprints, am I right?" Phil nodded in the affirmative. "You may never have the necessary equipment and may always rely on a lab."

The light beige machine wasn't as large as Phil thought it might be. It was portable and rested inauspiciously on a countertop at the far wall. The unit basically has two parts: the Gas Chromatography portion separates the mixture into pure chemical components and the Mass Spectrometry identifies and quantifies them.

Wendell retrieved the other swab and with a stainless steel knife-like object, scraped off the powdery residue onto a sheet of paper. He picked up the edges of the paper, shaking it until the residue fell into the middle of the paper. He then folded the paper into a crease and dropped the powder into the injection port of the machine. From there, helium, the carrier gas, transported the sample through the instrument where it was heated to 300 degrees Celsius causing the chemicals to become a gas. Chemical mixtures are separated based on their volatility and then sent to the Mass Spectrometer where the molecules are blasted with electrons causing them to break into positively charged particles called ions. The detector, or computer, counts the number of ions with a specific mass and then plots them on a graph called a mass spectrum where it is identified.

Wendell picked up the chart. "flunitrazepam."

CHAPTER 32

J acob's Creek really isn't a creek, more like a trickle from a spring—in this case seepage from abandoned mines that produce a mustard-like sediment on the creek's bed. Mononville sat on one side of the rusty mine water in Westland County. Two giant steps and a hop and you're on the other side into Morgan County and another legal jurisdiction where the Cozy Nook Hotel, also known as Wanda's Place, took root. Out of sight, out of mind, the two story building sat among pin-oak and locust trees in a country setting.

During the thirties and forties when the mines and mills were working full tilt, the hotel flourished when a Finlander named Sonafelder owned the hotel. Later, when the mills cut back and Sonafelder's consumption of Vodka increased, Earsoff Tecza made him an offer he couldn't refuse, especially with the muscle and financial aid provided by the LaBruscia Family.

Paul Andrews parked his Chrysler 300 under a pin-oak in the parking lot and headed toward the hotel. He walked heavy across the red dog slag, kicking at clumps of the steel-making residue, knowing that interviewing Wanda Obitko wasn't going to be easy or pleasant.

Paul had been to the Cozy Nook Hotel before. He participated on raids that were destined to fail because

Wanda had previously been tipped off. He remembered Wanda standing in the doorway, arms folded with a knowing and defiant grin on her face. He knew then and he knew now she was going to be a tough nut to crack.

Paul visualized the layout of the building as he walked toward the large southern style front porch. He remembered the main entrance opening to a hallway and steps to the second floor. On the right, a pocket door opened to a large sitting room with a spacious bar. On the left, a small door led to the office in the front of the building with a view of the parking lot. Three rooms, a bathroom and a closet occupied the second floor.

Paul looked to his left and noticed Wanda's pudgy face in the office window as he climbed the six recently sandblasted stone steps. Before he could walk halfway across the new decking of the porch, Wanda blocked the doorway with her wide body. She leaned against its frame as usual, with her arms crossed, but with a questioning look on her face, not the usual smirk.

"Business must be good," Paul said, pointing to the refurbished building's façade.

"Could be better," Wanda said, brushing cookie crumbs off her Muu Muu. "Whaddya want?"

Paul raised his hands in a submissive posture. "Just a few questions. Could we go inside?"

"No." Wanda's lips pursed into what looked like a miniature rosebud with her defiant retort. The close-cropped auburn hair that surrounded her face enhanced her green, but angry eyes.

"You've heard the Slasher's back? Bad for business? I'm trying to stop this guy. It would benefit us both if—"

"What do you want?"

"Information about some of your former...uh waitresses."

Wanda shot Paul a disgusted glance. What about them?"

Paul followed Wanda to the five rattan rocking chairs on the porch and they sat in the two nearest the door.

Paul figured Wanda had already heard about Earsoff's office being ransacked and the missing tapes, but he went over the information anyway.

"The R was probably for Roxanne Giannamore and the H for Hilary Jefferson, but the thief took some tapes under the letter D. Do you know any girl who might have a D for a first or last name?"

Wanda thought for a minute. "None of my girls... uh waitresses had names starting with a D."

Paul wrote notes in his pad. "What about J?"

Wanda slowly shook her head. "No. Only the last name of Hilary. Jefferson."

That's right, Paul remembered. The rolodex listed last names alphabetically. The letter J was for Jefferson. Hilary Jefferson.

"What do you know about Hilary Jefferson?"

"Nothing. Absolutely nothing."

Wanda didn't know a girl with the last name starting with a D and Roxanne was dead. "Who else worked at that time?" Paul asked.

"Just two girls. Linda Watkins and..." Wanda searched her memory. "Sylvia. Yeah, Sylvia Troupe."

Paul continued writing in his pad. "What happened to them?"

"Linda worked a few years and married a guy from Bratts Bridge."

"Sylvia?"

"She just up and disappeared."

Paul readied his pencil. "When?"

"Right after the murders." Wanda's face broke into a scowl. "Why are you asking me now? I gave this information to the police right after the murders."

Paul thought he knew the answer to the question he was about to ask, but he asked anyway. "Who did you talk to?"

"Antonelli. Lieutenant Antonelli."

Paul nodded and stood up to leave. "By the way, where did Sylvia go?"

"Don't know. Maybe back home?"

"Where was home?"

"A small town up north. Apollo, I think," Wanda said, walking to the doorway where she resumed her position.

"Do you have any records?"

"Naw, Earsoff kept them."

"Thanks," Paul said, and started to walk away.

Paul got what he came for except he wasn't satisfied with Wanda's information on Sylvia. The thief was obviously looking for the name of Hilary Jefferson in the rolodex. But why? And the name of Sylvia Troupe who went missing immediately after the murders was never brought up. Why? Did she know something about the murders? Or Hilary?

Paul drove back to DuCheck's thinking he had a trail to follow. Check Earsoff's rolodex for the names of Linda Watkins and Sylvia Troupe. And, of course, he thought there was something Wanda was hiding about Hilary Jefferson and Sylvia Troupe.

CHAPTER 33

The dark green Toyota Camry nested in its usual parking spot at the corner of Delaware and Donner, catty-corner from DuCheck's Bar. Karen Thompson drove today, although she didn't have to; she had seniority over Claudia Bianchi. But to be nice to a bitch with testosterone, Karen took turns driving.

"This is really boring," Claudia said. "I'm tired of watching this guy Wally and this old decrepit bar."

Karen met Wally only once and immediately liked him. She would rather sit in the car with Wally than *miss priss* twelve years her junior. Karen knew Claudia would rather be at a fancy nightclub listening to all those lying faces and their stupid pickup lines. That was Claudia. Always trying to impress. Always trying to get ahead— with as little effort as possible.

Karen's cell phone interrupted her thoughts. It was her brother Philip. He told her that Rohypnol was indeed in the wine bottle and glasses. She didn't repeat any of the information with Claudia present, just polite small talk to end the conversation.

Karen knew Wally couldn't have murdered anyone, and she felt relieved with the new information. She immediately wanted to help Wally, but with Claudia sitting shotgun her help was limited. And besides, she didn't trust Claudia. After all, Claudia's brother, Joe Sappone, was connected to the mob. She thought she'd better tell Wally of the test results. She grabbed her cell phone and started to open the door.

"Be right back," Karen said. "Got a personal call to make."

Claudia rolled her eyes and looked impassively out the window as Karen exited the car.

———————

Moldy placed the Elk hairs next to the standard dry fly hook and secured the wing with eight wraps of thread. He trimmed the hair with scissors and proceeded to finish the hackle and head. Moldy was a fly fisherman—just ask him. He dabbled in his hobby of tying flys whenever he had the chance. In this case, when the bar was empty, except for Wally and J.C.

Wally and J.C. discussed the possibilities of an affiliation between Albert Giannamore and Paden Tucker over a game of Rummy.

"I watched Tucker go into Chuckles. Sergei gave up Leonard Antonelli. The connection's there," Wally said.

J.C. spread kings. "How far does it go? The chief? The mayor? Don Vito?"

Wally picked from the deck when Caribbean Cruise music emanated from his cell phone. Wally flipped it open. "Hello."

"Wally it's me, Karen. Don't repeat my name. I don't want anyone to know I called."

"Okay."

"I'm outside. On the job. I called to tell you my brother called and you were right. Rohypnol was in the wine bottle and glasses. You were drugged."

"I knew it!" Wally said, discarding an ace.

"I've got to go. Claudia's waiting for me. Tell your nephew that Claudia Bianchi is Joe Sappone's sister. He'll know what that's about."

"Thanks for the info. I'd like—" Karen hung up.

"What's up Wally?" J.C. said, picking up the queen of spades.

"I just got confirmation that Giovanna and I were drugged."

"Makes sense. We knew it."

Wally opened his cell to the Caribbean Cruise music.

"Wally, Paul."

"Hey, I was just going to call you. I just got the results on the wine bottle and glasses."

"Good. I got an address on Linda Watkins. I'm on my way to Bratts Bridge. I've got a job for you."

"What's that?"

"Go to the Cozy Nook—"

"Cozy Nook?"

"Yes, the Cozy Nook. Wanda's holding out on me. I need more information."

"You don't understand. I can't—"

"Sure you can. Be a customer. Talk to one of the girls. I need info on Hilary Jefferson and Sylvia Troupe. Find out where they're from, where they live, their relatives. You know what to do."

"But—"

"It's important, Wally."

"Okay," Wally said, and closed his cell. "Damn it," he said. "I didn't tell Paul about being drugged."

J.C. spread queens ending the game. "Don't worry," he said. "Paul had to know you were drugged."

CHAPTER 34

Bratts Bridge is a small town. Very small, what's left of it, a former company-owned coal mining patch from the turn of the century. Most of the collapsed and run-down deserted buildings had been removed decades ago, leaving only a few dozen houses and a small concrete block post office.

Built on the ruins of Gettler's Grocery Store twenty-five years ago, the post office was the newest building in the community. Paul pulled off the two lane blacktop road into its parking lot. He entered the building to the sound of a bell, the kind old stores had above the door. At the counter, a huge man resembling a walrus sat behind a desk perusing Paul over his tiny spectacles. His balding head was pointed in contrast to his bulbous cheeks. His mustachioed fat upper lip protruded over his recessed chin.

"What can I do for you sir," he said, his beady eyes looking at Paul in apprehension.

"I'm trying to locate someone. A woman—"

Walrus man pushed himself away from the desk. A candy wrapper fell to the floor. "As a public servant and federal employee, I can't give you any personal information—"

"I don't need personal information. Just the location of this person so I can talk to her."

"Stalking."

"What?"

"Stalking. It's against the law to give information to the whereabouts of people because of these crazy people who stalk them."

"I'm sorry. I understand," Paul said, pulling out his shield. "I'm the law. I need to find a person that can help solve an ongoing case."

Walrus man inspected the badge. "Mononville. Okay, why didn't you say so? Who are you looking for? Name's Wilbur," he said, extending his hand.

"Paul. I'm looking for Linda Watkins. I was told she lives here."

Wilbur stroked his broom-like mustache. "Don't know of any Watkins here abouts."

Walrus man's appearance and his negative answer caught Paul off guard. "I'm sorry. Her maiden name was Watkins. She married a man from Bratts Bridge."

Wilbur scratched his head.

"Probably married and moved nine or ten years ago," Paul said. "First name Linda."

Light bulbs seem to shine in Wilbur's glasses. "Linda Fowler. Yeah. Married Earl 'bout that time."

"Does she live here now?"

"Yeah," Wilbur said, straining to stand up. He walked to the far window and pointed to a group of houses near a small ball field. "The gray one with the big porch."

"Thanks a lot, Wilbur," Paul said, and left.

Paul parked across the street from the gray house Walrus man said belonged to the Fowler's, and hopefully Linda Watkins' new abode. He walked leisurely across the road looking at their garage when a gust of wind blew dust from the ball field causing Paul to squint. He rubbed his eyes and took another look. It was unmistakable. The bright silver insignia of a Mercedes shown through the partially open garage door. Looked like a big sedan, Paul thought. It seemed to be out of place in this coal mining patch. For that matter, so did the large modern house.

Paul opened the wrought iron gate and walked on the cobblestone paved walk toward the house. The porch covered the width of the house and was deep, probably twelve feet. Flowering baskets hung along the porch's perimeter creating a charming, country atmosphere. Paul walked onto the porch thinking that the gliders, divans, chairs and bench seats could provide seating for the entire neighborhood. To his far right and in the shade of the hot, summer sun sat two rocking chairs. A thin, balding man, appearing to be at least sixty, sat in one of them.

"What can I do for you sport?" The man said in a resonant baritone voice.

The man might have been a good used car salesman thirty years ago, but the shiny store bought teeth would have caused slurred words and the wooden leg would have prevented him from hustling through a car lot.

The man's voice startled Paul. He didn't want to deal with the husband of a former hooker.

"Oh, excuse me. I didn't see you there. I'm looking for Linda Fowler. Is she at home?"

"She's on the phone," the man said as his teeth clacked together. "She's making arrangements with members of her card club for their annual tournament and dinner. Name's Earl. What's yours?"

"Paul. Paul Andrews. I'd like to talk to your wife about—"

"I used to know a Paul Andrews years ago," a husky female voice said.

The front door opened to an attractive woman with long shiny auburn hair. She wore a flowered print blouse over white slacks that emphasized her curvaceous body.

"Come in," she said while holding the door open.

She led Paul into a large foyer and turned left into a room lighted by skylights. Potted plants and flowers dominated the area.

"Linda Watkins. You want to talk to Linda Watkins, don't you?"

"Why yes..." Paul turned toward the porch "...but I didn't want to—"

Linda flipped her hand nonchalantly. "Earl? Don't worry about Earl. He knows my history. He's been to Wanda's Place. More than a few times." She looked questionably at Paul. "That's why you're here, aren't you?"

Paul nodded.

"Been in the paper. Those murders. The Slasher's back, isn't he?"

"Looks that way," Paul said, not wanting to discuss his theories about the murderer being a possible blackmail victim, or a revenge killer.

"What can I do? How can I help?"

"I talked to Wanda this morning. Seems Lieutenant Leonard Antonelli left a lot of information out of his reports on the Slasher murders."

Linda waited for Paul's question.

"Do you know of anyone who would want to kill Hilary Jefferson or Roxanne Giannamore?"

"Absolutely not! They were terrific girls. Didn't bother anyone. Didn't tell tales."

"Were they the type to blackmail someone? Maybe make some extra money?"

"Hell no. Wanda would have skinned them alive," After a few seconds, she said. "After she beat the shit out of them."

"Was Wanda a violent person?"

"No, not really. She ran a tight ship. No nonsense at the Cozy Nook. She didn't want any trouble."

"What about Hilary Jefferson? Any family? Hometown?"

"She started working after her husband left her. I don't know about family."

"She was married?"

"Yeah, a guy named Derrick. Worked in a mill when he got laid off. That's when he took off."

"Where's she from?" Paul said, writing in his notepad.

"Don't know."

"What about Derrick?"

"Not sure, I think Ohio."

"Ohio?"

She nodded. "Hilary went to school there, Steubenville, I think. Studied to be a paralegal in some college. She didn't finish. Got married and moved here."

"This Derrick guy sounds like an upstanding guy."

"Never met him. But no, a nice guy wouldn't leave his wife stranded in a strange city to fend for herself. She couldn't find a job so she came to Wanda's."

"What about Sylvia Troupe?"

"She took off right after the murders. Didn't even pick up her pay."

Paul was stunned at her last remark. "Do you think she knew something? Maybe saw something?"

"Don't know. She just disappeared."

"Wanda said she was from Apollo. Is that right?"

"No, Dysinger."

"Dysinger?"

Linda smiled. "Dysinger is a small village near Apollo. On route sixty-five."

Paul closed his pad. "Thanks for your help."

"Think nothing of it. Catch the bastard that murdered my friends."

As Paul walked onto the porch he heard teeth clacking over, "Have a nice day sport."

Paul walked to his car thinking he had a fruitful morning. There were plenty of leads concerning Hilary Jefferson: she married Derrick Jefferson; he may have been from Ohio; Hilary went to school to be a paralegal there and Derrick worked in a steel mill.

A little closer to home was Dysinger, near Apollo where Sylvia Troupe was from. He thought he's start there first.

CHAPTER 35

A miniature acorn from a pin oak pinged off the hood of the '98 Ford pickup. Wally didn't notice. He was deep in thought of how he was going to get the information he needed. He didn't like the assignment Paul had given him for a number of reasons: first, Hilary Jefferson was murdered ten years ago, who would remember?; second, if the Cozy Nook Hotel had kept records, they would have destroyed any incriminating ones long ago; and third, and most important, Wally thought this assignment might influence, in some way, his relationship with Karen.

But Wally made up his mind. He had to do it. He walked with vigor across the red dog parking lot and up the stairs to the hotel. Before he could knock, a tiny finger wedged open the door's curtain to Wanda Obitko's pudgy face. The inquisitive glare turned to a widened smile that exaggerated her bulbous cheeks and jowls. Her squatty beehive do remained intact.

"Well hello there, handsome," she said, opening the door. "Come on in."

"Uh, okay." Wally walked in as if the floor was covered with rubber cement. He stopped in the foyer. He noticed a stairway that led to the second floor.

Wanda motioned to a pocket door to the right with a wave of her arm. The fat under her triceps resembled a bat wing and jiggled when she pointed.

"Let's go in here blue eyes." She said, sliding open the door. "By the way, what's your name?"

"Uh, John."

Wanda slid him a doubtful glance. They walked into a large sitting room against the smell of smoke, alcohol, and various flowery fragrances. Two girls sat at a large bar to the left, and a third sat on a red flowered couch painting her fingernails.

"Girls, this is ah...John," Wanda said, smiling. She slid her arm around Wally's narrow waist and pulled him toward the bar.

"This is Raven," she said, gesturing toward the first girl.

Raven stood up to a tall five foot ten inches, slender with very dark hair, a beautiful pointed face and nose that contrasted with full lips.

"And this is Amber," Wanda motioned to the second girl.

Amber stood next to Raven. The two of them together resembled the number ten. She was very full-figured; some might say she was fat. She had flaming red hair and her round face was punctuated with a small pug nose.

Wally nodded.

Wanda walked him to the couch where the third woman sat and thumbed her hand toward her. "Vanilla's sprucing up her nails."

Vanilla didn't stand up. She continued painting her nails. She was al least a decade older than the other two girls. She had stringy, bleached blond hair and skinny vascular arms.

Wally thought her nickname could be "Geritol". He knew she would be the one of the three who might know Sylvia Troupe or Hilary Jefferson—not the high school dropouts.

Wanda had walked back to the girls at the bar waiting for Wally's choice. She stood next to Amber increasing their visualized number from ten to one hundred.

"I'll take this one," Wally said, pointing to Vanilla.

Vanilla calmly put her nail polish away and stood up to Wally's waiting hand. Wally escorted her past the silent number one hundred.

Wally and Vanilla climbed the staircase, slowly walked down the hall and into the last room on the left. The room was adequate for its intended purpose—a sheeted bed, a chair, a table with a wash basin, and a small mirror on the wall above the table.

Vanilla sat on the bed and patted it with her scrawny hand, inviting Wally to sit next to her.

"Have a seat," she said. "Wanda will be coming in to make arrangements."

"Look. All I want is to—"

Wanda knocked on the door as she opened it. "Okay handsome, what do you want? Straight? Around the world? Blow job? Sixty nine? Something kinky? Half hour? Hour—"

Wally interrupted. "I'm kind of new at this. What will a half hour cost?"

"Doing what?"

"Whatever I want."

Wanda looked at Vanilla. Vanilla nodded. "Two fifty," Wanda said.

Wally opened his wallet and pulled out two one hundred dollar bills and a fifty. "Time starts when I'm undressed, right?"

Wanda stuffed the bills in her moo moo pocket as she walked out the door. "Right."

Wally walked to the door and locked it. He heard the closet door open and close they had passed earlier in the hall. The closet was behind the wall the table and wash basin were on—and the mirror on the wall.

Wally stared at the mirror. Could it be a two-way mirror? He remembered Paul explaining what he had he learned at a police seminar about two-way mirrors. A patented chemical vapor process deposits a product known as *mirropane* on the surface of glass that reflects the image off of it. A regular mirror is painted on its back, reflecting the image from the back of the glass.

The test to tell the difference, he remembered, is to touch your fingernail to the mirror. If there is a quarter-inch gap between your fingernail and its reflection, it's a regular mirror. If they touch, the reflection is on the surface of the mirror indicating a two-way mirror.

Wally walked closer to the mirror. He remembered Paul saying that regular mirrors hang *on* the wall. Two-way mirrors are built into the wall.

"Time starts after I disrobe," Wally said, acting as if a normal business transaction was about to take place in front of a two-way mirror and that somebody was actually watching.

"I've got time," Vanilla said. "Your half hour has to start within five minutes though. House policy."

"No problem," Wally said, walking closer to the mirror, taking off his shirt to a cut, muscular build with defined pecs and abs. He quickly noticed the mirror wasn't hung; it was built into the wall.

"Boy, I'm getting old. Look at these wrinkles," Wally said, pointing to the reflection of crow's feet around his eyes. He touched he mirror and his fingernail touched its reflection.

He thought fast. "I can't look at myself anymore. I hate mirrors," he said, and covered the mirror with his shirt.

Vanilla was in the process of undressing; she had already taken off her blouse when Wally walked to the bed. He held his hand in a halting motion to stop her progress and sat on the bed beside her.

Wally cupped his hand around his mouth and whispered in Vanilla's ear. "Is there a microphone in here?"

Vanilla recoiled in surprise. "What?"

"I just covered the two-way mirror with my shirt. Is there a microphone in here?"

Vanilla relented. She shook her head. "No."

Wally relaxed and leaned away from Vanilla. "Look. I didn't come here for sex. I came for a few much needed answers."

Vanilla looked pissed. "What?"

Wally pulled a fifty from his wallet. "Just a few questions."

Vanilla hesitated for a split second and then snatched President Grant from Wally's fingers.

"Did you work here ten years ago?"

Vanilla seemed to think Wally's question odd. "Yes."

"Did you know Sylvia Troupe?"

"Yes."

"Can you tell me where to find her?"

Vanilla closed her eyes as if trying to activate deeply hidden memory cells. "Dysinger... yeah, Dysinger."

"Where is Dysinger?"

"Dysinger is a small town north of here. Somewhere around Apollo."

"She live's there?"

"Don't know. She did in the day. Haven't seen or heard from her."

"What about Hilary Jefferson? What can you tell me about her?"

"She's dead. Had her throat slashed about ten years ago."

"I know. Where was she from?"

"Somewhere out west."

"Where out west?"

"Don't know. She didn't say. She married a guy while she was going to school."

"What kind of school?"

"Business school. Don't remember the name. In Steubenville, I think."

"Steubenville, Ohio?"

"Yeah. Married a steel worker. A welder I think."

"Do you know where he worked?"

"No."

"I take it she took his last name, Jefferson?"

"Far as I know."

"Do you remember his first name?"

She closed her eyes again. "Derrick. Derrick Jefferson."

Wally thanked her for her help and explained just a bit of his situation for the next fifteen minutes and left.

CHAPTER 36

Bernard Eisner sat in his Mercedes S 550 Sedan across the street from the "Grapefully Yours Wine Shop" waiting for a few remaining customers to leave. Bernie could see a man dressed in wrinkled, baggy clothes standing impatiently at the counter with a bottle of wine in each hand. His bulbous red nose contrasted with his shaggy white beard. The owner of the store was attending to a well dressed middle aged couple at the rear of the store.

With the radio on, Bernie pressed a button on the steering wheel that activated the command system's telephone. The command system, standard in every Mercedes S550, has an eight inch display on the dash that offers precise control of the audio, telephone, navigation system and numerous vehicle settings by merely pressing an icon on the screen. Since he had already saved DuCheck's number to the call list, Bernie merely rotated the chrome selector knob to the bar's number on the command center's screen and tapped it.

After a few rings, Bernie heard J.C.'s voice through the car's speaker system. "Ducheck's".

"J.C. this is Bernie. Is Wally there?"

"Yeah, hold on."

After a few seconds, "Bernie, what's up?"

"Do you have the wine bottle that you and Giovanna drank from?"

"No, but I can get it for you."

"I really don't have time...do you remember the brand name of the wine and who made it?"

"Yeah. Yeah I remember. Tuscan Ridge. Gigi always bought Tuscan Ridge Wine. It's imported from Italy."

"But what kind of wine? Merlot? Rosé? Tuscan Ridge has a large selection of wines, I'm sure."

"No, but it was red. And hearty. Had a kick to it."

"Okay, Wally, thanks. You've been a great help. I'll get back to you."

Bernie touched the audio button and "Unchained Melody" vibrated through the speakers. He opened his laptop computer and *Googled* Tuscan Ridge. After finding the information he wanted, he watched the last of the customers leave the "Grapefully Yours Wine Shop".

Bernie entered the wine shop at the tinging sound of an overhead bell. A chubby, red-haired woman rushed to greet him.

"Good afternoon sir," she said. "What can I do for you?" Her smile broadened over her round face, her perfect white teeth sparkled as did her blue eyes.

"I'm interested in a wine," Bernie said, looking around the shop as if he had never bought wine before. "Imported."

Bernie couldn't help notice the backside of Mrs. Matilda Tucker as she ambled toward the far wall. Very large and rhythmic, he thought, like watermelons on a see-saw.

"I have some excellent chardonnay from Australia," she said, gesturing toward a half-gallon bottle."

"No, I don't think so. Maybe something from Italy."

Matilda Tucker turned left and headed down the aisle. She stopped and waved her arm across a four foot expanse of shelves.

"These are our imported Italian wines. Do you have a preference?"

"Red."

"Red? We have many red wines. What—"

"A friend of mine, a customer of yours, suggested a wine. Imported red."

Oh, that won't help. Did your friend say who made the wine?"

"Yes. Tuscan Ridge," Bernie said, looking for any expression on Mrs. Tucker's face.

"Okay, that would be Rosé di Primitiva," she said, her voice slowing and dropping in volume. The muscles in her prior jolly face seemed to sag.

"Here it is," she said, reaching for a bottle.

"That's it," Bernie said, smiling. "You must know my friend Giovanna Antonelli; you're familiar with her brand."

Matilda abruptly turned around, her mouth open. "Why...yes. Yes, she was a regular customer. Terrible thing that happened to her. Did you know her well?"

"Yes," Bernie said, grabbing the bottle from Matilda. "I've handled some cases for her."

Matilda didn't answer. She looked down and to the left. Bernie noticed her drawn and ashen face. "I'm an attorney. Bernard Eisner," he said, walking toward the check out counter and placing the bottle next to the register. Matilda walked slowly behind the counter. She punched the register keys.

"By the way," Bernie said. "Does your husband work here also?"

Matilda pounded a key on the register and the door flew open. She looked at Bernie with a stern face. She didn't answer as she took Bernie's Jackson and gave him his change. She put the bottle in a brown bag and plopped it on the counter.

Bernie could tell from her posture that he was to leave; and he agreed with her wishes. He got what he came for.

CHAPTER 37

The perky office secretary picked up the phone. "Triple A, Linda speaking. How may I help you?" The playful expression on her face turned to one of concern as she slowly slid off Paden Tucker's lap and stood up. "Why yes, he's available. Hold on please." The petite, middle-aged redhead pointed to the phone and mouthed the words— *it's your wife.*

Paden slowly reached for the phone, a *what the hell now* look covered his face. "Hello dear," he said, in a deep baritone voice while watching his secretary's ass as she sashayed across the room and out of his office. "What a pleasant surprise."

"It won't be pleasant for long," Matilda said, raising her voice. "I just had a visitor at the shop you should know about."

"Oh, who'd you run into?"

"Was there something going on between you and that Giovanna Antonelli woman?"

"What?"

"You heard me. Was there something going on?"

"Other than business, of course not!"

"There was a lawyer here today. Said his name was Bernard Eisner. Know him?"

"No. What'd he want?"

"He wanted a bottle of wine. Rosé di Primitiva. Sound familiar?"

"No, doesn't ring a bell."

"He said he was a friend of Giovanna Antonelli's. Any bells ringing now?"

"I don't understand."

"I don't understand either. This ambulance chaser intimates that there is some kind of connection between you and the late Gigi. What's going on?"

"I don't know."

"You bought her that wine for Christmas. Don't you remember?"

"It's her favorite wine. What's the problem here?"

"I don't know. This shyster lawyer seems to think there is. You had dealings with her husband—"

"Lots of people did. He ran the police force."

"But he's dead. And so is his wife. And this snake lawyer comes to my shop and drops a bomb on me. Why? Why not all the other people the Lieutenant knew?"

"I really don't know. I'll make some calls to see what's going on."

"Tell me you didn't have a fling with her."

"This is unreal. No! Absolutely not. I'll find out what's going on. See you later."

Paden slowly hung up the phone, picked it up again and punched in a number. "Meet you at the same place. Twenty minutes."

———

Paden Tucker sat on the top of a rotting picnic table watching an old black Cadillac drive up the serpentine, rutted dirt road.

Scenery Hill is really a plateau, perfect for a shooting range. Twelve weed infested firing lanes off to Paden's right were backed up by a forty foot high wall of slag, courtesy of the local steel mill. The burnt-out shell of the BRASS Sportsman's Club sat lifeless behind Paden. The club's name is an acronym for Breathe, Relax, Aim,

Squeeze, and Shoot. The building was struck by lightning twelve years ago. Half the members quit or joined another sportsman's club; the other half found another place to drink.

The Cadillac rocked to a stop next to Paden's Buick Luzerne. At six-foot four inches and two hundred and forty pounds, Albert Giannamore was quite agile; he seemed to float out of the car. Albert snatched his black Borsalino Fedora from the passenger seat, snugged it to his immense head, and walked up to Paden Tucker with the gait of a pro football linebacker, not the fifty-five year old man that played darts at the Four Aces Club. That's why Don Vito wanted Albert on the payroll. He was the muscle for the family. And he rarely had to use it—just his presence was enough to obtain needed results. And he always followed orders, a must for the Don. Loyalty. Above all, that's what the Don wanted—loyalty. Albert couldn't, and didn't want a real job. He was a follower; a perfect fit for the mob.

He looked at Paden with his huge black eyes that put fear in most men and said, "What's the problem?"

"I got a strange call from my wife today. Something Don Vito should be informed of."

"What's that?" Albert said, tightening the belt on his black Burberry double breasted trench coat. Albert always wore the black fedora and trench coat, even in the summer. Rumor has it that the hat and coat once belonged to Heavy Head Harrison, the man Albert murdered to get his *bones.* That was eighteen years ago.

"A lawyer came to my wife's wine shop today. Bernard Eisner. Know him?"

Albert pulled out a pad and pencil. "No. How do you spell that?"

Paden spelled the first and last name.

"Look," Paden said. "This guy was asking about Giovanna Antonelli and the Lieutenant."

"How do you spell that?"

Paden spelled the last name.

"The lawyer is suggesting there is a connection between me and Giovanna." Paden looked at Albert. "Are you going to write that down?"

"No, I'll remember that. Doesn't sound good. Don Vito will be concerned."

Paden's face reflected concern. "I don't think there's a problem here, but I would like Don Vito to look into this and see what this lawyer's up to."

"Okay, I'll tell him." Albert walked to the Cadillac, opened the door, flipped the fedora onto the passenger seat, and slid into the driver's seat. Two hundred and seventy horsepower kicked up stones and a roostertail of brown dust.

Paden sat motionless, looking out over the overgrown fire lanes and at the mountain of used up slag.

CHAPTER 38

Fifteen minutes earlier, Joey "Bags" Sappone had called Freddy Caruso to set up a meeting on behalf of Don Vito La Bruscia. "Don Vito say shaka the leg. Don't gotta all day." Freddy thought the call sounded like it might be important.

That was then, but now Freddy felt a sense of urgency walking toward the Four Aces Club. Guido, the lookout who usually stood on the corner, held the door open bypassing the usual time consuming pleasantries. Joey quickly ushered Freddy past the usual conspirators; Nark Manfreado, John Landucci and Walter "What's a Matta You" Matta who sat unusually quiet and aloof. Freddy confirmed his feeling about the importance of this meeting when he noticed that the usually closed door to Don Vito's office was open, smoke wafting into the hallway.

Joey joined the others at the bar, letting Freddy continue down the hall. Don Vito motioned Freddy in with his gnarly hand. "Come in," he said, and pointed his finger. "Close the door."

Freddy closed the door and sat on the edge of a chair in front of Don Vito's desk. He felt edgy waiting for Don Vito to speak.

Don Vito stubbed out his cigar in a burst of smoke and sparks, closed a notebook he was writing in and shoved closed the top drawer of his desk. He motioned to the door again. "Check the hallway, Freddy."

Freddy stiffened. The old man is paranoid, he thought, or there must be a huge problem. "Sure, Don Vito," he said, getting up. Freddy opened the door and checked the hallway. He closed the door and shrugged his shoulders and opened his palms suggesting the hallway was clear. Sitting down, he said, "What is it Don Vito?"

Don Vito leaned forward, his clenched hands on the desk. "We've got a dilemma."

Freddy's mind raced. What's wrong, he wondered? Wanda's place raided? crackdown on numbers? Protection? Did Don Vito find out that he skimmed a little on Wanda's payments? Freddy knew what happened to people when Don Vito was cheated or disrespected. Freddy felt the heft of the 9mm against his left side. "What kind of problem, Don Vito?"

"Tucker."

"Tucker?"

"Paden Tucker."

"Why Tucker. He's not one of us. How can he—"

"It's complicated. This problem with him will come back to bite us on the ass."

"How so, Don Vito?"

"Tucker's the right hand man for Representative Davis," Don Vito said.

Freddy's expression went blank.

"And we have a relationship with Davis."

"Yeah, well?"

"Well Tucker has knowledge of our relationship with Davis and therefore most of our businesses,"

"Has he become a danger?"

"Most recently...yes."

Freddy waited for an explanation.

Don Vito picked up a paper with notes scratched on it. "Tucker called a meeting with Albert Giannamore because he was concerned about a lawyer..." he referred to his notes. "...Eisner. Bernard Eisner is the lawyer. Anyway, Eisner went to Tucker's wife's wine shop asking questions about a wine preferred by Giovanna Antonelli, a wine he says was bought by Tucker and insinuated a personal connection between her and Tucker. And the captain as well."

"So, besides protecting our interests, Davis is concerned as well."

"Yes."

Freddy wondered why the sudden interest. "Does this have anything to do with the recent murders, or the Slasher? Or the murders of the two prostitutes ten years ago?"

Don Vito waved his arm. "Not now. All I know is Paden Tucker has to be stifled. *Permanently*. He peered over his glasses in a steady gaze. He knows too much.

Freddy knew Don Vito would do anything necessary to protect his investment—his family. He felt a pang in his stomach. "Yes Don Vito, I understand. I'll take care of it."

"Joey Bags has the same kind of car as Albert, doesn't he?"

"Yeah. Both are old black Cadillacs."

"Good. Call Joey tonight at six-thirty," Don Vito said, touching his forehead with his forefinger. Freddy knew the Don didn't actually "order" a hit, he had someone else pick the guys to set it up, insulating himself from the crime. "Usual method."

Years ago, Don Vito set up a communication system for his lieutenants that involved using pay phones throughout the city. When calling someone at home, the caller would say "I'll meet you in fifteen minutes on fourth street." Which meant the number four phone in fifteen minutes. To avoid the cops from obtaining the numbers, Don Vito would change the contact phones every month at the regular meetings.

"How do you want this done, Don Vito?"

"Have Joey call Tucker and set up an eight o'clock meeting at Wanda's parking lot."

"I don't think Tucker will want to—"

Don Vito pounded his desk. "I don't give a shit! Have Joey convince Tucker to meet him there." After a few seconds Don Vito settled down. "Make sure he drives his old Cadillac. Have him smear some mud on the license plate." He paused. "That's where I want it done." And with his finger he made a slicing motion under his chin. "I want his throat cut. Just like the Slasher."

"Whoa." Freddy said. "What's this—"

"Never mind. Later. Have Joey fire two shots before he takes off. One in Tucker, and the other in the air."

Freddy tried to think of a possible explanation, but couldn't. "Anything else?"

"Yes. Call Albert and have him stake out Tucker's house from seven o'clock to eight o'clock."

"Tucker's House?"

"Yes. Tell him if no action, leave at eight thirty. You can leave now. Don't talk to Joey until tonight."

Freddy figured out the connection. He got up and left, feeling like a thick, gooey weight had just fallen on him.

CHAPTER 39

At seven p.m. an old black Cadillac turned onto Dogwood Drive and slowly lumbered ahead, averting potholes caused by previous winter's freezes. Albert Giannamore looked for an opening in the trees from which to view the road below, Carradam Drive, and a view of Paden Tucker's house. He rotated the switch for the windshield wiper a few notches as the rain increased in intensity. The large heavy droplets pelted the expansive area of the vehicle's roof and hood, making a drumming noise as if tiny toy soldiers were marching over his car.

Albert found a break in the trees that provided the view he wanted. He pulled in the driveway of a small two-story brick house. A "house for sale" sign was in the yard giving Albert a sense of security that no one would be at home.

And suddenly the rain stopped. Albert let the wipers oscillate a few times before shutting them off and the night became very quiet. The windshield cleared and Tucker's small English Tudor came into view. Light emanated from the ground level of the house. Albert opened the glove box and pulled out a set of Tasco 6 X 30 mm field glasses. He put them to his eyes, turned the adjusting screw, and scanned the house, stopping on the window at the right side of the house. Mrs. Tucker was wiping dishes in the kitchen.

———————

A large black Cadillac, identical to Albert Giannamore's, crossed the Morgan County Line when the rain increased. The fog also increased, decreasing the visibility on old route seventeen. Joey "Bags" Sappone squinted as he looked for the Jacob's Creek exit. Good idea, he thought, doing it in another jurisdiction, keeping it away from the *family* and its political protection. The Cozy Nook Hotel, or Wanda's Place as it was known, was perfect for the job to be done. Earsoff Tecza had bought it with the help of the LaBruscia Family's money and he knew the job would be safe as Wanda would do anything Don Vito asked.

Joey pulled into the lot, the tires on the heavy Caddy crunched on the red dog. He drove to the left side of the lot, farthest from the hotel and turned off the engine. Joey noticed Wanda pulling the curtain aside and peering out the office window. He had a lot of time while driving to Jacob's Creek to think things over. He figured Wanda had received instructions over the phone. He wondered why he was to fire two shots after the job. Was it the time for Wanda to call the cops? Why did Don Vito want the police to know the time of the murder? Why was he instructed to slash Tucker's throat? These questions made him nervous.

———————

The new District Justice's Office occupied a small, one story brick building in the middle of the Fourth District, across the street from the Union Grille. The former office burned to the ground in '97. Sammy "dumpster" Durkacz set the structure ablaze hoping to incinerate the documents that were to be used against him in an arson case. Ironically, the evidence he torched wasn't needed at all. An infirm grandmother, confined to a wheelchair who lived in a low income high rise a few doors away, videotaped the entire incident from ignition to extinction. Sammy could be a possible candidate for the Darwin Award.

Paul, Wally and Bernie arrived at the Justice's office fifteen minutes early and sat in the last row on the defendant's side of the court. On Friday, Steitzer had Internal Affairs file a complaint against Paul as a suspect in Earsoff Tecza's murder. District Justice John Conte was running a little late with a case that involved a plaintiff who was accused of robbing a Seven Eleven Store. He had a stubby red Mohawk doo that contrasted with black eye makeup on a chalk white face. He appeared to be defending himself. He wore an Army field jacket with an Eighty-Second Airborne patch on the upper sleeve that prompted Wally to whisper a derisive comment in Paul's ear.

Three character witnesses had already given their version of the defendant's citizenship and were seated in the first row of the defendant's side of the court. The youngsters, late teens and early twenties appeared to be homeless. They were dressed in old and dirty disheveled clothes and had an odor surrounding them. The two men had hair as long as the female, and just as oily. Wally said they were trolls and lived under the Viaduct Bridge near Tarpley's Bottom.

Justice Conte asked the People's representative, and arresting officer Detective Stahlman for the facts in the case. He referred to a written statement by a customer in the store at the time of the robbery who said he noticed the stubby red Mohawk under the pantyhose that covered the thief, a videotape of the theft, and a statement by a clerk who recognized the perpetrator's voice as he was in the store fifteen minutes earlier.

All the evidence was repudiated by the defendant's lawyer until Detective Stahlman produced the robber's note that was handed to the clerk. The note read: *Put all the money in a bag. I've got a gun.* Justice Conte looked at the note, turned it over and said, "This case is held over for court and the defendant is remanded into custody."

As Detective Stahlman led the defendant out of the room, he showed the note to Paul who couldn't stifle a chuckle.

"What's that?" Wally said, nodding his head toward Stahlman.

Paul cupped his hand over his mouth. "He wrote the note on the back of his Colonel Sander's pay stub. *Another candidate for the Darwin Award.*"

Justice Conte motioned for Bernard Eisner to approach he bench. After a few minutes with the justice, Bernie came back and said that the matter had been postponed and that it would be rescheduled.

"Also," he said, "We have an appointment at City Hall."

"When," Paul asked.

"Now."

CHAPTER 40

Albert Giannamore popped open another diet soda. He watched his weight and stayed in shape. At six-foot four inches and two hundred and forty pounds, he was feared by bigger and decades younger men. He had been parked in the driveway of an abandoned house for nearly an hour watching Paden Tucker's house through a set of Tasco field glasses.

Mrs. Tucker is a handsome woman, Albert thought. Nice smile. She always smiles. And her cheeks puff up when she smiles making her eyes almost close, only a glint of sexuality shines through. Her breasts weren't large for a big woman, but her ass was. He loved to watch women's asses—big asses, watch them jiggle, alternately heave up and down, side to side. Albert is a certified *ass man* and he put Matilda Tucker's ass at the top of his top ten list.

Albert wondered what it would be like if her husband, Paden, was out of the picture. He thought of five different ways to kill a man—all of which he had used. His favorite was a sharp twist of the head. Paden had a pencil neck and it wouldn't take but a split second to snap it and end his ass-wipe career.

He watched Matilda walk into the living room and sit at a small table near the stairway to the second floor. She opened a wicker basket, pulled out a ball of yarn and started to crochet.

What a waste of time, he thought. And flesh. She could be sitting with him on the couch doing things only he could think of. He could sense his hands gripping her meaty ass as he kissed and tongued her full tender lips.

And then, he thought, maybe Don Vito's going to whack Paden. That's why he was watching the house—to check on him. And then he'll be in that house and on the couch with Matilda. But then the wistful smile disappeared from his face. Paden didn't show and it was eight thirty and he has to leave.

Albert started the Caddy and pulled out of the driveway. As he drove away a smile reappeared on his face and he thought—maybe...

———

Joey couldn't figure out why Don Vito LaBruscia wanted Paden Tucker eliminated. But why worry about it, he thought. Don Vito had others whacked for petty reasons—or none at all.

Joey didn't like Tucker anyway. Suck-ass, he thought, squirrelly pencil-necked little puss. Never worked a day in his life, he just worked his jawbone. And that political job Davis gave him at the Triple A wasn't a job; the secretary did all the work, Paden showed up an average of three days a week. He had more reasons to dislike Tucker, but he had fired himself up to the point where he wouldn't hesitate to do his duty.

The rain had stopped a few moments earlier, giving the windshield a translucent view of Wanda's Place. It was seven fifty-five when a dark blue Buick Luzerne slowly pulled into the lot, inching up next to the Caddy. Tucker got out of the Buick, opened the passenger door of the Caddy and slithered in.

"What's this about?" he said, wiping a few raindrops from his forehead.

"What? Chu don know?" Joey thought he would amuse himself for a while and maybe find out why the Don wanted Tucker whacked.

"No. I got a call from Freddy. Said I was to meet you here."

"Yousa telling me he dida no say why."

"No." Tucker looked confused.

Joey stared at him for a long minute.

"Maybe," Tucker said, pursing his lips, "maybe it had something to do with the meeting with Albert."

"Coulda be. Ifa you tella da trute."

Tucker's normally small slitty eyes suddenly opened large. "I told Albert the truth,"

"Maybe you makka some things up. You know, what'sa the word...embellish."

Tucker sat back in a defensive posture. "Absolutely not. Everything Matilda told me I relayed to Albert. I thought you guys should know."

"Didda you tink it wasa important?"

"When a lawyer asks questions about Giovanna and Leonard Antonelli's murders, I think it's important."

Joey hesitated. "Thisa lawyer...a...what'sa his name?"

"Eisner. Bernie Eisner."

"Yeah, yeah, thatsa right. Eisner. I donta tink...look, maybe it's notta that important."

"Well he thought so. He claims Giovanna's wine was drugged before she was murdered. That the bottle came from my wife's shop."

Joey felt Tucker was lying. He had all the information he thought he could get from Tucker. He figured he'd put it all together later.

"You hundren percenta right," Joey said. "We havea info that that shyster lawyer's a perv-sicko. Our person saysa he goesa to Wanda's Place for sex with animals."

"You're shitting me!" Tucker said, turning his head to look at Wanda's place as if he could see the horrible act Joey had just described.

That's when Joey reached over and grabbed Tucker's head with both hands and, with one quick twist, snapped the pencil-thin neck of Paden Tucker.

Joey laboriously lumbered out of the Caddy, walked around the car, opened the passenger door and yanked Tucker's body out dropping it to the ground. The switchblade opened to a metallic click, a sparkle of moonlight reflected off its blade as it slashed across Paden's throat, turning it crimson. He wiped the blade on Paden's jacket, retracted the blade and put it in his pocket. He pulled a 9mm Beretta from the holster under his left arm. Two shots rang out. One bullet blasted through the forehead of Paden; the other in the air.

Joey looked at the Cozy Nook Hotel and saw Wanda's face in the office window before she yanked the drape closed. He got in the Caddy with the satisfaction that he had completed his assignment.

Doubt hung heavy in the air when Paul, Wally and Bernie arrived at City Hall's parking lot. Bernie lingered a few moments wondering what Mayor Majewski was up to and exited black beauty last.

Wally kicked a stone in the parking lot, watching it bounce in an unexpected direction. "I wonder what the Mayor's up to," Wally said. "Why'd he want me here also?"

"Strange," Bernie said, "This meeting is out of the ordinary, it's after regular office hours."

"Some kind of Deal?" Paul asked.

"No, I strongly doubt it," Bernie said, opening the main door. "But something's up."

They took the elevator to the third floor, all three watching the floor indicator. The door opened to a dimly lit hall, four wall sconces of low wattage provided the only illumination. The noise of Bernie's hard leather soles and heels of his imported shoes set the tempo of their walk on the sixty foot marbled hallway.

Bernie stopped suddenly and held out his arm in a halting motion. "That sounds like Representative Darby Davis."

They looked at each other. Bernie could see fear creeping on Paul's face and he felt it breeze past him as well. Why would Davis be here? Is this going to be a political lynching?

Bernie wrapped his arm around Paul's shoulder. "Don't worry, I won't let things get out of control."

Wally looked straight ahead. "I won't either."

The translucent glass door opened to the reception room and the crooked smirk on Lieutenant Algie Steitzer's face. "Welcome gentlemen," he said through capped teeth. "The mayor's waiting." Algie waved his arm in the direction of the door leading to the Mayor's office.

They walked in and sat in chairs facing the Mayor's desk. Bernie was on the far right and noticed the monitor on the polished mahogany desk. Representative Darby Davis sat to the rear and right of the mayor.

The mayor picked up a handful of papers and referred to them as he spoke. "You were suspended Friday, Paul. We are investigating the slashing murder of Earsoff Tecza. We have written statements from Rusty, the bartender at Chuckles Bar and Grille, and four other gentlemen that witnessed the altercation last Thursday evening that resulted in the injuries to Mister Tecza."

"May I see those please?" Bernie said reaching over the desk.

"Certainly," The mayor said, "keep them, I have copies." Bernie started to peruse the documents. Mayor Majewski continued. "We intend to file a complaint with District Justice Conte and have him issue an arrest warrant."

In accordance with Pennsylvania State law, the first steps of any criminal prosecution takes place before the minor judiciary, called district Justices, or magistrates.

Bernie interrupted. "But you don't have any evidence that Paul committed a murder, only statements by a local bartender and four drunken card players."

"They weren't drinking," Steitzer said.

"When I get them on the stand, they'll admit to drinking," Bernie said, thinking Steitzer's comment stupid. "Justice Conte will dismiss the complaint. It won't get to court."

"I think it will," Darby Davis said. "The people are ready for justice in this county and I intend to see this *Slasher* thing solved."

"The arraignment will be in about three days," Majewski said through clenched and crooked teeth.

Bernie couldn't believe what he was hearing. "Why put this man through a court trial? A jury will never convict Paul without any evidence."

"Maybe not," Majewski said. "But it'll look good for the city to prosecute these crimes. And one of our own too. A dirty cop—"

Paul jumped out of his seat. Bernie grabbed him "I object," Bernie said. "This man—"

Majewski pounded his desk. "Order in this room. This man is not on trial yet. Maybe we could come to some kind of agreement and settle this whole mess."

Bernie composed himself. He couldn't believe that the Mayor and State Representative would want to make a deal without any evidence. But just for curiosity sake he said, "What do you have in mind?"

Majewski pulled a sheet of paper from the top drawer of his desk. "Paul resigns with full pension and serves a two year suspended sentence for aggravated assault."

Bernie waited for the mayor to continue. "And...?"

"And that's it."

"Why would I let my client accept this preposterous offer?"

Darby Davis leaned back in his chair. "Things could get sticky if this problem is not resolved right now."

"Sticky?" Bernie asked in disbelief.

Majewski took the ball. "The Representative is certain that Paul could be charged with Tecza's murder and that he and Wally conspired together in the recent slashings"

Bernie straightened in his chair. "This is preposterous. They're not—"

Davis interrupted. "The public wants this Slasher thing cleared up. They don't care if it ends with a cop resigning in disgrace or the both of you going through a long court case."

Wally spoke up. "It'll look like Paul was the Slasher and couldn't be caught because I helped him. In other words, you'll look like a good public servant and get elected as the new Pennsylvania U.S. Senator."

Darby and Wally had a brief staring match. Wally won. Darby stammered, "I just want to protect my—"

Wally interrupted. "Ass."

Darby smiled one of those smiles that said *I've got you by the short hairs.*

Steitzer's phone must have vibrated. He took it out of his pocket, excused himself and left the room.

Majewski clasped his hands together on his desk. "Well gentlemen, do we have to do this the hard way or the easy way?"

Paul looked at Wally.

Wally said, "You can take your offer and—"

Steitzer burst into the office, extremely agitated. "Mayor. Representative...Representative Davis. I'm so sorry."

Majewski threw the pencil he was holding on the desk. "What the hell is it Algie?"

"It's Paden. Mister Tucker. He was just murdered a few minutes ago."

"What?" the Mayor said. "How? Where?"

"In The Cozy Nook's parking lot. His throat was slashed. And he was shot."

Darby Davis sat back in his chair and slowly said, "Well gentlemen, our business here is over. The complaint will not be filed with Justice Conte. And Mayor," he looked at Majewski and sternly said, "I suggest you lift Detective Andrew's suspension immediately."

Wally and Paul congratulated each other as they left. Bernie didn't buy the performance. He gave Representative Darby Davis' performance a *three* out of a possible *ten*. What did he think he was doing? He knew he couldn't put a deal like that on the table. And he was calm about Tucker's murder, looking like he knew it was going to happen. It was a stage show alright.

CHAPTER 41

Joey "Bags" Sappone sat alone at the Four Aces Club watching reruns of "Baywatch". He had downed half a dozen shots of Old Overholt with Stoneys chasers. All of a sudden he jumped up and left the bar in such a hurry that wafted cigar smoke followed him in a jet stream out the bar.

As the door closed, Walter "What's a matta you" Matta said, "What's up with Joey?"

"Play the damn card, will ya," Mark Manfreado said, "Trump that ugly king of hearts."

Walter slid the queen of hearts on the table. Mark rolled his eyes in annoyance and his nose increased in redness.

Albert laid off by dropping the nine of hearts on the table, leaving the trick to his partner John Landucci.

John led the left bower, drawing the ace of spades from Manfreado, who slapped it down on the table. That left the ace of spades which John led and took the fourth trick. John led again, throwing down the queen of trump for a clean sweep. "I've got to call it a night," he said. "Got some early collections tomorrow."

"Yeah, me too," Manfreado said. "I've had a long day."

One by one the card players left, followed by Albert who put on his Burberry trench coat and Borsalino fedora. He locked up, as usual, and drove off in his old Cadillac.

Albert started to drive home when he abruptly turned onto Delaware and circled around on Watson a few blocks from the club. He backed his Caddy into a deserted gas station. Five minutes later he was in the alley in back of the Four Aces Club. His dark clothes blended with the night as he hunched over trying to unlock the bottom of two locks on the metal back door. The bolt finally clicked and Albert swung open the door. Once inside, he turned the two levers locking them and then closed the two slide bolts he had purposely left open.

Albert knew the only way anyone could enter the bar would be through the front door. Only a small armored vehicle could break down the back door; and that's the way Don Vito wanted it. Light from a corner street lamp squeezed through the narrow window near the ceiling illuminating a small portion of the bar. Albert checked the dimly lit area, walked behind the bar and opened a black metal box under the counter. He pulled out a small .32 automatic pistol. He looked around, put the pistol in his pocket and walked down the hallway into the storeroom and closed the door. He snapped the light on and arranged cushions that he had previously stashed behind cases of beer into a comfortable seat next to the hallway wall. From that position, and with the stockroom door open a few inches, Albert had a good view of the front door as well as the bar.

Earlier that evening, Don Vito grabbed Albert when he came back from watching Tucker's house and told him someone had been in his office. He didn't go into detail, but he said he had ways of knowing. Don Vito was a secretive man. He didn't trust anyone and surely wouldn't tell anyone of his methods.

Albert turned the light out and snuggled into his cushioned seat. His watch registered 3:30 a.m. when Don Vito's suspicions came to fruition. Albert perked up at a clicking sound. And then another. Albert watched the front door open. Both locks had been opened. The intruder had both keys. The man stood frozen, listening, and then slowly walked behind the bar. He climbed up on the beer cooler and screwed open a ceiling exhaust vent and installed something in it. He carefully lowered himself to the ground and walked to the other side of the bar area. Albert couldn't see what he was doing, but heard similar noises the intruder made with the exhaust vent.

Albert heard the man step down from whatever he was standing on and then heard his footfalls in the hallway. Albert put his hand on the .32 pistol as the man approached the storeroom door. The intruder walked past and stopped at Don Vito's door. Albert carefully stood up and inched to the storeroom door. He heard keys jingle and saw the man put a key into the door. That's when Albert dashed out and slammed the man into the wall. Albert couldn't see who it was, just a dim, gray outline of a man. The man tried to swing, but Albert was too fast and too strong. That's why Don Vito wanted Albert for the job. He was the *muscle* for the Family—and he had a lot of it. Albert hit the man with a left hook knocking him down. Albert stopped momentarily thinking he had knocked him out but the man tackled Albert, knocking him down. The man tried to get on top of Albert but to no avail. Albert threw him to the side, picked him up and executed a rear naked choke hold on him. Soon after, the man's arms and legs stopped shaking. Albert violently twisted his neck making sure he was dead and then checked the man's pulse before frisking him. He found a small electronic device in his pocket. He took his wallet and all the contents from his pockets.

Albert went to the bar and retrieved similar devices from two ceiling exhaust fans. He left the bar through the back door. He came back minutes later with the Caddy and loaded the corpse into the trunk.

Albert Giannamore had been down this road before, sometimes with others, sometimes alone, but always when it was under the cloak of darkness and always when it was expedient. It had only been forty five minutes since he broke the intruder's neck. He turned off Skillet Hill onto a dirt road that descended a steep grade to Flaggart's Bottom and Ralph Imbrogno's Salvage Yard. The rusted hulks of automobiles, trucks and other assorted metal carcasses stretched for a half mile along the Youghiogheny River.

Albert drove slowly through the yard, avoiding potholes and rusted scrap metal until he came to a small opening near the end of the yard. That's the place, a good place, he thought, and threw the Caddy into reverse. In a few days, the area will be covered with junks, stacked two high and then another location will be selected. He backed halfway into the opening and stopped. Albert got out and opened the trunk. When Albert rolled the body over, the moonlight illuminated the face of Walter "what's a matta you" Matta.

"Holy shit," he said. "Damn."

Albert stood there for a moment staring at the corpse. Dumb bastard, he thought, he deserved it snooping around the Don's office. He did the right thing with Matta. After all, the Don said someone was trying to get into his office. He wanted Albert to surveill it, and he did. He didn't do anything wrong. Asshole deserved it.

Albert found the shovel where he had left it from a previous hit. He shoveled in the moonlight, thinking about Walter Matta, the good times, the jokes, and the family at the club. Almost finished, he wondered why Walter would want to be an undercover cop, disgracing the brotherhood. The thought pissed him off as he speared the shovel into the ground. His shoveling became fiercer, faster until he broke out in a sweat.

He finished the death bed for Walter, and walked back to the Caddy. He picked up the body like it was a sack of potatoes and threw it over his shoulder. He walked back to the hole and disgustedly threw the corpse into it. A few minutes later, the bed was covered and stamped down. Albert dusted himself off as if the evening's job was a minor annoyance.

CHAPTER 42

The throaty sound from the Chrysler 300 echoed off the concrete buildings in the town of Arnzen. Paul had installed special mufflers that produced the deep-throated sound he wanted from the powerful Hemi engine. It would take another hour to reach Dysinger and the home of Sylvia Troupe where he hoped to unearth much needed information to the Slasher's murders. He got the time he needed to investigate when he had asked for and was granted leave after last night's strange meeting at City Hall.

After driving for an hour and a half Paul passed Seton Hill University. He continued farther north on route 65 where the buildings became less obvious and were being replaced by trees and farmland.

Paul relaxed in the rural atmosphere and thought about last night's events. He'd been a police officer for seventeen years and never heard about a deal anything like the one offered to Wally and himself. It was incredulous, he thought, not having a shred of evidence against either one of them. Majewski didn't have the stones to initiate this bazaar undertaking. Representative Davis had to be behind it. But that didn't make any sense at all. Davis was a master politician running for U.S. Senate. Why would he muddy his reputation in a case that would blow up in his face? Paul's mind visually went over the last few minutes of the meeting in slow motion. Davis didn't look surprised, he thought, the bastard seemed to know Tucker was going to be murdered. Was it a setup? Could Tucker have something on Davis and was blackmailing him? Did Davis have him eliminated by a copycat Slasher?

Paul considered the names of a number of felons who could be possible suspects, not zeroing in on any of them. He pulled out his pad and wrote a note reminding him to check on recent prisoners released or paroled from prison.

As Paul drove into the town of Dysinger, he felt confident that the Mayor, and Davis at the very least, knew something about the Slasher murders. It didn't take long to find the local police department located in the rear half of the local Post Office.

Paul walked around the building into the one room office. It consisted of one cell in the rear at the far left side, a possible storage room next to it, and a restroom on the right side of the room. A large desk to Paul's left had a nameplate on it that read: Chief Sean McKenna.

The desk immediately in front of Paul was probably for a dispatcher or patrolman. A gray-haired man with silver stars on the lapels of a gray police shirt sat behind it. Before Paul could identify himself the man stood up and extended his hand. He said, "Chief McKenna. How can I help you?"

Paul flipped his shield. "Paul Andrews. Detective at Mononville."

The Chief pointed to a chair at the right side of his desk. "Whoa, Nellie. What's so important that a detective from Mononville comes all the way up here to Dysinger?" He inched up to the front edge of his chair. "Something big?"

Paul pulled a folded sheet of paper from his breast pocket. "I don't know yet. I wondered if you could give me information on a Sylvia Troupe. Maybe came back here around ten years ago."

"Name's familiar," the Chief said, sliding across the room in his wheeled chair to a file cabinet next to his desk.

Paul walked over, his blood rushing in anticipation of a lead. He watched the Chief slowly prod through the manila folders.

"Here it is. Troupe. Yes, now I remember. Sylvia Troupe."

Paul hunched over the Chief's shoulder. "What can you tell me about her?"

The chief's face registered annoyance as he swung his chair around to face Paul. "Well, let's see here. Yeah, here it is. She came back home August first in nineteen ninety-eight."

"Excellent record keeping Chief. How can you be so sure as to the exact date?"

"Because that's the date she also disappeared."

The "Oh shit" look fell on Paul's face.

"What happened? Was there an investigation?"

"Of course. You city boys aren't the only ones to investigate a crime," the Chief said, flipping a page of his notes. "Her mother reported her missing the next day. Too bad. Old woman was sick. Said Sylvia sent her a check every month."

"Is she still alive?" Paul asked, wondering if she kept letters, notes, anything.

"Nope. Died a few months later."

Paul started getting nervous with all the small chit-chat. "Well, what happened? Any trace of her?"

"No. She was last seen at *Grumpy's*, a bar at the end of town.

"She goes to a bar the first day she comes back home?"

"Yeah," the chief said, referring to his notes, "you'd think she'd spend some time at home. I guess she preferred the company of the stranger she was with than being with her mother."

"Stranger?" Paul sat upright and pulled a pencil from his pocket. "Did you get an I.D. on him? Did he pay with a credit card?"

"No. The bartender, Bridget, remembered that he was handsome, tall about six foot four." He squinted at his notes. "And he had a scar on his right temple."

Could this be, Paul thought. Maybe. I'll ask anyway. "What color hair did he have?"

The chief ran his finger down the page. "Oh yeah, hair was black with a thin streak of silver in it."

Paul's face broke into a smile as he put his pencil in his pocket. He knew the identity of the stranger.

CHAPTER 43

On Tuesday morning, at precisely 9:00 a.m., Don Vito LaBruscia walked into the Mononville Post Office and opened the brass door to post office box number 365. Most businessmen, politicians, civic leaders and others that had privacy issues, used post office boxes in addition to their regular mailing address. Don Vito pulled out a small envelope, read it, and put it in his pocket.

Albert parked his Caddy in the rear of the Four Aces Club at 9:05 a.m. He walked toward the Mononville Post Office knowing that Don Vito would be walking back from picking up his mail. They met halfway between the Post Office and the club, in front of Veteran's Memorial Park.

Albert nodded toward the park as he turned onto its cobblestone entrance. He walked toward a bench near the central fountain, visually checked the area and, finding the area secure, he sat down.

Don Vito walked behind the bench and leaned on it. "Albert, you're up early this morning. What did you find out last night?"

"You were right, Don Vito. Someone was trying to get into your office."

Don Vito sauntered to the front of the bench and sat on the end opposite Albert. "Who? What happened?"

Albert slid Walter Matta's wallet across the bench. "What's a matta you."

The Don's face opened in surprise. He opened the wallet. "Shit. How could this happen?" He fumbled through the cards and pictures in the wallet. "Anything else?" he said, apparently not finding what he was looking for.

Albert reached into his pocket and slipped over Walter's keys and the three electronic devices. He neglected the loose change he found in his pocket.

"Uh huh," Don Vito said in a low voice. "What we have here is an undercover cop. Good thing you got to him before he planted these devices." The Don quickly became annoyed. "Where is he now?"

"Where no one can find him."

Don Vito lurched forward. "You killed a cop?"

"I surprised him. He fought back. I couldn't help it. It was him or me."

"You could have subdued him, knocked him unconscious."

"His neck broke," Albert lied.

Don Vito sat back in resignation. "What's done is done. Who brought him into the family anyway?"

"Joey."

"Joey. Yeah, that makes sense. Look. That brings up another matter. Information recently divulged to me." Don Vito slid closer to Albert. "This information is from my special source. When I tell you, try to compose yourself, okay?"

Albert looked like a light bulb lit above his head. "You mean—"

"Yes, my source told me the name of the Slasher."

Albert was reaching for the Don. "You've got to—"

Don Vito waved him off. Albert relented like a schoolboy. "I know you want the man who murdered your sister, and I'm going to give him to you."

Albert looked like he was ready to jump out of his skin. "Thank you Don—"

"I wasn't sure until now. I didn't want to believe that someone close to me...to us would do something like this. But with this information and recent events...it makes perfect sense."

"Who Don Vito?"

"It could have been an accident. Maybe he tried to cover it up. Maybe Leonard or his wife was blackmailing him." Don Vito waved his arm and bowed his head. "But when he brings it into the family...he has to be stopped."

"With the family?"

"Joey."

"Joey? I don't—"

"He murdered Paden Tucker. There's a witness. I want to get rid of Joey before the witness comes forward."

"When?"

"As soon as possible. I'll hold off the witness until the time is right. Okay?"

"Absolutely. I can't wait to get my hands on—"

Don Vito held up his hand in a halting motion. "I know how much you want to get your hands on your sister's killer, but you're important to me. I don't want you to get caught or involve yourself in this."

"But I have to—"

"Listen Albert. Why do you think it's important to eliminate Joey before the police get him?"

Albert hesitated. "So he won't turn."

"That's right. That's why I don't want you involved. Understand? You're too important to me."

"How's this going down?"

"I want you to meet with Lieutenant Steitzer. It's arranged. You coordinate with him for a time and a place and I'll have the witness make the call after you've made the arrangements."

"I would really—"

"I know Albert, sometimes it's hard to refrain, but in this case it's best for you and for the family."

Albert lowered his head. "You're right Don Vito."

"You can piss on his grave afterward."

Albert managed a faint smile. "I still can't believe Joey would do such a thing."

"Like I said Albert, maybe it was an accident, maybe it was a mistake and he had to cover it up. We'll never know. It's over." The Don stood up. "I've got to go now. Good job Albert. I don't know what I'd do without you"

Don Vito walked down the cobblestone path and out onto the street. Albert sat on the bench digesting the information he had just heard.

———————

Don Vito walked two blocks to the *Prince of Peace Roman Catholic Church*. At precisely 10:00 a.m. he climbed the steps to the church, a Chihuahua nipping at his heels. He pulled open the heavy oak door and entered the sanctuary. He paused at the holy water font, dipping his trigger finger in the liquid and dribbled the water on his forehead. He genuflected, and at the same time made the sign of the cross as he walked into the church. He repeated this ritual as he stopped at the fifth pew, and then turned left and sat in the fifth seat from the isle. Three old women made mumbling noises in the first pew. Don Vito pulled back the kneeler and assumed a prayer position. After about thirty seconds he sat back and looked around the church. He slowly reached under the seat and retrieved a small envelope that was taped there.

———————

Very few people would be in the Mononville Municipal Library at eleven o'clock, and today wouldn't be any different. Only Representative Darby Davis sat at a table in the mystery section of the east wing. He was thumbing through an old mystery novel by Ross Macdonald when Don Vito walked around a corner of shelving and spotted him.

Don Vito slowly navigated his way up the isle appearing to browse through book titles. Davis got up and walked up the isle on the other side of the shelving and stopped opposite Don Vito.

"Joey Sappone will have to be responsible for Tucker's murder," Davis said, "that's what we agreed on."

Don Vito scanned the area with suspicious eyes. "Yes, that's right. Everything is arranged."

"Joey can't make it to the police station."

"I know," Don Vito sadly said, "He was a good soldier. One of my family but he'll flip. Under pressure, he'll flip," Don Vito gestured by turning his hand over.

"Do you have a plan?"

"I'll have someone take care of it," Don Vito said. He didn't divulge more than he had to. That's why he wasn't in the same predicament as Joey.

"When?"

"Shortly after I give Wanda the go-ahead. She'll call the cops and give them a statement."

Davis looked hard into the eyes of Don Vito. "This won't leave a bad taste in your mouth, will it?"

"No. Like you said, he's the only one who could be the Slasher. He's caused me a lot of grief and jeopardized the business."

"I'll leave a note if we have to meet again."

"This was a good place," Don Vito said. "But not again. I can't be seen too many times in a library. People might think I'm trying to get wise." He smiled and slowly walked away.

CHAPTER 44

On Tuesday morning Claudia Bianchi walked into Essey's Coffee Shop. The clock on the wall above the cigarette machine showed 11:00 a. m. Her brother, Joey "Bags" Sappone, had called her earlier for a meeting. She looked older than her twenty-eight years, and walked older yet, slow with a slight limp. Her buxom chest bounced as she plopped down in the seat across from Joey.

"What's up bro?"

"Housa the job goin' sis?" Joey asked, smiling. Even though he hated cops he loved his little sister. He watched her grow as a person—a person on the right side of the law.

"You didn't ask me to come here to ask about the job. What's on your mind?"

"Whatsa matta? Can'ta big brudder see lil sis oncea inna while?"

Claudia leaned forward. "What's the problem Joey? You in some kind of trouble?"

Joey pinched his thumb and forefinger together. "Maybe...lil bit."

"What's a little bit, Joey?" Claudia grabbed her brother's huge hand.

"I dunno for sure. Maybe no," Joey said, tilting his head to the left and down, not wanting to say what really bothered him.

"What aren't you sure about? Surely you know—"

Joey fought the urge to lose his temper. "Look. I'ma tell you whatta I know." He paused, thinking how to word his explanation. "I thinka Ima ben set up. Whadda they call it? Patsy? I tink maybe."

"Patsy? Patsy for what Joey?"

"I canna no tella you. You the law. You geta in trouble wit your job."

"But I can't help if—"

"Yessa you can," Joey said, grabbing both his sister's hands. "Ifa I have to leave town, or if I canna not be found," Claudia started to cry. Joey regretted the choice of words. "Donta cry Claudia, I mean notta at the clubba." He put his hand of her shoulder. "I always takea carea myself. I be okay. I takea carea the familia all these years, no? I justa might hafta suddenly go away."

Claudia settled down. "What can I do?"

"Youa know Vaccari, the shyster?"

"Ron? The attorney?"

"Yeah, thatsa him I givea key to shyster for boxa ina bank. He givea to you...maybe. Understand?"

Claudia nodded. "I understand, but—"

"No buts. "Thisa you bigga brudder aska you. Okay?"

Claudia reluctantly left. Joey felt a sense of relief knowing things would be taken care of if anything went wrong. What could go wrong? he thought. He was a good soldier. He did everything that was asked of him. But why did the Don want Tucker eliminated—in front of a witness, no less.

And then he remembered what Tucker had said. Eisner. Bernard Eisner the attorney; he was the problem. I'm good at solving problems, he thought. I'll get back in the good graces of the Don.

CHAPTER 45

A lazy day would describe the atmosphere in the City of Mononville. Not much going on; the day before the arrival of social security checks and the silver sneaker brigade of shoppers meandering the streets. Lazy described city hall also except for Claudia Bianchi who walked nervously into the women's room. She approached Karen Thompson who was combing her auburn hair to the hip-hop music of "Dynamite".

"Karen, you got a minute?" Claudia said nervously. Even though they were partners there was a distance between them. Claudia went by the book and tried to prove to herself that she wasn't like her brother, Joey. Karen was the opposite; she was at ease with herself and the job.

Karen slid her comb into her purse. "Sure, Claudia. What's up?"

"Have you seen Paul?" Karen's face went blank. "Detective Andrews."

"Oh, I'm sorry. I wasn't thinking. Yeah, Wally said he drove up north early this morning. I don't remember the name of the town."

"Did he say when Paul was coming back?"

"A little after lunch," Karen said, looking at her wristwatch. "Around now, I guess."

Claudia pursed her lips in thought and then said, "He eats at Johnson's. I've already eaten. Can you cover for me Karen?" She looked at Karen's expressionless face. "It's important."

"Absolutely. Sure, go ahead. If anyone asks, I'll say you took the cruiser to the car wash."

"Okay, thanks. I'll be back as soon as possible."

———————

Open twenty-four hours a day every day, Johnson's Restaurant attracted shift workers for breakfast, business people, shoppers and cops for lunch, family members for dinner, and evening revelers when the bars closed.

A large grille and cooking area occupied half the length along the left side of the restaurant. A counter with red leather covered stools faced the grille and ran the same length. A chubby waitress with a hairnet worked feverishly flipping burgers. Round tables sat neatly in the rear of the room. The opposite wall housed a long line of booths. Paul sat in the last one.

Claudia hiked to the back of the restaurant and stood at the booth where Paul was sitting and said, "Paul, I'd like to talk to you. Mind if I sit down?"

Paul looked up, hesitated a moment, and pointed to the seat across from him. He said in a tone that expressed his being annoyed. "Yeah, have a seat."

Claudia slid into the booth. "I'm sorry to bother you. Do you have a few minutes?"

Before Paul could answer, the waitress arrived with an Italian hoagie and a cherry coke. She placed his order in front of him, slid the check under the salt shaker, and left.

"Well, I haven't eaten yet. I'm running late. Just got back."

"Karen told me. Up north somewhere?"

"Dysinger," Paul said, looking for a reaction from Claudia. Paul knew her brother Joey Sappone and wondered if Claudia knew anything about the Slasher murders and if she was connected to the family.

Claudia seemed to look into her memory. "Never heard of it. Anyway, I have to talk to you about my brother. I think he's in trouble."

"Joey?"

"Yes. Joey." Claudia told Paul about their earlier meeting. She said Joey seemed nervous and said he was being set up for something but wouldn't tell her. She also said that Joey gave attorney Ron Vaccari a key for a safety deposit box in case he disappeared.

Paul's face reflected amazement at what he was hearing. It sounded as if Joey had given an attorney the key to incriminating evidence in case somebody whacked him. The world would be better off without Joey, Paul thought, but the evidence might be about the Slasher murders, maybe even a name. That would clear Wally and restore Paul's reputation at the same time, and that gave Paul some relief.

"What can I do?" Paul said.

"There's something going on with that crowd Joey hangs with. Maybe you can find out what it is and what trouble Joey got himself into?" She put her face into her hands, her eyes welling up. "Have you heard anything?"

"No, not really," Paul said. He didn't want to divulge information about Leonard Antonelli's connection to the Slasher murders. He felt Antonelli got rid of Sylvia Troupe who was a possible witness, or knew something about the slayings. After all, she disappeared immediately after the murders. "But if I do, I'll let you know."

Claudia grabbed Paul's hand. "Thanks Paul." She stood up and left.

Paul watched her leave, thinking something really big was right around the corner. He thought about getting a court order to open the safety deposit box, but he realized that no judge would sign the order without probable cause—and he didn't have any. All he had was hearsay from the sister of a reputed mafia figure.

Paul remembered what Claudia had said about something going on with the crowd Joey hung out with, meaning the Four Aces Club. Paul flashed back to the club when he went to meet with Don Vito. There was a new guy sitting at the bar with, what Paul thought, a strange look about him. Could he be a cop?

Before digging into his hoagie, he made a mental note to visit his friend, George Rixie, at the local F.B.I. Office.

Paul didn't waste time after lunch. He called Stahlman and said that he'd taken a detour and would be late getting back to the office. He drove as if he were going to a fire across town to Pennsylvania Street and Twenty-Third Avenue.

The elevator doors opened on the twenty-first floor of the U.S. Federal Building. Paul turned right and walked down the long marble hall and then made a left. He didn't need directions to Agent George Rixey's office. Twenty years ago they served as military policemen at Fort Bragg, North Carolina. They both ended up in law enforcement. Paul, being a local boy and tied to his family, opted for a job in Mononville. Rixey had bigger ambitions. He went to night school while serving in the military and after discharge went to law school on the G.I. Bill. He'd been an agent for twelve years, stationed in Mononville for the last four. They had always kept in touch with E-mail and snail mail, but the last four years were like old times.

When Paul walked into the office, the secretary wasn't surprised; she just motioned with her arm toward Rixey's door.

"Hey sarge, what's new in the bureau?"

Rixey had been looking out the window. He swung around in his plush leather covered chair. "Paul, what a coincidence. I was just thinking of you."

"Thinking about the last lunch tab I picked up?"

Rixey grinned. "No, I think I picked up that tab. It's your turn."

"First thing to go is the memory, George."

"That's right, you forgot to call. I have an important job. People don't walk in unannounced."

Paul grabbed a chair, pulled it close to Rixey's desk and sat down. "Hear anything going on at the Four Aces Club?"

"Every now and then rumors surface about Don Vito and the usual suspects. Why?"

"Anything significant? Anything ongoing?"

"If there was, I couldn't tell you; you know that."

"What if it's really important to me?" Rixey opened his hands in a disappointing gesture. "That's not being a good friend," Paul said. "What if I had some spicy information for you and didn't tell you?"

"Do you?"

"Do I what?"

"Do you have information for me?"

"I might."

"Something I'd like?"

"How about linking a cop to the Slasher murders?"

"Rixey leaned forward, his friendly mask turned somber. "Really?"

"I do, and it possibly goes to city government. How about it?"

"I'm interested. What do you want?"

Paul leaned forward and whispered. "Do you have a man in the Four Aces Club?"

Rixey smiled. "I was wondering when you were going to ask."

Paul suddenly realized it was true. "Wow, I thought—"

"You made a good assessment. You're good Paul. You were there only once."

Paul's forehead wrinkled in puzzlement. "How'd you know I was there? Keeping tabs on me?"

"No. It was in the agent's report."

"Okay. What's going on there?"

"He's been there four months. The Don's very secretive. Don't know anything yet, but things are about to change."

"How so?"

"Visual and listening devices."

"But nothing yet?"

"No, I'm sorry. What do you have for me?"

Paul told Rixey about his trip to Dysinger and the information he received from Chief McKenna and Bridget's statement. The bartender said the last person seen with Sylvia Troupe was handsome, tall about six foot four, had a scar on his right temple, and a silver streak parted his coal black hair.

"Perfect description of Captain Leonard Antonelli," Paul said, obviously happy with himself.

"She must have known something," Rixey said.

"That's the way I figure it. He knew the identity of the Slasher and helped cover up the murders. But why was he killed? And his wife?"

He was killed after his wife, right?"

"Yes, and tried to put the blame on my uncle Wally."

"She knew who the Slasher was and probably tried to squeeze him in some way. Blackmail comes to mind."

"Giovanna was Leonard's ex. Maybe he got pissed off and approached the Slasher and he got whacked. But why kill Earsoff Tecza?"

"A lot of questions have to be answered," Rixey said, "if I hear anything at he Don's club, I'll let you know."

Paul left with a renewed feeling that things were going to work out.

CHAPTER 46

A n unmarked Ford Crown Victoria slowly bucked across the railroad tracks that led to the abandoned Koehler's Wire Mill. The vehicle turned left, past the scrap yard and drove into the decaying carcass of what was the former galvanizing building. Sunlight shone through gaping holes in the corrugated roof and siding, highlighting the remains of the number two patent furnace, the caved-in lead pan, and the rusted spindles and blocks that had once held bundles of wire waiting to be processed. The Crown Vic parked close to the wall behind waist high weeds

As Steitzer got out of the cruiser, a stiff breeze blew through the building's skeleton mussing his hair.

Albert Giannamore leaned on the hood of his old Caddy. "What kept ya'? You're five minutes late."

"I try to be careful."

"Being careful is being on time. We can't risk being seen together," Albert said, pointing a finger at Steitzer. "It's timing. It has to be precise and involve as little time as possible. Understand?"

Steitzer nodded. "Right. I'm told you have a project for me."

"That's right," Albert said, putting his arm around Steitzer's shoulder leading him away from the cars to the side of what used to be the foreman's office. "Were you told about the project?"

"No." Steitzer portrayed the definition of nervous, looking around as if he *were* the project.

"We found out who the real Slasher is—"

Steitzer turned in surprise, breaking away from Albert's arm. "What!"

"True. And as a much as I'd like to kill the bastard myself, I can't."

Steitzer's expression revealed that he understood. "Because of your—"

"Sister. That's right. That's why someone else has to do it, and legally."

"Legally?"

"You're going to do it." Steitzer said, leaning against the doorframe of the office. "You'll be a hero, the man who captured and eliminated Joey "Bags" Sappone." Albert patted Steitzer on the shoulder.

"Joey? But why? And how?"

"Why? Because a witness will call in a report saying she saw Joey shoot and cut the throat of Paden Tucker."

"But the body was discovered early this morning. There were no witnesses."

"There will be. She will come forward when we want her to. And she will identify Joey as the Slasher."

"Did he do it? Joey, I mean."

"Hell yes. That's why we want to get rid of him. He's one of us. What if he rolls over for a deal and shoots his mouth off about the family? Doing it this way isolates us from him completely. If we had known about Joey being the Slasher, don't you think the public would have expected me to get rid of the slimeball? No, it has to be this way."

"Okay, that's the why. What about the how?"

"I'll let you know when the call will come in. Be near your dispatcher. You'll be the first one on the scene and you'll pick up Joey."

"And then?"

"And then you shoot the bastard when he tries to escape."

"I don't know—"

"He's a known felon. He carries a gun. Who would question a perfect shooting like that? Besides, you'll be the town hero. Promoted to captain, I'm told."

Steitzer straightened his shoulders and managed a faint smile. "When?"

"Tonight. Stay in the station," Albert said, as he turned and started walking to his Caddy, leaving Steitzer to mull over his new project.

Joey drove to Ebensville, twelve miles out of town to Geno's Restaurant for lunch, but couldn't finish his stromboli. He had to leave. He had a feeling of paranoia. On the way back to Mononville he thought the Don had put out a contract on him. But why? He always was a loyal soldier. Was it over the Slasher thing, the politics of it? He wondered why he was ordered to rub out Paden Tucker in such a strange manner. Why fire two shots and then cut his throat? And why in the parking lot of the Cozy Nook Hotel? Wanda saw him. Was she supposed to see him? Was she going to be a witness? Maybe he should get rid of Wanda. No, she was under the protection of the Don and he would get someone else to take her place as a witness. But again, he didn't do anything wrong. And if he did, it couldn't be that bad. Bernard Eisner is the problem. He remembered what Tucker said the night Joey shot him.

Joey crossed Mononville's city limits into the south side by way of Knox Avenue. He drove past Cupper's Gym where he had toiled and sacrificed to become a golden gloves boxer. He wondered what would have happened if he had pursued a boxing career instead of being wooed into the mob as a *strongarm*. The scars and dark bags under his eyes were testament to the many blows he took to his head. That's probably what clouded his thinking.

Could he get back in the good graces of the Don by getting rid of Bernard Eisner? He drove to Fall's Lake and relaxed on a picnic bench, thinking about what he was going to do next. An hour later, he made up his mind.

Joey drove back into town and stopped at a Quick Stop convenience store where he got Eisner's address and telephone number from a telephone book.

The magnificent English Tudor home sat on a slight knoll at 433 Stanton Lane. Dark oak post and beam construction framed the brilliant white exterior. Azaleas, rhododendrons and evergreens enhanced the lines on the three story house which sat on a one-and-a-half acre plot.

Joey quickly drove by noting the Mercedes parked in the governor's drive. Earlier, when he was at the Quick Stop convenience store, Joey made a phone call to Bernard Eisner's home pretending it was a wrong number making sure Eisner was home. Joey had also entered Stanton Lane in the direction heading into town as not to drive by the house unnecessarily. He pulled over at the intersection of Stanton Lane and Willow Road, and the entrance to the Willow's Golf Course. He pulled into the parking lot and found a space facing the intersection. He pulled out an old newspaper and pretended to read it.

Joey became more nervous with his soaring paranoia. He figured he'd have to eliminate Bernie today —and soon. The sooner the better, he thought. Then he'd be back in good standing with the Don. His wish was about to come true when the black Mercedes S 550 Sedan drove down Stanton Lane, through the intersection, and headed for Mononville.

The Caddy's 280 horsepower yanked the car away, leaving rubber stains on the asphalt. Joey quickly caught up with Bernie when he realized that the timing was bad; it was still daylight. He'd have to follow him and wait for darkness.

CHAPTER 47

B ernard Eisner walked through DuCheck's door at 6:00 p.m. Moldy leaned on the working side of the bar entertaining Ten Quarts with tall tales. He motioned to the back room with his thumb and mouthed the words, *they're in the back*.

Paul, J.C., Wally, and Harvey sat around a five foot diameter table J.C. had salvaged from a second hand store.

Bernie strode around the corner while pulling a notepad from his jacket pocket. "Sorry I couldn't meet yesterday, I was up to here in work." He motioned with his hand under his double chin. He grabbed a chair and sat down.

"Yesterday was hectic, all right," Harvey said. "Paden Tucker was found murdered...with his throat slashed. That'll take the heat off Wally and Paul."

"That's right," Wally said. "We were at the District Justice's office Monday about the time of the murder."

"And in the Mayor's office when the call came in," Paul said.

J.C. smiled broadly. "Terrific. I also heard the Mayor and Representative Davis offered you guys a deal. Too bad it fell through," J.C. said, stifling a laugh.

"What was that about?" Harvey asked Bernie.

"Apparently Representative Davis wanted some good press for the upcoming election. Paul and Wally would be the sacrificial lambs with Paul resigning from the force and serving a suspended sentence for a year for the lesser charge of aggravated assault. Of course Wally would be thought of a co-conspirator and guilty as well in the Slasher murders."

"He's still going to get good press, I think," Paul said.

"How so?" Wally asked.

"I talked to Joey Sappone's sister Claudia, this afternoon," Paul said. "She's worried about her brother being in trouble. Joey told her he gave a safety deposit box key to Attorney Ron Vaccari, in case he disappears."

"Or maybe he's being set up for murder," Bernie said. The others waited for Bernie to continue. "I went to the Grapefully Yours Wine Shop Monday afternoon and asked Mrs. Tucker some questions about the Tuscan Ridge Rosé di Primitiva wine that Giovanna always bought. She got rattled. She knew something and I believe she told her husband."

"I don't get the connection," Harvey said.

Bernie slid his chair closer to the table. "Well, with what's transpired recently, it looks like Tucker notified the *goodfellas* about my visit, and predictably the mob would want to eliminate any connection to them. Joey must be involved somehow."

"I don't know Joey's connection, but the mob is definitely involved," Paul said. "And Leonard Antonelli was as well." Paul told about his trip to Dysinger to check on Sylvia Troupe and how he found out that Leonard was the last one to see Sylvia alive.

"Wow," J.C. said "How far up the ladder does this corruption stretch? The Mayor?"

Bernie answered. "I'm convinced it stretches to Darby Davis."

Paul nodded. "I agree. They're starting to run scared. The old Slasher murders have stirred up a hornet's nest of exaggerated controversy and a lot of unwanted publicity. Even the Fed's are interested."

"Really?" Harvey and Wally said simultaneously.

"Really," Paul said. "I talked to George Rixey at the regional F.B.I. Office." He looked around to each person and said, "You can't repeat this, but they've got a man on the inside."

"That's great news," Harvey said.

"Great news for eliminating some of the mob and their soldiers, but will the Slasher's identity be revealed?" Paul asked.

"The Feds will prosecute on recently obtained evidence," Bernie said. "The Slasher murders were a decade ago. I don't think—"

"That's right," Paul said, "we still have to pursue the Slasher."

"What's next?" Wally asked.

"I'm glad you asked," Paul said. "I think a trip to Steubenville is in order."

Wally remembered that Hilary and Derrick Jefferson were from Ohio. "You're right. We don't know anything about Hilary Jefferson. It might turn out to be a lead. I'll leave tonight and get an early start tomorrow morning."

"What do you expect to find, Paul?" Harvey asked.

"Don't know. Anything will help. Maybe we can dig up her ex-husband. Maybe he still works at a mill. Hilary went to school there; somebody knows them."

Joey checked his watch for the umpteenth time; it registered 7:30. He had been sitting in his old Caddy for the one-and-a-half hour meeting in DuCheck's. Joey parked one block away on Delaware behind an old International Scout with an unobstructed view of Bernie's Mercedes.

Nervous, Joey's sweat crept down his face. He felt he was in the tenth round and behind on points. Don Vito's reach was long and the only counterpunch Joey felt he could muster was the elimination of Bernie Eisner. That would be enough for a decision and a reprieve, he thought. He wanted it to be over—and soon.

Another tick of the minute hand passed when Joey saw Paul leave DuCheck's and drive west on Donner in his Chrysler 300. A few minutes later, Bernie left the bar and drove off in the same direction.

———

Dusk hung over Jackel's Restaurant when Bernie pulled into the parking lot. The restaurant was a popular suburban eatery and meeting place as evidenced by its nearly full parking lot. Joey slowed as he watched Bernie pull into an empty spot on the lot's rear right perimeter. Joey drove to the other side of the lot and parked where he could view the restaurant's entrance.

After waiting for five minutes, Joey decided Bernie had ordered dinner. Twenty minutes later, and under the cloak of darkness, he knew Bernie would be leaving soon. He wondered how he would get the job done. He could catch him at the entrance and stab him. No, breaking his neck would be better. His thinking became clearer. Not at the entrance, he'd wait for him at his car. Nobody would see him.

Joey circled around to the back of the lot to where the Mercedes was parked. A large, new model pickup truck was parked next to it. Joey sat on its rear bumper. He thought it wouldn't be a good idea to kill Bernie there as it would create unwanted publicity. The Don wouldn't like the notoriety that a prominent attorney's death would inevitably bring his way. No, he had to be smart about it. Bernie had to disappear—permanently. Joey fixed his eyes on the Mercedes. Nice car, he thought. He'd like to take it for a spin.

Joey quietly sat listening to footsteps on the pea-gravel lot and couples' chatter as they left the restaurant, but nobody came his way. An old man mumbling to himself shuffled into a Volkswagen within twenty feet of

Joey and certain death. Joey would snap the neck of anyone who came close enough to identify him.

Finally Joey heard louder footsteps coming in his direction. He peeked around the side of the pickup's bed and recognized Bernard Eisner in the darkened light. Joey felt like a ray of sunshine had shown down onto his life, that his problems soon would be over and that the Don would again hold Joey to his bosom.

Kill him first? No, Joey thought, I'll have to keep him alive—for a while anyway. That's what Albert had always instructed Joey to do. *Don't get caught with a dead body in the car. That's stupid. Wait until you're ready to dump him in the hole. That's when you kill him.* That's what I'll do, Joey mumbled under his breath as Bernie approached with the keys to the Mercedes in his hand.

A knockout straight right hit Bernie's jaw as he turned toward the noise of Joey's heavy footfalls on the gravel. Joey grabbed Bernie before he hit the ground. Why'd I do that, he thought, he'll be dead within the hour. A few bruises won't matter. Joey threw Bernie into the car and wrestled him into the passenger seat. He strapped Bernie in the seat with the seatbelt harness and pulled out two plastic wire ties. He secured Bernie's hands to the shoulder strap and secured his ankles together. He didn't gag Bernie as someone might see it, and besides he figured he was going to be out for a while anyway.

———

Bernie came to when Joey turned the radio on. He knew he was in his Mercedes and someone was driving it. He didn't know what exactly had happened, except that his jaw throbbed with pain. He felt panicky when he felt the plastic ties on his wrists and ankles, but knew he couldn't let the driver know he had regained consciousness.

Who was this person, Bernie thought, why was he being kidnapped? Was it because he was helping Paul and

Wally? His head hung slumped against the passenger window, blocking his view of the driver. He waited until the Mercedes drove over a fairly rough portion of road to wiggle his torso slightly to the left as if the car's motion had caused it. One more stretch of bad road, he thought, and I'll be able to position my body and turn my head to see the driver. In less than a minute Bernie got his wish. He maneuvered into position and slowly opened his left eye. He wasn't surprised to see Joey Sappone behind the wheel of his Black Beauty. He wasn't stealing the car he thought, he would have left him in the parking lot. Or would he? He wouldn't leave him there to call the police. He knew he was being taken somewhere to be disposed of. His work had invaded the premises of the mob and they had put out a contract out on him. But how could he get away. Bernie thought it was hopeless. He knew Joey's reputation, how he had been a boxer and the work he had done for the mob. Getting away from him would be a miracle, a miracle Bernie couldn't fathom in his wildest imagination.

Bernie felt the car pull off the road onto gravel. Oh shit, he thought, this is going to be it. But it couldn't be; there's light and noise. He wouldn't be murdered around people. Bernie slowly opened an eye when the car came to a stop. A restaurant? Joey stopped at DiSalvo's Restaurant? Yes. Bernie remembered it, out on Wyano Road, heading west out of town.

Joey stopped the car and left the engine running. He quickly opened the door and struggled to get out, passing gas as he did. He has to use the restroom, Bernie thought. He figured he had a few minutes to figure out how to get out of this mess.

CHAPTER 48

Steitzer paced back and forth on the dispatch center floor like an expectant father wondering if he should make the call. His nerves finally got the best of him and he dashed into his office. He picked up the phone but quickly put it down. No, he thought, he couldn't use the office phone; the call could be traced. He opened the bottom right desk drawer and pulled out a disposable phone he had taken from the evidence locker earlier that day. He punched in a number.

"Albert, it's me. What's the—"

"Who?"

"Me. Algie. I haven't heard—"

"I told you to never call me, it's too dangerous."

"I have a disposable. It can't be traced. I was careful."

"What about my phone asshole? Ever hear of a wiretap?"

Steitzer froze at the thought that the feds might be listening to the conversation. The fact that Albert's phone might be tapped bypassed his fragile ego. "Yeah," he managed to say in a low submissive tone. "I was just wondering about...you know—"

"We haven't located him yet. Don't call again. Take care of your job. Don't bother me," Albert said, and hung up.

Steitzer slowly slid the phone back in the desk drawer and slumped into his chair. He stared at the opposite wall trancelike for what seemed like endless minutes mulling over his predicament. The noise of a door slamming shut jerked him back into reality. He slowly walked back into the dispatch room. He peered through the door's window into the darkness, hoping that the call wouldn't come at all.

———————

In addition to leaving the car running, Joey left the radio on also. That's it, Bernie thought, the phone in his shirt pocket is voice activated. He could call the police but he didn't have their number stored in the command center. DuCheck's, he thought, would be the best bet. Paul and Harvey could be reached by J.C. and he trusted them all.

Bernie felt he had to act fast but his hands were bound to the shoulder strap with a plastic wire tie. He certainly couldn't reach the steering wheel to tap the phone button. But maybe, he thought, he could reach the command center or the buttons on the front of the consol. Bernie strained to slide his hands up the strap to where he could be in a position to lengthen the strap and reach for either of the buttons. A few drops of perspiration later, he managed to extend his arms forward to where his index finger barely touched the telephone button on the consol—and the music stopped.

Since the number was already on the call list, all Bernie had to say was, "Call DuCheck's." The wireless interface did the rest.

Bernie heard the soft audible dialing of the digits followed by two rings.

"Hello, DuCheck's," J.C. said.

"J.C. this is Bernie I've—"

"Bernie, glad you—"

"J.C. listen! I've been kidnapped by Joey Sappone. I'm in my car and tied up. I'm calling on my command center—"

"What can I—"

"Don't interrupt. He can come back any second. Just listen. Stay on this phone and don't hang up. Call the police on your cell phone and tell them I'm being kidnapped and then call Paul and tell him what's happening. Right now I'm in the parking lot at DiSalvo's Restaurant and we're heading west. Don't talk on this phone or he'll hear you. I'll talk to him and indirectly give you locations of where we are. Do you understand?"

"Yes."

"Good," Bernie said as he noticed Joey coming out of the restaurant. "Not another word, he's coming toward the car."

———

Algie Steitzer almost jumped out of his skin when the phone rang. He tried to appear calm, but noticed that his hands were trembling.

"What's that?" the desk sergeant said. "You say Bernie who was kidnapped? By Joey Sappone?"

"Kidnapped?" Steitzer said, trying to sound as if he was the only one who could handle an emergency. He was expecting a call from a witness to a murder that implicated Joey. Not this. He extended his arm toward the sergeant. "I'll take that sergeant." He put the phone to his ear. "Who is this please? Uh huh. Okay, spell the last name. By who? Okay, where are they? Do you know where they're going? Okay, I'll take care of it. Thank you."

Steitzer rushed off before the desk sergeant could ask who was kidnapped. He dashed into his office, opened the bottom drawer of his desk, grabbed the cell phone and punched in a number.

"Albert it's me. I know I shouldn't be calling but there's a problem."

"This better be good Algie."

219

"Joey went berserk. He kidnapped Bernard Eisner, the attorney."

"He what! Why?"

"I don't know why, but he was last seen at DiSalvo's Restaurant heading west."

"That dumb shit. What's he trying to prove? He must have lost it. He's working this on his own. We had nothing to do with it. You have to stop him. Now!"

Steitzer thought he was off the hook. "What can I do? I don't know what he's up to or where he's going."

"He's headed for Imbrogno's Junkyard. Follow the road to the end of the yard. Go there and finish the job."

Albert hung up. Algie's trembling hand replaced the phone in the drawer. He slumped down in his chair wondering what was worse—taking a chance with Joey Sappone or Albert and the mob. To do nothing surely would be fatal. Shooting a fleeing felon from a kidnapping would be a good shoot. He checked his revolver and hesitantly walked out of the building.

———

When Joey slid into the car, Bernie didn't hesitate to act as if he was becoming conscious because he didn't want Joey to think about the radio being off. Bernie faked a moan and struggled with his wrist restraints. He didn't want Joey to think about the possibility that he was being tricked.

"What the hell? What's going on?" He looked at Joey with pretended surprise.

"We're a goin' for a ride, yousa and me."

"Where? Why am I tied up?"

"Causa yousa ben a bad boy, mista fancy pants attourney."

"What have I done? I don't even know you."

"Yousa know mya bossa, mya friendas, mya familia."

"I know your name's Joey. Joey Sappone, right?"

"Thatsa right. Anda I'ma the lasta person yousa evr gonna see."

Bernie slouched in the seat. He didn't want to hear those words; they sounded permanently fatal. Shit, he thought, this is more than a kidnapping. He had to act fast. He looked out the window for a minute. "Can I have one last request?"

Joey had a smirk on his face. "Surea, what'sa you pleasure?"

"I'd like an ice cream cone."

"Icea creama makea you fat."

"Come on Joey, Porter's Dairy Delight is coming up soon. How about it?"

"No."

"At least tell me what I've done to you, your friends and your family."

"Yousa causea trouble. That'sa what."

"What trouble? I'm helping a friend who is falsely accused of murder. Doesn't have anything to do with you."

"Yessa it does. Trouble startsa when you butta youra big nosea into Tucker's busaness."

"That has nothing to do with—"

"Enda story."

Bernie couldn't figure out the connection Joey had just made with Tucker; he had too many troubles in front of it. "Is that the Hemming's house? I thought is burned down last year."

"No, thata wasa ol' lady Crawford's house."

"Did you hear that, Paul? They're on route one-twenty-two heading west."

"I heard, J.C. I'm converging on that location." When Paul had received J.C.'s call he had been home for ten minutes. He lived twelve miles northwest of DuCheck's. Joey was heading west and hoped with Bernie's directions he could intercept them before Joey stopped to fulfill his contract.

J.C. pressed the phone to his chest. He talked into the cell phone. "They're coming up on Porter's Daily Delight, Paul."

"All right. Maybe I can intercept them shortly. Stay on the phone." Paul hoped J.C. didn't make a noise that Joey could hear; it would blow the whole operation. He needed Bernie to help prove that he and Wally didn't have anything to do with the Slasher murders.

"Paul, Joey said Bernie stuck his nose into Tucker's business. Does that mean anything to you?"

"Not at the moment. I'm concentrating on catching up with them."

A few minutes later, J.C. spoke into the cell phone. "Paul, they're at the Crawford's house. Do you know where that is?"

"Yes, I'm triangulating on that location."

"Skillet Hill? I never heard of it. Where are we?" Bernie said, nervous that anyone coming for help would know of it either.

"Ina tha kitchen. You'ra gonna' be ina fryin' pan soon or maybe tha skillet."

Bernie felt a little relieved when he saw the sign. "Flaggart's bottom? Never heard of that either."

"Good. Youa won'ta be hearin nuttin ina lilla while."

A few minutes later, Bernie said, "Imbrogno's Salvage yard?"

"That'sa junk to yousa. Gonna be, what tey say, recycled. Yeah, you'sa gonna be recycled."

"Paul, have you heard of Skillet Hill?"

"Yeah, I know where it is."

"How about Imbrogno's Salvage Yard?"

"That too."

"That's where they're going."

CHAPTER 49

Algie Steitzer picked out a police cruiser from the station garage instead of one of the Ford Crown Victorias commonly used by detectives and officers. He felt the Ford seemed too official for him; he wanted the world to know everything was being done by the book. He didn't want any slipups with Albert; that's why he took the cell phone from his desk.

The wheels of the cruiser chirped on the concrete as 310 horsepower yanked the car from its parking space. Steitzer activated the cruiser's emergency lights knowing he had to make it to the auto *boneyard* before Joey left. After all, he thought, a desolate junkyard would be the perfect place to put Joey down. He'll say Joey resisted arrest and was in the process of attacking him.

Algie caught route one-twenty-two on the outskirts of town and headed west. He felt more relaxed knowing that this new situation would work out for the best.

He visualized the process of eliminating Joey when he said, "Shit! Bernie." It dawned on him that attorney Eisner would be there also.

What would he do with Bernie? Algie wondered what Albert would do. No, he wondered what Albert would *tell* him to do. Damn it, he said to himself. I might have to kill Bernie as well. Bernie, a prominent member of the community would be a witness to a perfect shoot. If Joey has a gun on him, He could use it on Bernie and say Joey had killed Bernie before he got there.

Steitzer passed a sign that read Skillet Hill; he was minutes away from the hardest decision he had ever made—and he didn't yet know what that decision would be.

———————

Paul sped down the steep grade to Flaggart's Bottom kicking up stones and dust rounding sharp curves. He knew Imbrogno's Salvage Yard was minutes away and hoped he would make it in time. He figured by the timeline J.C. had given him, Joey couldn't have arrived much earlier.

Paul turned the lights off before entering the yard. The splinter of moon provided enough light for him to navigate over deep ruts and potholes that might swallow small foreign cars. The car heaved and twisted slowing Paul's momentum. A few minutes later he saw a dim light in the distance above the dark silhouette of a mound of stacked vehicles. He saw an opening in the scrapheap and pulled off the road. He shut off the engine, got out of the car and shut the door carefully without making any noise. He walked fast and then jogged toward the light. The light brightened as he got closer and he heard intermittent soft scraping sounds but couldn't make out what they were. And then he heard voices, but not distinguishable words. He slowed his gait as he neared the mound of junk. He crept closer, careful not to step on anything that would create noise, and made his way to a point where he could peer around the bumper of a '78 International Scout.

The first thing Paul saw was Joey's large mass leaning against the fender of Bernie's Mercedes. Joey was looking off to his right where the sound was coming from. Paul slowly edged forward to see what Joey was looking at and what was making the sound. Holy shit, Paul said to himself, it's Bernie shoveling dirt. He stood knee deep in a hole digging his own grave. Paul pulled his Glock 9mm from its holster and carefully walked into the opening.

"Don't make a move, Joey," Paul said, pointing the automatic at Joey's head.

Joey whirled around; an astonished look appeared on his face. "What?—"

Bernie turned around. "Paul, am I glad to see you," he said, crawling out of the ditch. "What kept you?"

"I thought you could use the exercise," Paul said. Joey made a move toward Paul. "Don't try it Joey. I know you're fast, but you're not faster than a nine millimeter bullet."

Joey slunk back on the fender. "How'sa you know I wasa here? Who'sa told you? One a my guys?"

"No I did," Bernie said. Joey looked at Bernie as if he had lost his mind. "On the phone in the car." Bernie explained how the command center worked.

"Shit," Joey said. "Teckanonlogy bitesa me inna tha ass again."

"Assume the position," Paul said, walking toward Joey.

Joey turned around and placed his hands on the roof of black beauty.

After Paul frisked Joey, he pulled out a set of handcuffs from behind his back and snapped one cuff on Joey's right wrist. He pulled down Joey's right arm in back of him. He reached up and grabbed the left arm to perform the same operation when Joey whirled to his left, elbowing Paul in the left temple knocking him to the ground. His pistol went airborne into the metal jungle. Paul was dazed, trying to clear his head. He was on his hands and knees struggling to stand when Joey kicked him in the chest. Paul couldn't talk or breathe, but was able to move enough to deflect the second kick. Paul rolled to his right, trying to maneuver under the chassis of an old truck and away from Joey's kicks. Joey bent down and grabbed Paul's leg and tried to pull him back into the opening.

Paul heard a loud *thunk* and felt Joey's grip release. He rolled over and saw Bernie standing over Joey brandishing a shovel in the ready position. Paul moved as quickly as he could to finish the job of handcuffing Joey. Bernie pointed to a spot near a rusted fender where the glock had landed. Bernie stood over Joey while Paul retrieved his weapon.

"Thanks Bernie. I owe you one."

"My pleasure," Bernie said. "By the way, there's a fresh grave over there." Bernie pointed to a mound next to the hole he was digging.

———

Algie Steitzer drove down the twisting, potholed road wondering what he would find. Did Joey help him by finishing Bernie off or would he have to go to plan "B" and use Joey's gun? Wait a minute, he thought, what if Joey doesn't have a gun? He didn't want to think about it as he was confused and just wanted to put it all behind him. He quickly drove to the end of the yard as Albert had told him, bouncing over the potholes and twisting and turning to maneuver around old junks and deep holes. He felt better when he saw the glow of light directly in front of him.

What's this? He thought, as he entered the opening. Detective Andrews and Bernard Eisner? What the hell are they doing here? And what's that? Joey sitting on the bumper of an old wreck? And handcuffed? Algie's imagination went wild wondering what Albert and the mob would do to him now. He couldn't kill Joey now. Not with two witnesses present. Maybe he could kill all three, his mind raced in desperation. He'd have to get Joey's gun first and then shoot Paul. That would leave an old Bernard Eisner and a handcuffed Joey to deal with. He was satisfied with his plan.

"Nice work, Paul," Algie said, getting out of the cruiser. "How'd you get here before me?"

"I was already home when J.C. called me. I was closer, I guess."

Algie looked sheepishly at Joey and then directed his question to Paul. "What's this all about? I got a call about a kidnapping."

"We'll settle this back at the station," Paul said, walking away with Joey. "Bernie can fill us in there." Bernie got in the Mercedes and started it.

Algie had to think fast. "I'd like to see Joey's weapon, please."

Paul kept escorting Joey to his vehicle. "He wasn't carrying."

Shit! Double shit! Algie said under his breath. What would he do now? He stood there in the darkness and watched his life slowly drain away from him. As much as he hated to, he felt the only thing he could do was to call Albert again.

CHAPTER 50

Albert slammed the door to Don Vito's office and walked down the hall into the bar. Freddy Caruso, and Mark "Rudy" Manfreado were seated at the bar discussing what variety of tomatoes had the best nutritional value. John "Slick" Landucci sat at a table hovered over a *Guns and Ammo* magazine.

Albert grabbed Landucci by the arm and said, "Let's take a walk." Slick left his reading material on the table and followed Albert out the door.

Landucci caught up to a fast walking Albert. "What's goin' on Al?"

"Not here," Albert said, motioning with his head toward the park. "In the park."

Albert led the way. John Landucci followed him to a secluded bench in the middle of the park.

Albert scanned the area before they sat down. "I've got a job for you. Paul Andrews is bringing in Joey—"

"What! I thought Steitzer was—"

"Steitzer screwed up. I knew we couldn't trust him," Albert said shaking his head. "It was a simple job. Simple." He looked up to the heavens for spiritual help. "Anyway, he has to be eliminated. Now."

"But I thought Joey—"

"Steitzer first. He'll snap like a twig. Once he gets in front of an assistant district attorney, he'll sing like a bird. He'll roll over on all of us."

"You want me to—" Landucci gestured with his hand a swiping motion across his throat.

"Tonight. Now! They've just left Imbrogno's. You've got to hurry. Get your rifle and don't miss."

"What about Joey?"

"We'll get to him later if you can't erase him tonight. Joey is the Slasher, remember? Nobody will believe him anyway. But Steitzer is first."

John "Slick" Landucci dashed home and picked up his rifle. He drove in a three block radius around City Hall to find a suitable spot to shoot from. An abandoned watch repair shop on Lenawee and 27th Street looked perfect to him. Slick felt he could park unnoticed in the rear of the building and shoot from a rear window that faced the station's parking lot.

John turned off the vehicle's lights and backed up close to the building. He retrieved his gun case from the rear seat. A swift kick opened the weather-beaten door. He scampered up the stairs to the second floor. A narrow hallway led to the back of the building and a small room that was probably once used as a bedroom. He forced open a rear window that was swollen from moisture damage and checked his line of fire. He found an old folding chair, dusted it off with a rag he found and placed it in front of the open window. He sat in the chair with the case across his lap. He swiftly zipped it open and removed the Remington 700 VS rifle. He quickly opened a side pouch on the case and pulled out a Leopold VX-111 4.5-14X 40mm varmint scope. He precisely attached it to the rifle, loaded four .308 caliber cartridges into the magazine and checked the field of vision with the scope. He figured the distance to the station's parking lot to be four hundred and fifty yards. He watched the leaves in the trees that bordered the lot for wind and adjusted the elevation and windage knobs on the scope.

John "Slick" Landucci earned his nickname because of the easy, nonchalant way he performed his work. Nothing seemed to bother him, even under the most extreme circumstances—and tonight was one of those times. He didn't have time to get nervous because at that moment Paul's car pulled into the lot followed by Bernie's Mercedes a few moments later.

Landucci watched Paul pull Joey out of the Chrysler. Paul held Joey firmly with both hands as they walked toward the station. Slick focused the scope's crosshair reticle on Joey's head and found the trigger with his index finger. He had a perfect shot, but held off on Albert's orders: *Steitzer first.* Just then, Steitzer's cruiser pulled into the lot. Slick thought he could whack Joey first and still get a shot off at Steitzer, but Joey was nearly at the door and Steitzer was still in the patrol car. As Algie exited his vehicle, Paul was opening the door to the station house.

"Shit," he said, wanting to shoot a double. He felt somewhat relieved wanting to take his frustration out on Steitzer; he always wanted to shoot a cop anyway.

It was a long shot. He liked long shots, they showcased his shooting ability and the distance provided plenty of time for him to make a clean getaway. Steitzer hesitated for a moment to slide his car keys into his pocket—that's when the crosshairs centered on his right ear and a shot rang out.

When Paul heard the shot he instantly pushed Joey through the door. He turned around to see Lieutenant Algie Steitzer drop to the ground. Bernie was halfway to the station when he heard the shot and dove behind Paul's car.

Sergeant Alan Fiore, on duty at the desk, ran over to assist Paul. "What the hell's going on?" he asked. "Is that Joey Sappone?"

"Yeah. Call all units in our vicinity. Officer down, call E M S," Paul said, pointing to the parking lot. "Lieutenant Steitzer's been shot. Do that immediately and then book Joey on kidnapping."

"Kidnapping?"

Paul crept cautiously out the door while looking in the direction where the shot had come from. "You okay, Bernie?"

"I think so," Bernie said, looking back at Steitzer. "The Lieutenant's been shot. Is it safe to check on him?"

"No, I'll do it. You stay there." Paul continued toward Bernie, carefully avoiding being in the open He sprinted across the lot and slid up to Bernie in a cloud of dust. Algie lie prone, spread out for all to see. Paul didn't want to expose himself not knowing what the shooter intended. "Fiore! Are there any units coming?" Fiore didn't respond, but the sound of sirens was more of a relief to Paul than Fiore's reply.

A patrol car sped up with screeching tires as the vehicle slid to a stop in front of the Lieutenant. Corporal John Walters opened the door and fell out onto the ground with a revolver in his hand. "Who's hit?" he asked.

"The Lieutenant," Paul answered. "Stay put. I'll check on him." Paul crawled on his hands and knees to the lieutenant who lay face down in a pool of blood. He checked his carotid artery for a pulse. Finding none, he rolled him over and stared at the gaping hole in his head. Paul began to wretch. "He's dead," he managed to say.

Paul pointed to where he thought the shot came from. "John, coordinate your efforts in the row house area. Get back to me as soon as you can."

Walters took off, spraying stones from his fast getaway. Paul waited with Bernie until the E M S ambulance arrived before entering the station.

Fiore came back from locking Joey into a cell and said to Paul, "What did you say about kidnapping?"

"Book him on kidnapping. He kidnapped Bernie."

"In addition to the murder charge right?"

Paul stared at Alan. "Murder. What murder?"

Alan Fiore slapped his forehead. "I forgot. You weren't here when the call came in. Wanda Obitko at the Cozy Nook Hotel called in saying she saw Joey shoot Paden Tucker and then slit his throat." He went to his desk and handed Paul the report.

"When was that?"

"About eight thirty. She said she would have called earlier, but was scared."

"Scared my ass," Paul said, motioning Bernie to follow him. Paul walked down the hall to his office holding the door open for Bernie. "Doesn't make sense. Joey's not the Slasher. He's not smart enough. And besides, he's not the type to be with prostitutes. And he certainly wouldn't slash Albert's sister."

Bernie stepped forward. "If you can check on Joey's whereabouts when the recent slashings occurred, it would prove Joey wasn't the Slasher."

"Someone with power had to have ordered Joey to kill Tucker making it appear that the real Slasher did it," Paul said, looking at the report Fiore had given him. "Wanda said there were two gunshots before she saw Joey slit Tucker's throat."

"Sounds like Joey signaled Wanda with the gunshots."

"She had to be in on it," Paul said. "The shots were meant to alert a witness."

"So someone ordered Joey to kill Tucker and make it appear that the Slasher did it—or to set up Joey."

"Maybe both," Paul said. "Maybe the real Slasher set it up. Or someone who knows who the Slasher is set Joey up to take the heat off the Slasher."

"Joey could be a liability to this person. Setting him up would kill two birds with one stone. The Slasher *and* Joey both go away."

"That's what I'm thinking," Paul said. "Stay here I'm going to talk to Joey."

The iron door clanked open. The cellblock guard waved Paul into the holding cell area. Joey sat on a two inch thick mattress leaning against a concrete wall. He wasn't surprised to see Paul.

"You're lucky. They wanted Steitzer first," Paul said, watching Joey's reaction—and it betrayed him.

Paul could tell by Joey's expression that he would be the next to go. The shooting of Steitzer, the way Tucker's murder was reported, and the fact that Joey's sister had asked Paul for help on Joey's behalf reaffirmed Paul's previous conclusions.

"Bullashit," Joey said.

"They set you up as the Slasher, Joey. You're getting the real one off the hook, don't you know that?"

"Doublea bullashit."

"You have information, Joey. You know who the real murderer is."

Joey shrugged his shoulders. "Maybea that'sa my acea in the hole."

Paul looked into the eyes of Joey Sappone, the eyes that told Paul he was going to be a loyal soldier to the end.

233

CHAPTER 51

W ally sat at a window table in the dining room of the Hampton Inn in Steubenville, Ohio. He had already eaten breakfast and slowly sipped a cup of hot coffee while staring out the window onto University Boulevard. He pondered over the events of last night's meeting at DuCheck's Bar. He felt that Tucker's murder, obviously done by the Slasher, took the heat off himself and Paul, but doubt remained in some people's minds and the murderer's identity had to be revealed. He was unaware that Joey Sappone had performed the murder and that Paul suspected Joey had been ordered to carry out the hit and make the murder look like the Slasher's handiwork. Wally was also unaware of Leonard Antonelli's possible participation in the disappearance of Sylvia Troupe, a friend and co-worker of Hilary Jefferson and Roxanne Giannamore. The fact that Steitzer was assassinated would have prompted Wally to believe that the mob was involved, and that a possible end to the Slasher murders would be close at hand, especially when Paul said a Fed had infiltrated the mob. But Wally had to follow every last lead. He noticed when driving through the city last night that the mills were empty and rusted. That eliminated looking for the only living person left, Rick Jefferson, Hilary's husband who was known to be a welder. The only lead left for Wally was Hilary Jefferson. He had to dig up all the information he could about her to find the answer he was looking for.

A waitress scuffed her feet across the floor as she walked to Wally's table. She threw down the check and started to walk away.

"Nice town, Steubenville," Wally said.

"Yeah, I guess so," she said, through chomps of chewing gum.

"I wonder if you could help me out," Wally said, smiling that smile he had perfected over the decades to the pleasure of many young ladies. "A friend of mine wants to be a legal secretary. I wonder if there's a school here she might attend."

"Your granddaughter?" she said with a straight face. "How nice. I heard that's a good job. Don't have to walk a lot or put up with old geysers who like to grope."

Wally groaned. He waited for a response. "A school?"

"Oh yeah. Let's see. They teach that secretary stuff at the Jefferson Community College."

Community College? Wally chuckled to himself. He thought of the local college, Westmoreland County Community College being known as *We Can Count and Color.* And then he remembered the outstanding programs they had to offer.

"Where is it located?"

The waitress pointed out the window. "See this road right here?" Wally nodded. "You follow it that way, right behind that red truck. Let's see, about a mile. And then the road changes into Sunset Boulevard. About two more miles and you're there."

"Right on the road?"

"Can't miss it."

Wally dropped a dollar for a tip, picked up the check and left.

———

The community college looked new and the parking lot was full. Wally walked into the business office fifteen minutes later. A bespectacled middle-aged woman, wearing what one might call a tent dress, addressed Wally.

"Can I help you sir?"

"Yes, I'm interested in some information on one of your former students."

"Oh, we can't give out any personal information of our students. We're required by law—"

Another one of those damn laws. "She's dead. I'm looking for next of kin."

"Well...I don't know."

"Law applies to students, doesn't it? She's not a student."

"Well, she was."

"*She* doesn't exist anymore. I just want to contact next of kin."

The tent woman squirmed in her chair. "Well, okay, if you put it that way. What's her name?"

"Hilary Jefferson."

The secretary massaged the computer keys. "I don't have any record of a Hilary Jefferson. One L?"

"Yes."

"What department? What course was she taking?"

"She was studying to be a legal secretary."

The secretary's pudgy face looked up in surprise. "Not here."

"What?"

After recapping what Wally had said to the waitress at the Hampton Inn, the secretary pulled out a large notebook and fingered through it. "Franciscan University," she said. "That's where they have a legal secretary program."

"I think I passed it a few miles back," Wally said.

The secretary gave Wally directions to the university and typed out a note for him. "Here," she said. "This will help with your next stop. Ask for Helen at the registrar's office."

Wally grabbed the note. He smiled in appreciation. "Thank you," he said sheepishly, and left.

The university looked completely different than the community college. Wally felt the atmosphere provided more of an atmosphere for learning. He stopped three times asking for directions and arrived twenty minutes later at the registrar's office. He asked for Helen and handed her the note. She looked at Wally with suspicious eyes, but dumpster dived into a file cabinet retrieving a manila folder.

"Her next of kin?" she said. "Let's see. Her husband's name is Rick. 1223 Curry St. Wait a minute. This address doesn't exist anymore. It's part of the West End Redevelopment. Maybe you can check a new phone book."

Wally thought that could be a possibility, but if Rick was a welder he would have left the area a long time ago. He decided on Hilary's next of kin. "What about her maiden name and last address. That might help."

Helen thumbed through the last page. "Here it is. Her maiden name is Stuhl. 102 Woodcrest Avenue, Yakima, Washington."

CHAPTER 52

P aul walked down the cellblock corridor two hours later than he had planned. Paperwork, reporting to the mayor and Representative Darby Davis, and finally spitting out a mix of truth and political spin for reporters, kept him from searching for the real Slasher.

Paul stopped in front of Joey's cell. The guard on duty clanked open the iron door. Joey sat on his bunk hunched over a tin tray pushing scrambled eggs and sausage into his mouth when Paul walked in.

"What'sa thisa stuff? Tastes likea shit!"

"Not your regular home cooking, that's for sure," Paul said, sitting down. Joey grumbled something under his breath as he gobbled another huge bite of sausage. Paul slid forward on the chair. "Who gave you the order to kill Bernard Eisner?"

"No one."

"You kidnapped him. Someone ordered you to do it. Who?" Joey didn't answer. "Algie Steitzer was assassinated last night. Your friends will be after you next."

Joey opened his mouth to say something, but didn't.

"Who gave you the order to kill Paden Tucker?"

Joey waved his hand in a negative manner.

"You were set up, Joey. Wanda gave you up. She's going to testify."

Joey looked at Paul as if he didn't believe him.

"Think about it Joey, why did you fire two shots before you slashed Tucker's throat? Are you the Slasher Joey?"

The expression on Joey's face confirmed what Paul already knew. "You're not the Slasher, Joey. You don't want your family to live with that, do you?"

Joey pushed his tray aside and leaned back on the bunk.

"You know who the Slasher is, don't you? Tell me and spare your family the humiliation."

Detective Stahlman walked in with a piece of paper and gave it to Paul. Paul quickly scanned it and said, "The fresh grave next to the one you were digging contained the body of an F B I agent. Now it's the murder of a federal agent, Joey. Tell me what you know. I'll try to help you."

"Don't say another word, Joey," a man standing in the hall warned.

Stahlman shrugged his shoulders as if he didn't have a choice but to bring the man into the cell block.

Paul turned and looked at the man. "Who are you?"

"Oscar Stillatano, consigliore for the LaBruscia Family. My client has nothing more to say to you."

Paul's face took on a disgusted look.

"And I'd like to talk to my client," Oscar said. "Now, please."

Paul and Stahlman walked out of the cellblock area.

"What rotten luck," Paul said. "Timing couldn't have been worse."

"He looked like he was ready to crack."

"A few more minutes," Paul said, "and we would have had Don Vito LaBruscia by the short hairs. He's behind everything. He knows the identity of the Slasher and who killed Steitzer."

"And we can't subpoena Ron Vaccari for Joey's safety deposit key either."

Paul dropped his head. "No judge would issue paper without cause. We don't really know if Vaccari has the key. Joey's sister told me about the key, that's hearsay.

"Looks like our hands are tied."

"The Don's attorney will make sure Joey doesn't sing. All the people involved have been eliminated."

———

Wally strode into Paul's office fifteen minutes before noon. "How's everything goin'?" Wally said, cheerfully.

Paul recounted Bernie's abduction by Joey Sappone, Steitzer's assassination in the parking lot, and that a federal officer's grave was uncovered next to the hole Bernie was digging.

"Holy shit! I missed all that?"

"Yes, and more," Paul said. He recounted the conversation he had with Joey earlier and the interruption by the Don's lawyer. He was sure Joey would never offer any information about the Slasher or any of the recent murders.

"So, you don't know who the real Slashers are, do you?"

"Slashers?" Paul asked

"That's right. Let me tell you what I found out in Steubenville. All the mills were gone or shut down, so I concentrated on Hilary first. I went to a school where one would go to study to become a legal secretary. At the Franciscan University I found Hilary Jefferson's maiden name."

Paul looked puzzled. "Okay...so?"

"So her maiden name is Stuhl. And guess what, she's from Yakima Washington."

"No," Paul said, sliding into his chair. He closed his eyes and held his head as if he had a migraine.

"Yes. And she's the sister of the one and only Harvey Stuhl we so love and adore."

"I'll be damned," Paul said. "But what information do you have on the Slasher?"

"Slashers, remember? As soon as I got back, I went to Harvey's apartment and found a box he had addressed to me."

Paul interrupted. "What was in it?"

"Hold your horses. Two notebooks from Antonelli's safe, a twenty-five automatic pistol, four manila files, eight video tapes from Earsoff's club, and a note from Harvey that I just finished reading," Wally pulled the note from his pocket.

Paul looked like he could hardly contain his emotions. "What's in the note?"

Wally straightened the paper and began to read the note:

> *Dear Wally. I'm addressing this letter to you as you'll probably be the first one to read it after your trip to Steubenville. My deepest apologies to both you and Paul for the trouble I've put you through. As you know by now Hilary was my sister. When I heard of her death, and the circumstances that surrounded it, I came to Mononville to find out who murdered her. It took years of searching through police files and talking to people only to come up with rumors and innuendo. The three names that kept coming up in my investigation were Captain Antonelli, Giovanna Antonelli and Earsoff Tecza. Sorry again Wally, but I thought by killing Giovanna and putting the blame on you, Paul would be forced into action on your behalf, after all she was involved in the business as well as Leonard. When you decided to go it alone and not*

involve Paul, I decided to up the ante by killing Leonard and making it look like the Slasher did it thus pointing the dirty finger at you for both murders and for being the Slasher. I thought Paul and you would intensify the investigation, but I found out that higherups were involved and that it would be impossible for that to happen. I decided to go it alone with the information I found in Tecza's office and Leonard's safe to terminate the people involved at the top of the totem pole. Everything I found to prosecute the bastards is in the box. I really didn't think you would discover me. Sorry I have to leave so soon, I really loved you guys. Don't look for me, I'll be invisible. Harvey

Paul leaned back in his chair. "So he murdered Giovanna, Leonard, and Tecza. What else is in the files?"

"Like he said, he found evidence in Leonard's safe that led to Earsoff's club where he found the tapes, files loaded with other information that led to those further up the ladder."

"Where's the box with the evidence?"

"In my car."

"Bring it in and—"

"Hold on," Wally said. "You don't want to bring the evidence in here. The mayor is involved also."

"We'll go to the Feds first. I'll give the evidence to Rixey. I trust him.

Darby Davis' hometown constituents packed the auditorium of the C.I.O. Hall in anticipation of his campaign speech. Five more rallies were scheduled throughout the district before next Tuesday's election.

Paul Andrews, Agent George Rixey, and two federal marshals entered the rear door of the building to the sound of Councilman Bill "brown-nose" Bouilliard's oratory warming up the crowd for Davis.

The posse ascended a stairwell and walked briskly down a narrow hallway toward the auditorium. They approached the doorway as Bouilliard finished a glowing introduction of Darby Davis.

Agent Rixey, the two federal marshals, and Davis arrived at the microphone simultaneously. The crowd went silent as Rixey read Davis his rights as a federal marshall handcuffed him. Paul stood in the doorway watching the best performance he had ever seen.

J.C. poured a shot of Old Overholt into Ten Quarts' glass when Paul and Wally walked in. Business looked good. The old timers seemed to come out before an election—not so much in celebration, but what seemed to be a feeling of despondency for what the next four years would bring.

"I'll have a shot and a beer," Paul said.

Wally looked at Paul, amazed. "Ditto," he said.

J.C. looked from one to the other. "What's the celebration?"

"Tell him," Wally said.

"I defer to you. You have the honors."

Wally couldn't contain a grin. "Davis was led off in handcuffs tonight by the F.B.I., and it happened in front of all of his constituents."

"All right," J.C. said, leaning closer. "Give me the scoop."

"He was the original Slasher," Paul said.

"Original?"

"Yeah," Wally said. "There were four in all."

"Four, holy shit! Who?"

Paul threw down a shot and said, "Well, let's start with Representative Davis. He had rough sex with Hilary Jefferson and accidentally killed her. Roxainne Giannamore was eliminated because she witnessed the murder."

"Davis murdered them both?" J.C. asked.

"No, just Hilary. Antonelli and Paden Tucker took care of Roxainne, making the murders look like a transient serial killer slashed their throats. Antonelli also murdered Sylvia Troupe who fled to Dysinger. He found her and whacked her the next day."

"That's three," J.C. said, "who's the fourth?"

Paul and Wally looked at each other, neither one wanted to speak.

"Come on guys. I can't—"

Wally spoke up. "Harvey."

"Harvey? No way man. Harvey couldn't—"

Paul spoke. "His sister was Hilary Stuhl Jefferson."

"Oh my God! How'd you find out?"

Wally went to Ohio and checked out where Hilary went to school. He found her maiden name and that she was Harvey's sister.

"What about the others? How'd you get the evidence?"

"Harvey packed up all the evidence when he knew Wally would discover Hilary's identity. Tecza had tapes and files on Davis. Antonelli had two notebooks implicating the whole gang. And Harvey left a note. You can read it after the police are finished with it."

"Great job, Wally."

"Harvey lied," Paul said. "Everything he did or said was a lie. But he did get rid of those corrupt bastards."

"Giovanna didn't have to be murdered," Wally said, "he's a vigilante. But I don't blame him for what he did. I'd do the same thing."

Paul stared into his glass. "Are you going after him

Wally?"
There was no answer.

Printed in the United States
217188BV00001B/1/P

9 781602 643802